When It Snows
In Sarasota

Dr. Kevin Kremer
Illustrated by Richard E. Capes

First printing, July 2004

Copyright © 2004 Snow in Sarasota Publishing
P.O. Box 1360
Osprey, FL 34229-1360
www.snowinsarasota.com

ISBN 0-9663335-2-7

Printed in the United States of America
by Serbin Printing, Inc. – Sarasota, Florida

Available at

www.snowinsarasota.com

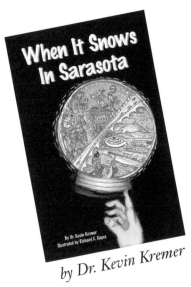

by Dr. Kevin Kremer

by Patricia Ladd

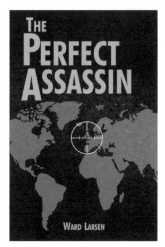

by Ward Larsen

*This book is dedicated to all the people,
past and present, who have made the
Tampa Bay-Bradenton-Sarasota-Venice
area such a terrific place to live!*

*Two of those people, Otto Graham and
David Weeks, have recently passed away.
They are an inspiration to this author and
are both characters in this book.*

Special thanks from the author:

- To Richard E. Capes, an amazing person and an incredible artist, for illustrating this book!
- To the Kremer Family for their constant love and support!
- To Robin Clark for all her help!
- To Judy Webster for her terrific graphic design work!
- To Adam S. Westcott at the Sarasota County History Center for his assistance!

To the following for reading the third draft and giving me advice regarding possible improvements:

Warren and Judy Rider
Jim and Janice Gallogly
Jim and Vi Vranna
Mrs. Smith
Dr. Jan Jones
Mike Kern
Clayton and Carla Albrecht

Karol Volk's Class in
   Charleston, South Carolina
Dr. Roth's Class in Bismarck,
   North Dakota
Tyler Huschka's Class in
   Kansas City
Dr. Greg Gazebo

To the following friends for their gracious help:

Kari Wise
Aundrea Haverlock
Jan Feeney
Jessie Angell
Coach Kevin Feeney
Chad Renner
Nick Hillman
Dr. Jamie Martinson
Ron Ladd
Gary Wilbur
John Gates
Jack Collins
Will Volk

Karen Underdahl
Kelly Kremer's U of M
   Gopher swimmers
PGA Golfer Bo Van Pelt
Thomas Ladd
John Wanner
Kelly, Kizzy, Linda, Alley,
   Deborah, Marissa, Amanda
   and all the other employees
   at Barney's Coffee in the
   Westfield Mall in Sarasota
   who made my mochas each
   morning!

Treatment of Wild Dolphins

Although dolphins like the one in this book are extremely smart and charismatic, the National Oceanic and Atmospheric administration encourages people to admire dolphins from a distance. Petting, feeding, or teasing dolphins is against the law. According to marine biologist Kathy Wang, "When people regularly approach a dolphin with food or for petting, it causes the animal to lose its natural wariness toward people and it can become aggressive. Also, a dolphin's newfound comfort with people makes it more likely to get hit by boat propellers or the boat itself."

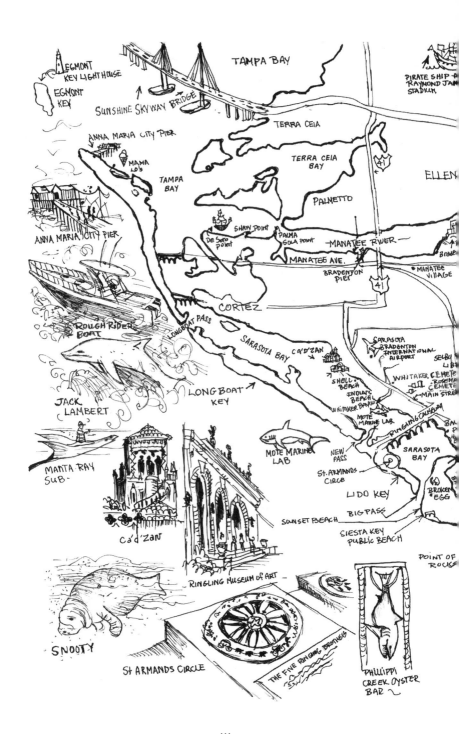

EGMONT KEY LIGHTHOUSE

EGMONT KEY

SUNSHINE SKYWAY BRIDGE

TAMPA BAY

PIRATE SHIP - RAYMOND JAM STADIUM

ANNA MARIA CITY PIER

MAMA LO'S

TAMPA BAY

TERRA CEIA

TERRA CEIA BAY

PALMETTO

ELLEN

ANNA MARIA CITY PIER

SHAW POINT

De Soto Point

PALMA SOLA POINT

MANATEE RIVER

MANATEE AVE.

BRADENTON PIER

41

MANATEE VILLAGE

Brade

ROUGH RIDER BOAT

LONGBOAT PASS

CORTEZ

SARASOTA BAY

CA'D'ZAN

SARASOTA BRADENTON INTERNATIONAL AIRPORT

SELBY LIB

WHITAKER CEMETE

ROSEMA CEMETE

MAIN STRE

SHELL BEACH

INDIAN BEACH

WHITAKER BAYOU

MOTE MARINE LAB.

RINGLING CAUSEWAY

JACK LAMBERT

LONG BOAT KEY

MANTA RAY SUB.

MOTE MARINE LAB

NEW PASS

ST. ARMANDS CIRCLE

SARASOTA BAY

BROKEN EGG

LIDO KEY

CA'D'ZAN

SUNSET BEACH

BIG PASS

SIESTA KEY PUBLIC BEACH

POINT OF ROCKS

RINGLING MUSEUM OF ART

SNOOTY

ST ARMANDS CIRCLE

THE FIVE RINGLING BROTHERS

PHILLIPPI CREEK OYSTER BAR

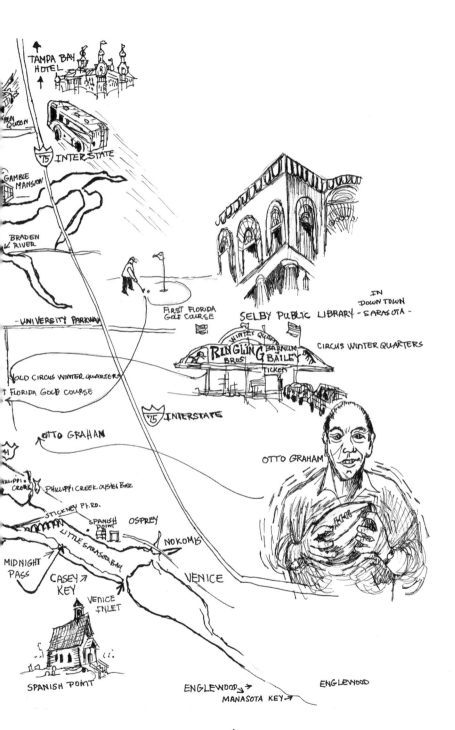

TAMPA BAY HOTEL

HEN QUEEN

75 INTERSTATE

GAMBLE MANSION

BRADEN RIVER

FIRST FLORIDA GOLF COURSE

UNIVERSITY PARKWAY

OLD CIRCUS WINTER QUARTERS

FLORIDA GOLF COURSE

75 INTERSTATE

OTTO GRAHAM

PHILIPPI CREEK

PHILIPPI CREEK OYSTER BAR

STICKNEY PT. RD.

SPANISH POINT

OSPREY

LITTLE SARASOTA BAY

NOKOMIS

MIDNIGHT PASS

CASEY KEY

VENICE INLET

VENICE

SPANISH POINT

ENGLEWOOD

MANASOTA KEY

ENGLEWOOD

SELBY PUBLIC LIBRARY - SARASOTA -

IN DOWN TOWN

RINGLING BROS BARNUM BAILEY

WINTER QUARTERS

Tickets

CIRCUS WINTER QUARTERS

OTTO GRAHAM

1

Sarasota, Florida, definitely got more zippy after Prez moved to town!

Prez was born with the name Mike Gold in Bismarck, North Dakota. After doing a report on Teddy Roosevelt in the second grade, Mike told his teacher and classmates he wanted to be President of the United States someday–just like Teddy. After that, some of Mike's second grade friends started calling him *Prez* and the nickname stuck.

As time passed, Prez's desire to become President continued to grow. Now almost an eighth grader, Prez knew he had about 22 years before The United States Constitution would allow him to run for the world's best job–and he couldn't wait.

Prez brought new meaning to the word precocious. His brain was like an enormous sponge. He loved learning, exploring, and inventing. At times Prez could be a little scatterbrained, but that was understandable. His brain was working on so many things at the same time.

A month ago Prez and his parents moved to Sarasota after Prez's dad's software company won a big military contract from Central Command in Tampa, and Prez's dad decided to relocate his company to nearby Sarasota. Although Prez loved living in Bismarck, the move to Sarasota was easier because one of his best friends, Chad Renner, moved there with him. You see, Chad's parents both worked for Prez's dad, and the two families had been good friends for a long time.

Making things even better, Prez's parents and Chad's parents found new homes on the same block on the north end of one of the most beautiful beaches in the world–Siesta Key Beach. There was only one house between Prez's and Chad's.

Prez and Chad were playing catch with a football after breakfast in front of Prez's house on the last day of May, just 25 yards from the beach and the calm water of the Gulf of Mexico. The two friends were both wearing swimming shorts, T-shirts, and had bare feet. Both boys were wearing their Pittsburgh Steelers caps which they rarely took off their heads.

Watching these two play catch, it was obvious Chad was a much more gifted athlete than Prez. Chad was taller, slimmer, and more muscular than Prez, and looked like the natural athlete that he was.

Prez's interest and participation in sports had grown over recent years, however, influenced greatly by his Bismarck friends–sports fanatics all. Prez had even gone out for seventh grade football this past year, and had done quite well playing on the offensive line.

"Hey, Chad," Prez said, throwing the football to his friend 20 yards away, "besides the beach–what are your favorite things about living in Sarasota so far?"

Chad threw a perfect spiral to Prez, thought for a few

seconds, and said, "Let's see ... there's all the cute Florida girls ... You've got the boating, the kayaking, and the fishing ... Of course, there's those Tampa Bay Buccaneers season tickets your dad got for us ... Did I mention the cute girls?"

Prez chuckled. "I think so," he said, throwing a wobbly spiral a little high so Chad had to jump to catch it. Chad jumped up and caught the football with ease.

Chad held the ball and kept thinking a little longer. He was quiet for several seconds before he said, "You know I miss Bismarck and all our great friends there, Prez, but I'm having a blast here in Sarasota. Everything's like a big adventure–it's all so new. I even like all the new names around here."

"What exactly do you mean by that, Chad?"

Chad fired the football to Prez and explained, "Do you remember in sixth grade when Dr. K made us find out how we got our names, and after that, we studied how places in North Dakota got theirs?"

"Sure, that was extremely interesting," Prez replied.

"Well," Chad said, walking closer to Prez to continue the conversation, "since we moved here, I've been thinking about the names and where they came from."

"Like what?" Prez inquired.

"You know, like Florida to start with. Like Sarasota and Manasota and Stickney and Bradenton and Tampa and tons of others. I'm curious where all those names come from."

Prez tried to sound serious. "Chad, you've become so much more than an ignorant athlete." Both boys laughed.

"I've been hanging around you too long," Chad said. "You've always said I need to develop my mind–not just my *superior* athletic skills." Chad and Prez giggled at Chad's faked conceit.

Prez gave his friend a light punch in the arm and said, "Mr. Superior Athlete, if you want, we could start researching some of the origins of the place names around here."

"How do we start?"

"We could do it several ways, but I suggest we go to Selby Public Library downtown. I heard they have a huge aquarium inside, built right into the structure somehow. We can take a look at that and research some place names, too."

Prez's dad came outside at that moment, and Prez asked, "Hey, Dad. Do you mind if Chad and I take the boat and go to the public library downtown this morning?"

"Sounds good to me," Mr. Gold replied. "Give me a call on the way, though, all right?"

"Will do, Dad," Prez said.

Chad got a mischievous grin on his face, and asked, "Mr. Gold, are you gonna dump the Pittsburgh Steelers and become a Buccaneers fan now that you've moved down here?"

Chad asked the question knowing both his dad and Prez's dad were huge fans of the Steelers for life–just like Chad and Prez were.

Mr. Gold gave the boys a funny look, and replied, "Maybe when it snows in Sarasota on Christmas." He paused briefly and added, "Or there's a major hurricane in North Dakota."

"Funny, Dad," Prez chuckled. "A hurricane in North Dakota has a zero probability."

Then Prez got an intensely inquisitive look on his face, a sure sign his brain was working. After a few moments, he said, "I wonder how many times, if any, it's even snowed here on Christmas?"

"I doubt if it's ever snowed in Sarasota," Chad guessed, "but we can look that up when we're at the library."

Mr. Gold walked toward the house, and said, "Let me know what you find out. I've got to get to work. You two boys have a fun day."

After Mr. Gold had gone back in the house, Prez blushed a little, and asked Chad, "Should we ask KT to come along to the library?"

Katy Heidebrink, who they both called KT, was their next door neighbor. She was a cute, blonde girl, the same age as the two boys, who had recently moved to Sarasota from Fergus Falls, Minnesota. KT's parents bought a jet ski, bicycle, boat, kayak, and parasailing business on Siesta Key called Siesta Key Water Fun.

Chad teased his friend, "You have a little crush on KT, don't you?"

Prez's face flushed some more, and he said, "I may have a slight crush on her, but I think we really could use her help."

"Hey, Chad," Prez said, trying to change the subject quickly. "Speaking of names of things, I'll give you a dollar if you can give me the names of five types of birds down by the beach."

Chad looked that way, studied the birds carefully, and confidently said, "You're on, Prez."

"Begin anytime you're ready," Prez said.

"All right," Chad began. "The pelicans, of course."

Prez held up one finger, and said, "I think brown pelicans would be more accurate, but that's one."

"The seagulls."

Prez held up two fingers and said, "I don't think technically they're known as *seagulls*, but I'll give you credit. Actually those are gulls–more specifically *laughing gulls*–but that's two. Three more for the money."

Chad pointed at two other birds and said, "You've got the great egret *there* and the snowy egret over *there*."

Prez held up his third and fourth fingers and said, "Very impressive! That's three and four. One more, and you get the thumb–and a dollar."

Chad wasn't sure about the next one, but it was his best chance. "The little nervous dudes running around in unison at the edge of the water are ... *shandelearrings*."

Prez started laughing when Chad said *shandelearrings*. While he was still laughing, he tried to talk like a crazed game show host. "You win, Chad! It's actually *sanderlings*, but I'm not going to be picky. You win!"

When he was done laughing, Prez continued speaking, doing his best game show host impression. "By the way, a sixth type of bird, the one standing on that old cement post out there that looks like a black duck, is a cormorant, and it's been seen diving as deep as 100 feet below the surface. Now, Chad, would you like a sports bonus question for an extra quarter?"

"Bring it on!" Chad answered confidently.

Prez added some suspense to his game show host voice. "What was the Tampa Bay Buccaneers' record in their first year in the NFL?"

Being a true sports fanatic, sports trivia was a passion for Chad. This was an easy question for him. He answered Prez doing his own impression of Howard Cosell, famous sports analyst, as he'd heard him speak many times on The Sports

Classic Channel. "Prez, you insult my sports intelligence. The year was 1976. They only played 14 games back then. A pitiful Tampa Bay team lost all of them. Their record–a dismal zero and fourteen. By the way, the next year the pathetic Bucs lost their first 12 games before finally beating New Orleans 33 to 14."

Speaking in his super-enthusiastic game show host voice, Prez said, "You're not nearly as dumb as you look, Chad–and you win a quarter!"

Several hundred yards out in the Gulf of Mexico, a man stood near the back of his boat, pointing an advanced parabolic listening device in Chad and Prez's direction–listening intently to their conversation.

"The Selby Public Library," he said out loud to himself. He smiled. "Let's see how smart this Prez guy really is."

KT Heidebrink walked next door to Prez's house after she ate breakfast. Chad and Prez were already standing in the boat–still on a trailer in the driveway more than 30 yards from the beach.

"Hop in, KT," Prez said.

With a puzzled look on her face, KT asked the obvious question, "Uh ... don't you think we should put the boat in the water first?"

Prez smiled and said, "I've got that covered, KT. Jump in."

KT reluctantly climbed up on the trailer, and the boys helped her into the new 37-foot boat named the *Rough Rider*. Then, Prez casually reached into his swimsuit pocket, pulled out a small remote control device, and pushed a few buttons.

KT could hear the sound of an engine starting, and soon the trailer and boat were moving slowly in reverse toward the beach. The whole time this was happening, KT had a wide-eyed look, partly in awe of what was happening, partly anxious about what was going to happen *next*.

She didn't have to wait long. When the trailer got to the edge of the water, Prez pushed a button, and they stopped.

Then he pushed another button and the boat slowly rose approximately a foot above the trailer–like it was a hovercraft. After that, Prez used a small joystick to guide the *Rough Rider* over deep enough water, then he slowly lowered the boat to the surface.

By this time, KT's eyes were huge, and it looked like she was either going to scream or faint! With an astonished look on her face, KT said, "I've been around boats and marinas in Minnesota all my life! Where did you get that gizmo, Prez?"

Prez smiled and said, "Just a little something I invented."

KT was amazed. "Excuse me," she said. "You invented this gizmo, Prez?"

"It's no big deal," Prez replied.

"Sure!" KT exclaimed. "You've made your boat into a hovercraft, and it's no big deal!"

"It really isn't a hovercraft," said Prez. "We can talk about it sometime if you'd like."

Prez started the boat's three 250-horsepower outboard motors, and soon the three of them were headed north in the beautiful, calm, sparkling coastal waters off Siesta Key. Prez was sitting in the captain's chair, while KT and Chad sat in comfortable padded seats near the front of the boat.

As they got underway, and KT had settled down a little, Chad said, "KT, this morning Prez asked me what I liked about living in Sarasota. How would you answer that?"

It didn't take KT long to answer. "I really love living on the beach and helping my parents run their new business."

Chad asked, "Is there anything you miss about Minnesota?"

"Sure ... I miss my friends most, but I e-mail them almost

every day, so that helps. Some of my friends might even get to come down here this winter and next summer."

Prez said, "Chad and I feel the same way about our friends, KT. We have some great friends back in Bismarck, too. Fortunately, Governor Ed is going to fly some of them down here this summer."

"Excuse me," KT said, looking a little astounded. "Are you talking about Governor Ed, as in the governor of North Dakota?"

"That's right," Prez answered nonchalantly. "Governor Ed is a good friend of ours."

"And how did that happen?" KT asked.

"We met him when we were in Dr. K's sixth grade class at Dorothy Moses School in Bismarck," Prez explained. "Governor Ed challenged all the students in North Dakota to get in better physical shape, and our sixth grade class took on the challenge in a big way."

Chad added, "Prez even built a cool spaceship we called *The Starship Exercise* that got a little out of control and ended up flying over most of North Dakota, but that's a long story."

KT's eyes got bigger. "*You* are the ones who chased that spaceship all over the place? That was even on the front page of our Fergus Falls newspaper–and in the national news. What really happened with all that, anyway?"

"It's a pretty long story," Chad said.

"We've got the time," KT insisted. "I'd like to hear it–and please don't leave out any important details."

"Well," Chad began, "it really started the first day of school when Governor Ed got on television and challenged all the kids in North Dakota to come up with ideas to help people in the state get in better physical condition. After that, our sixth grade class did tons of cool stuff to promote fitness–then Prez came up with the idea of building *The Starship Exercise* which would fly over a fitness float we were going to enter in a huge parade they have in Bismarck called the Folkfest Parade. With lots of help from our parents and everyone else in our class, Prez got the spaceship ready just in time, and we got the fitness float ready, too. We even talked Governor Ed into riding on our float in the parade."

"Is that how you first got to know Governor Ed?" KT asked.

"Yup. A group of kids from our class, including Prez and me, went to Governor Ed's office at the Capitol to ask him to ride on our float," Chad explained.

"So, what happened during the parade?" KT inquired.

"The parade started out great," Chad said. "On our float, Governor Ed, Dr. K, and most of our sixth grade class were demonstrating various ways to stay fit. Prez was standing on the float, using a remote control device to fly *The Starship Exercise* above us. It was really cool."

Prez chuckled. "Not for long, though."

"What happened next?" asked KT.

"A big orange happened," Chad answered, laughing. "A huge papier-mache orange came loose on the float in front of us and came rolling toward the SUV that was pulling our float. It startled the driver–he hit the brakes–the float jolted and so did everyone on it–then a girl in our class named Michelle who was demonstrating the balance beam on our float fell off the beam and landed on Prez–who dropped his remote control onto the street–and it broke into several pieces."

"Oh, my gosh!" KT exclaimed. "Is that when *The Starship*

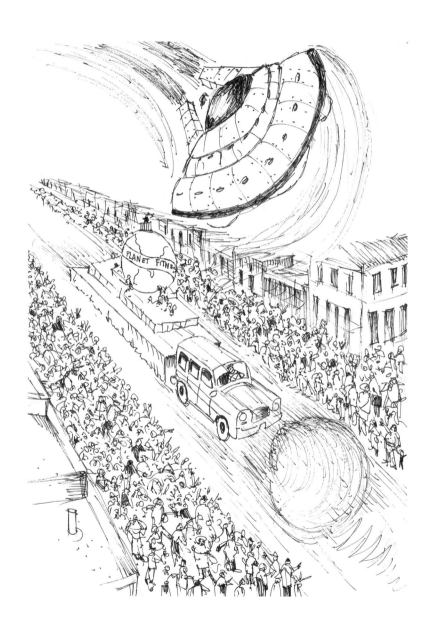

Exercise started flying all over the place?"

"Yup," Chad replied. "After that, our whole sixth grade class, along with Governor Ed, Dr. K, and some of our parents, got in a bus and followed the spaceship as it flew all over North Dakota."

"Sounds like a real blast!" KT observed.

"Actually, it was one of the best times *ever*," Chad said. "Prez was in the back of the bus trying to build another remote control device so he could regain control of the spaceship. A huge caravan of cars started following our bus and *The Starship Exercise* on the crazy journey–there were even military helicopters in the air ready to shoot Prez's spaceship down if it flew too close to a building or something. Fortunately, that wasn't necessary, and Prez regained control of *The Starship Exercise* and landed it safely ... Hey, I just thought of something! All our problems back then happened because of an orange ... and what's pictured on most license plates in Florida, I ask you?"

KT and Prez gave Chad really strange looks, and then they all three started laughing.

KT said, "I have a feeling Sarasota is never going to be the same with you two North Dakota boys in town."

Prez gave KT a big smile. "I think I can almost guarantee that."

Prez continued driving the boat at a moderate speed through Big Sarasota Pass, then into Sarasota Bay.

KT observed, "You two never mentioned the names of any of your friends who are flying down here this summer–besides Governor Ed."

"That would be Jan, Kari, Jessie, Mike, Nick, and Kevin," Chad noted.

"How did you all become such good friends?" KT asked.

"It's a little complicated," Chad began. "We all knew each other since kindergarten at Dorothy Moses School, but we became really good friends in the sixth grade when we all ended up in the same class—then there was *The Starship Exercise* thing plus that little election thing."

"What little election thing?" KT inquired.

"Well," Chad explained, "we had a simulated country deal where our class wrote a constitution. We had two political parties, we made laws and everything—but the election for president got really competitive and maybe a little out of control when Prez ran against Jan."

"What happened?" asked KT.

"The election campaign was a lot of fun, but it might have gotten a little too real," said Chad. "Jan and the other people in her political party—like me—got in some real good battles with Prez and the people in his party. It was wild, but through it all, Jan and Prez became really good friends, and the rest of us all got to be great friends, too."

"Who won the election?" KT wanted to know.

"Prez did—by one vote."

"Tell me more about Jan, Kari, Jessie, Mike, Nick, and Kevin," KT requested.

"We can do better than that, KT," Chad offered. "Next time Prez and I conference call them, we'll introduce them all to you."

"Promise?"

"I promise," said Chad. "Hey, Prez—you never had a chance to tell us *your* favorite things about living in Sarasota."

Prez thought about that for a few seconds. "I like many

of the things KT and you mentioned, but I've got a few others," he said.

"Like what?" KT asked.

"Well, the *Mother Goose and Grimm* comic strip in the newspaper to start with. The Bismarck people don't know what they're missing. It's the first thing Chad and I read each morning."

"I like it, too," KT said. "The Fergus Falls newspaper didn't have it either. My dad says the guy who does *Mother Goose and Grimm* lives right on Siesta Key."

"I'd sure like to meet him sometime," Prez said. "Anyway, besides that, I like the fact that my mom finally gets a chance to use her marine biology degree at the Mote Marine Laboratory here in Sarasota. There really wasn't a huge demand for marine biologists in Bismarck, you know."

"Prez, where does Mote Laboratory get its name?" asked Chad. "There's no moat around it or anything."

"Mote is the last name of the man, Bill Mote, who did so much to make the place successful."

"That makes sense," Chad observed.

KT asked, "Prez, what else do you like about Sarasota?"

"I don't want to bore you too much, but Sarasota is an exciting place to be if you're interested in politics like I am."

"I'm not bored at all," said KT, "but what do you mean exactly?"

Prez answered, "Well, Florida seems to be where the action is when it comes to politics. That presidential election excitement in 2000 took place down here. Besides that, Congresswoman Katherine Harris is one of the most famous politicians in the United States, and she's from Sarasota. Also, I realize my chances of becoming President are greater if I'm a candidate from a larger state like Florida as opposed to a small state in population like North Dakota ... Are you bored yet?"

"Not at all," KT replied. "I was president of my seventh grade class in Fergus Falls, and I'm interested in politics, too."

Chad chimed in, "Has anyone from Florida ever been elected President?"

"Not really," Prez explained, "although Andrew Jackson, our seventh President, was governor of Florida for about 11 weeks back when Florida was a United States territory. Jackson was from Tennessee, though, so Florida can't really count him."

"Why was Andrew Jackson only governor for 11 weeks?" Chad asked.

"From what I remember reading, Pensacola was the capital of the Florida Territory, and it wasn't much of a place to live back then," Prez answered. "Jackson and his wife were anxious to get out of there."

"Is Jacksonville named after Andrew Jackson?" KT asked.

"Sure is," Prez replied.

"Has there ever been a President from North Dakota?" KT inquired.

Prez answered, "Lots of North Dakota people like to say Teddy Roosevelt was a North Dakotan, and he did live there awhile, but he was actually from New York. To answer your question, no true North Dakotan has ever been elected President."

"What about Minnesota?" Chad asked.

KT said, "We've had a couple of Vice Presidents from Minnesota that I know of–Humphrey and Mondale–but we've never had a President."

KT looked at Prez and asked, "Anything else you like about living here, Prez?"

"Well, Sarasota has a boat festival called the Suncoast Offshore during the Fourth of July week where all sorts of fancy speedboats are put on display and then they race. This year they're adding a cool Creative Boat Parade, where people can design just about anything that floats, and I want to enter ... if we can find the time to finish our boat by then."

"I'll help you if you'd like," KT offered.

Prez felt his heart beating faster. "Thanks, KT. Chad and I can use all the help we can get."

KT asked, "When are you guys going to tell me exactly what we're going to be doing at the library?"

"Right now," Prez replied. "First, we want to find out if it ever snowed on Christmas Day in Sarasota or if it's even snowed here at all. Second, we're going to try to find the origin of some of the place names around here."

"What place names?" KT inquired.

Chad reached for his backpack and found the notebook where he'd listed the names Prez and he had talked about earlier, along with a few others he'd added since. He said, "Here are some of the ones we thought we could start with–Florida, Sarasota, Manasota Key, Stickney Point, Siesta Key, Venice, Bradenton, Osprey, Nokomis, and Tampa. Are there any others you can think of right now, KT?"

"How about Tamiami Trail?" KT said. "It's the major road through Sarasota, and it has such a funny name."

"Good one, KT," said Chad. "I'll add that to my list. Any others you can think of?"

"What about *Seminole*? It's all over the place down here. You've got the Florida State Seminoles nickname–and streets, businesses, high schools, a town, and tons of other stuff have the name *Seminole*. I think the Seminoles were a group of Indians, but I'd like to know more."

"Another good one, KT," Chad remarked, as he wrote it down. "Any others?"

KT thought for awhile longer, and said, "I know it's not a place name, but have either of you noticed the *Michael Saunders* signs on almost every house or business for sale around here?"

"Yeah, he must be a rich dude," Chad said.

"Uh, actually *she* must be rich, Chad," Prez pointed out. "I've seen her picture on the society page of the paper a few times. She's an extremely elegant woman, and I read where she actually grew up on Longboat Key."

"I'd like to hear how she got Michael for a name," Chad said. "Uh ... do you think I'm elegant, Prez?"

"More like *elephant*," Prez said, and all three of them laughed.

KT suggested, "Why don't we get one of those free tourist maps they have of the whole Tampa Bay and Sarasota Bay area, and maybe we can eventually find out how all the important places on the map got their names."

"Great idea, KT," Prez said.

"Super idea," Chad added. "I'll bet they'll have some copies of that map at the library or somewhere near there. They're all over town. By the way, KT, do you know how Minnesota got its name?"

"Sure do. Minnesota comes from two Sioux Indian words meaning *sky-tinted waters*. I just studied it this year in school.

What does *Dakota* in North Dakota mean?"

Prez said, "I think it's named after the Dakota division of the Sioux Indian tribe that once lived there. The word *Dakota* means *friend*."

"So, how do most places get their names anyway, Prez?" KT asked.

"Most of the names of towns were taken from the names of the little post offices that opened when a community was just getting started. The people, or postmasters, who were chosen to run the post offices by the national government got to pick the names. They could name them pretty much whatever they wanted."

"Anything?" asked KT.

"Pretty much," Prez affirmed. "Some postmasters used Indian names, historic names for the area, or their own names. Others used names of wives or girlfriends or kids. Some towns were named after animals, war heroes, early settlers, lakes or mountains nearby, or whatever. I think some postmasters were just trying to be funny when they picked their names."

"What do you mean?" KT inquired.

"Like Zap, North Dakota, for example," Prez said. "Or Boring, Oregon, or Okay, Oklahoma."

"Well, we have a town in Minnesota called Embarrass, and that's embarrassing," KT said with a giggle.

"I saw a town on a Florida map named Ace of Diamonds," Prez added.

Chad asked, "Did the first postmasters get paid anything?"

"Yes, a little," Prez replied, "but many times the post office was part of a general store, and it brought in all sorts of extra traffic. It was good for business."

"Can a town change its name if they don't like it?" Chad inquired.

"Sure," Prez said. "In fact, remember Bismarck was called Edwinton once, and then the people changed it to Bismarck–hoping the leader of Germany, Chancellor Otto von Bismarck, might invest some money in the town."

"Did he?" asked KT.

"No, but the name still stuck," Prez answered.

Chad said, "I remember some people in North Dakota even wanted to change the name of the state several years ago because they thought the word *north* brought too many cold thoughts to people's minds or something, and that's what's kept people from moving there."

"I remember hearing about that," KT said. "Why didn't North Dakota's name get changed?"

"It's really hard to change a place name that most people like and have gotten used to," Prez replied. "Just imagine how much it would cost just to change all the maps and signs."

"Besides," Chad said with a laugh, "who were those people in North Dakota trying to fool? It *does* get pretty darn cold in North Dakota, but it keeps out the riff raff."

"Speaking of North Dakota," KT said. "What's the first thing people down here say when you tell them you're from North Dakota?"

"COLD!" Prez and Chad answered at exactly the same time.

"Or a few mention the movie *Fargo*, or they ask if the faces of the Presidents carved in the mountain are in North Dakota," Prez added.

Chad asked, "What happens when you tell them you're from Minnesota, KT?"

"Mostly, they say *cold*, too," said KT. "A few people mention the Minnesota Vikings or the lakes or the huge mosquitoes. One guy asked me if we really had a professional wrestler as our governor once—which we did, of course—good old Jesse Ventura."

Chad's eyes got really big, and seemingly out of nowhere, he said, "I just thought of something. Do you realize KT's from Minneso–ta, and we're from North Dako–ta, and we all moved to Saraso–ta. Coincidence–or more than that?"

"You're scaring me now, Chad," KT said with a giggle.

Prez changed to his most enthusiastic game show host voice and said, "Chad, I'll give you a dollar if you can tell me the names of four other prominent places that end in the letters TA."

"If I can get help from KT."

"Sure," Prez said, "but then you each get only 50 cents if you answer correctly. I'll give you one minute starting right *now*."

Prez started the timer on his watch.

Before two seconds had passed, KT said, "Atlanta!"

"That's *one*!" Prez said, holding up one finger.

Less than five seconds after that, KT said, "Alberta, Canada!"

"Two!" Prez said, holding up the second finger.

"Augusta, the capital of Maine!" Chad said within seconds.

"That's *three*!" Prez exclaimed. "You two are amazing!"

"How about Augusta, *Georgia*?" KT said right after that. "Home of the Masters Golf Tournament, I believe," she added.

"You win!" Prez exclaimed, continuing to use his game show host voice. "And you still have tons of time left! Now, how about a sports bonus question worth 13 cents for each of you?"

"Bring it on!" Chad exclaimed.

"This is a good one my dad told me," Prez explained. "There's a college in Florida called Stetson University. What's the nickname for their sports teams?"

"I don't have a clue," Chad said.

KT decided to give it a try. "My grandpa wears a Stetson hat, so I'm going to guess the *Hatters*."

"You're absolutely right, KT!" Prez said excitedly. "By the way, the college was founded by the maker of those Stetson hats! That's absolutely amazing!"

"Way to go, KT!" Chad exclaimed.

Then, Prez said, "Hey, we're almost at Bayfront Park. We'll tie the boat up at the marina there and walk to the library."

"I think I may know how Bayfront Park got its name," Chad noted.

As soon as they got to Selby Public Library, they picked up a tourist map of the Tampa Bay and Sarasota Bay area inside the front door. Then they quickly entered the library, looking for the aquarium.

It didn't take them long to find it. Serving as the entrance to the youth library was a large arch-shaped aquarium loaded with at least 20 different types of beautiful tropical fish. Right away, Prez became fascinated with the uniqueness of the structure, and he suddenly became totally focused on its construction.

Talking to himself out loud, he said, "I'm estimating the entire arched aquarium structure is 12 feet tall and 16 feet wide. The arch itself appears to be approximately four feet wide."

KT pointed out, "The fish are pretty awesome, too, Prez, or don't you even notice them? Look at that pretty blue and yellow one over there."

Prez was oblivious to anything but the aquarium structure at that point as he kept thinking out loud. "I'm guessing at least 3,000 gallons of salt water. Four-inch-thick acrylic walls. The coral seems to be some type of fiberglass material."

Chad could tell his friend had gone into his own little world, and he decided to have some fun with him. Chad said, "I hope that mermaid doesn't get hit by that nuclear submarine."

"Me, too," Prez mumbled, as he continued to examine every detail of the aquarium's construction.

In a voice a little too loud for the library, Chad said, "There's Congresswoman Katherine Harris!"

"Where?" Prez said, suddenly snapping out of his trance.

Now that Chad had Prez's attention, he asked, "So, what's the game plan, Prez?"

"Let's go upstairs and find the reference section," Prez answered. "We'll grab all the books on local history, take them to a table, and dig in. We can bookmark any pages related to early snowfall or the place names around here with yellow Post Its. Anything else we find interesting, let's mark with blue Post Its. We've got our minicomputers, notebooks, and pens for any notes, and I've got some change if we want to Xerox anything. Oh, make sure you write down your source and page number when you take notes."

"Yes, *teacher*," Chad said with a smile. "How much time are we going to spend on this today?"

"Should we see how much we can do in two hours?" Prez suggested.

"Sounds good to me," KT said.

"Me, too," Chad agreed.

The three went upstairs, found the local reference section, and within a few minutes they'd found more than a dozen books they thought might be helpful. They took them over to a large wooden table near some windows with a great view, and sat down.

They started scanning the books intensely. Soon, notes were being taken, pages were being bookmarked, and interesting discoveries about the Sarasota area were being made by each of the three researchers.

KT found a reference to snow in Sarasota in a book on local history and showed it to Prez. After Prez read about it, he said, "I'm going to read the local newspaper articles on microfilm for the snow day mentioned here. I'll be back in a few minutes."

Not long after Prez left, Chad found the story of how the first post office in Sarasota got its name. "Look, KT," Chad said. "Here it says a guy by the name of Charles Elliott Abbe started the first post office on August 16, 1878. There were only about 40 families around here at the time. It says he put the name *Helena* on the post office application, but the Post Office Department in Washington, D.C. changed it to *Sarasota*–which was already the name of the bay nearby."

KT asked, "Where did Abbe get *Helena* from?"

"Apparently, the Abbes had a lot of land around here and they called it *Helena*. It doesn't mention how they came up with that name for their land though."

"Does it say where the first post office was located?" KT asked.

"Yup," Chad replied, "at the northeast corner of Arlington Street and Osprey Avenue, near where Morton's Market is located today. The Abbe family had their post office inside their general store."

"Have you found anyplace where the name Sarasota comes from?" Chad asked.

"It sounds like that's a mystery, but there are lots of theories."

28

"Like what?"

"Well, the name could have come from an Indian trading post on north Longboat Key called Saraxola, but that's not my favorite theory."

"Well, what is your favorite theory, KT?"

"It could have come after the Spanish word *zarzosa* meaning *briery*, but that's not my favorite theory, either."

"What's briery?" Chad asked.

"Thorny bushes and stuff," KT replied. "But that's not my favorite theory."

"What is, KT?"

"It could have come from the Indian word *Sara-se-cota* meaning *landfall easily observed*, but that's *still* not my favorite theory."

Chad and KT were having fun with this exchange. "You made that quite clear. What is, KT?" Chad asked with a big grin on his face.

"It could have come from the Spanish expressions *Sarao sota* meaning *place of dancing*, or it could have even come from the Indian words *sua* meaning *sun*, *ha* meaning *water*, and *zota* meaning *shadow*."

Chad asked, "Is *that* your favorite theory?"

"Not really."

Chad was holding back a big laugh at this point. "Well, what the heck is, KT?"

"It's explained in a wonderful romantic story I really like."

"You can't beat a little romance. Where did the story come from?"

"Well, the first family of settlers in Sarasota was the Whitakers. And William H. Whitaker hired a school teacher from Ohio after the Civil War named Miss Winifred

Harper. She was the first person who told the story, but who she heard it from or whether she even made it up is anyone's guess. Anyway, this Miss Harper told the story to the children, and they later passed it on to a guy named George F. Chapline who came here from Arkansas in 1902. He's the guy who wrote it down."

Chad said, "I'm ready to hear it."

"Do you want me to read it to you or tell it in my own words?"

"Give me the KT condensed version for now," Chad said. "We can Xerox the whole thing later if we want."

"Well," KT began, referring to a book where the story was written, "once upon a time ... long ... long ago, in the year 1539, Hernando de Soto, famous Spanish explorer, was exploring this area, and he had his beautiful, young daughter along."

Chad couldn't help himself. "Don't tell me! Her name was Sara, wasn't it? Sara de Soto!"

"That's right, Chad. Now, do you want to hear the rest of the story or not?"

"Go on. I *almost* promise not to interrupt again, KT."

KT giggled and then continued, "Anyway, Hernando de Soto's men captured a handsome, young Indian prince named Chichi-Okobee, son of a famous Indian chief named Black Heron. Chichi probably could have escaped, but he really didn't want to."

"Why not?"

"Because, one day he caught one good peek at the beautiful Sara de Soto, and he fell deeply in love. Sara, by the way, felt the same way about Chichi, too."

"It's hard to beat love at first sight," Chad said, giggling.

"That's true, Chad. Anyhow, sometime soon after that, Chichi got sick ... really sick, and he was near death, in fact. The Spanish doctors tried everything to save Chichi, but nothing worked. When the Spanish doctors gave up, Hernando de Soto allowed Sara to make Chichi comfortable in his dying hour. Well, thanks to Sara's loving care, Chichi got his health and strength back."

"The power of *love*," Chad interrupted. "Sorry, KT, I couldn't help it."

KT giggled. Then she forced herself to get serious again. "Anyway, then Sara must have caught what Chichi had because she got really sick after that. The Spanish doctors tried again, but they weren't able to help her."

Chad interrupted again. "A good Spanish doctor must have been hard to find 500 years ago."

"Probably," KT said, almost cracking up. "In any case, Chichi begged permission from Hernando de Soto to go to his father's camp, deep in the Everglades, to get the great medicine man, Ahti, who could possibly save Sara. De Soto gave his permission, so Chichi ran away as fast as he could. Days later, Chichi returned with the medicine man who gave Sara mysterious herbs, uttered strange incantations, and stayed for many hours at her bedside."

"What are incantations?" Chad asked.

"They're like magical phrases or something like that," KT explained. "So, anyway, Chichi waited. But it was no use ... Sara died."

Chad gave KT an overly exaggerated, agonized look. "KT, I needed a happy ending to this story," he said.

"Sorry, Chad ... Brokenhearted, Chichi went to De Soto and asked if Sara could be buried in the prettiest spot in

Sarasota Bay. He also asked to be allowed to take part in the ceremony. Hernando de Soto gave his approval and allowed Chichi to return to his camp to get some of his fellow warriors to make up an honor guard.

"The next morning, 100 Indian braves appeared, headed by Chichi-Okobee. They were in three large canoes, which were draped with dark mosses from the forest. All the braves were decked out in war paint, and they had their best bows and arrows. The canoes landed right up on the beach, paddled by Chichi's braves. After that, the body of Sara was gently placed in one of the canoes which was called the funeral barge. In the other two canoes were Chichi and the honor guard. Slowly, the fleet moved to the exact center of Sarasota Bay where Sara's body was lowered gently into the water.

"At a signal from Chichi, every warrior sprang to his feet, holding a tomahawk in his hand. In unison, the 100 braves chanted a sad, mournful funeral song. Then, the blades of their tomahawks crashed into the canoes."

Chad was surprised at this development. "You mean they drowned themselves so they could protect Sara forever?"

"Yes, Chad. Chichi and his warriors had gone to guard the resting place of the beautiful Sara de Soto in the clear waters of Sarasota Bay."

"I liked that, KT ... especially the way you told it."

Suddenly, Prez returned to their table–almost running–obviously anxious to share something with his two friends!

4

"You're not going to believe what I found!" Prez said excitedly, as he stood beside the table.

"What?" Chad asked.

"Give us some details!" KT pleaded.

"Well," Prez began, speaking faster than usual, "I was reading about a time it snowed in Sarasota–the old newspapers are on microfilm, so I was using a microfilm reader. Anyway, after awhile I noticed the machine next to me was on, but no one was using it, so I just got curious and took a look–you won't believe what the article on there was about!"

"What?" KT and Chad said at the same time.

"A super-strange event that happened during the 100th Anniversary Celebration of Sarasota!"

"Stranger than snow in Sarasota?" Chad asked.

"No doubt," Prez said. "On November 9, 2002, they had their Centennial Celebration here. They had a huge party downtown and a gigantic Boat Parade of Lights that night out on Sarasota Bay.

"After the boats had finished their parade route and had docked near Bayfront Park–right where our boat is parked right now–suddenly, a boat decorated in tens of thousands of lights came out of nowhere and slowly headed toward

shore as everyone watched!"

KT couldn't help herself. She interrupted and asked, "What happened next?"

"That's when it gets even weirder! It turned out no one was even on that boat. Fortunately, the boat was going so slow some guys were able to board it before it collided with anything, *but there was no one on it!*"

Chad asked, "Did they find out whose boat it was?"

"Yes," Prez replied. "it was owned by a mysterious old fisherman everyone called Captain Sarasota. He apparently lived on his fishing boat, the *Ponce de Leon*, out in the Sarasota Bay and Tampa Bay area as long as anyone could remember."

"Unreal," KT said.

"Strange stuff," Chad added. "Wasn't Ponce de Leon the Fountain of Youth guy?"

"He was," Prez answered. "Although many historians wonder if he really was looking for such a fountain at all. I do think he's responsible for naming Florida, but I can't remember any of the details. Anyway, this Captain Sarasota story gets even more bizarre. They looked for Captain Sarasota for months–but they never found a body or anything. After this all happened, no one could even find out Captain Sarasota's real name, his age, any relatives, or *anything*. It turns out he kept to himself all those years he had fished and lived out on the water around here."

"Didn't they find any clues at all?" KT asked.

"They did find some numbers carved on the wooden steering wheel of the *Ponce de Leon*," Prez replied, "but no one ever figured out what significance they had–if any."

Chad asked, "Did the article you read mention what

numbers were carved on the wheel?"

"Sure–487699," Prez answered quickly.

"Strange ... to say the least," KT said. "Prez, did anyone ever come back to the microfilm reader with the Captain Sarasota article on it?" she asked.

"No," Prez replied. "That was a little strange in itself. I was hoping someone would show up so I could talk to him or her about this whole thing."

"I think we've got to dig into this story a little deeper," Chad said eagerly.

"I think so, too," KT agreed. "What do you think, Prez?"

"I was hoping you two would be as intrigued about this as I am. I think this is something we've got to make the time for. Let's put these books away and head back to the boat. We can talk about this some more on the way. By the way, did you two find anything interesting while I was gone?"

"Lots," Chad replied. "Including a love story KT would like to tell you about Sara de Soto ..."

As they were walking down Main Street back to the boat, Chad asked, "Prez, did you find out if it snowed on Christmas here?"

"Not really," Prez answered.

Chad persisted. "What do you mean, not really?"

"Sorry, the Captain Sarasota story has me intrigued to the max. Actually, it almost snowed here on Christmas in 1989–but not quite."

"How close did it get?" KT asked.

"Well, it snowed on the night of December 23 for a few hours, but the snow didn't stay around very long."

"What was it like around here?" Chad inquired.

"Let's just say Floridians don't handle cold and snow like we do in North Dakota. It was in the mid to upper 20's with barely enough snow to make a tiny snowman or a few snowballs, but the cold weather raised havoc around here."

"Like what havoc?" Chad asked, not really quite sure what the word *havoc* meant.

Prez said, "Like power outages and millions of dollars of damage to the citrus trees and other plants. People were freezing, and most didn't have the right clothes to wear to stay warm."

"What was it like around the rest of the country?" KT inquired.

"It was amazing," Prez answered. "The article I read from the Sarasota paper mentioned it was 40 below zero in Bismarck, and a train even froze on the tracks in Minot, North Dakota. Really, almost the whole country was freezing cold. Some places in the South got their first white Christmases in over a 100 years!"

"Just think," Chad observed, "they had all that trouble in Sarasota from temperatures in the twenties above zero. We played football outside with no coats on in North Dakota when it was that cold."

"It's whatever you're used to, Chad," KT said. "Mom says after a few years here, we're going to become wimps in cold weather, too."

"We'll see," Chad said. "Oh–I just thought of something, Prez. What do you think of when I mention the name *Helena*?"

"Why?"

"KT and I found out the first postmaster of Sarasota, a guy by the name of Abbe, almost named the first post office

Helena, but then the Post Office Department in Washington decided on Sarasota instead."

"Interesting," Prez said. "Well, surprisingly, I don't think of *Helena*, the capital of Montana, first. I think of Napoleon Bonaparte, the famous Emperor of France."

"Why's that?" asked Chad.

"Well, after Napoleon lost the famous battle at Waterloo, he was exiled to the island of St. *Helena*, a remote island in the South Atlantic, where he died back in 1821."

"Cool," Chad said. "I wonder if that's where Abbe got the name?"

"I'll write it down, and we can check it out later," KT said. "By the way, I've got a sports question for you two I thought of when I was reading in one of the books about Sarasota's history. I'll even give you each 50 cents if either of you can answer it."

"Bring it on, KT," Chad said confidently.

"All right. What sport was played right here in Sarasota before it was played anywhere else in Florida and maybe anywhere else in the whole country?"

After a few seconds, Chad said, "I don't have a clue on this one, but I'll guess baseball."

"Good guess, but that's not right," KT said.

Prez said, "With a golf course every few blocks in Sarasota, I'm going to guess golf."

"You're right, Prez!" KT exclaimed, trying to sound like a game show hostess.

"Interesting," Chad said. "Did you two know the letters in golf stand for *gentlemen only ladies forbidden*?"

"Cool acronym," Prez remarked. "I heard the Scots didn't allow ladies to play golf hundreds of years ago when it got started, but now we even have ladies playing on the PGA Tour with the men once in awhile. You ladies sure have come a long way, KT."

"Maybe it's time to come up with a new acronym then," KT said. "But I'll bet it would *really* be hard to change the name of a sport."

"That's for sure," Chad agreed. "So, Prez, what do you think we should do first to explore this whole Captain Sarasota thing?"

"I think we might want to talk to a famous Sarasotan who they say knows pretty much everyone and everything that goes on around here. Maybe he can help us out."

"Who's that?" KT asked.

"I'll give you a few hints," Prez said. "He's a sports fanatic like us. He's on ESPN Radio and TV all the time. He has tons of enthusiasm and a super-loud voice. He likes kids, and he lives on Siesta Key."

"Dickie V!" Chad exclaimed, trying his best to do an impression of Dickie V's voice.

5

At 7:15 the next morning, KT, Chad, and Prez listened to *The Mike and Mike Show* on ESPN Radio. At that time, Dickie V was doing his usual phone-in radio interview on the program, calling from his home on Siesta Key. As he often did whenever he was in town, Dickie V mentioned on the air he was going to The Broken Egg restaurant for breakfast right after he got off the phone.

As soon as the ESPN interview was over, the three eager teens got on their bikes and rode to the restaurant, just four blocks from where they lived. Chad was toting his small backpack with a Dickie V bobblehead and a magic marker inside.

While they were riding down Avenida Messina, side by side, Prez glanced over to KT and Chad and said, "Our best chance for a conversation with Dickie V might be to catch him before he gets into The Broken Egg. When KT asks him to autograph the bobblehead, that might be the best time to talk to him."

"Why me?" KT asked.

Prez explained, "Dickie V likes young people, and you'll probably remind him of his own daughters when they were younger. Besides, you're by far the cutest of us three."

"Speak for yourself," Chad said with a giggle.

"Please, KT?" Prez asked kindly.

"Now that you're asking me politely, I guess I'll do it," KT replied.

When they got to The Broken Egg, they parked their bikes near the front of the restaurant and started looking for a car driving up with Dickie V inside. They didn't have to wait long. In less than three minutes Prez spotted Dickie V's familiar bald head, as a new, dark blue convertible turned the corner and approached The Broken Egg. Since there were no parking spots left directly in front of the restaurant, Dickie V drove half a block further down the street to a public parking lot.

KT, Chad, and Prez took off running after him. As they got within 20 yards of Dickie V's car, they slowed down, trying not to look so obviously eager.

They watched as he got out of his car. Then they approached him. KT was leading the way with the bobblehead in one hand and the marker in the other. Prez and Chad were following close behind.

When Dickie V spotted the three of them coming toward him, with KT holding the bobblehead, he smiled and said in his booming voice, "Awesome, baby! Dipsy do dunkaroo! Heck, don't you kids think I'm better looking than my bobblehead doll?"

KT, Chad, and Prez giggled. They'd heard Dickie V speak in his own unique way many times before on radio and television, but actually seeing and hearing him in person was an incredible experience!

As KT held the bobblehead and marker toward him, ready to ask for his autograph, Dickie V asked, "Do you three have time for breakfast? I'll buy even–then we can have a good chance to autograph my bobblehead and have a prime time talk! If you like a great breakfast, The Broken Egg is the *creme de la creme*! Heck, it's flat out fantastic–with a capital F!"

"Sure, that would be great," KT said, speaking for the three of them.

As they were walking toward the entrance to the restaurant, Dickie V asked, "So, are you three kids in beautiful Sarasota for a prime time vacation?"

"No," KT replied, "all three of us recently moved to Sarasota. By the way, I'm Katy, but these two guys call me KT. Their names are Chad and Prez."

There was no time to talk any further, as Dickie V got to the door of the restaurant and held it open for the three teens to enter.

The first thing KT, Chad, and Prez saw when they got into The Broken Egg, right by the door, was a plethora of Dickie V stuff on display for sale including Dickie V bobbleheads, Dickie V mini-basketballs, Dickie V posters and pictures, books by Dickie V, and T-shirts and hats with Dickie V's likeness on them. There was even Dickie V salsa and Dickie V shampoo!

KT laughed out loud when she picked up a bottle of Dickie V shampoo with his big bald head pictured on the bottle. "Give me a break! I can dream, KT!" Dickie V said with a booming laugh.

As they walked further into The Broken Egg, it turned out to be even better than they'd anticipated. It was a friendly, noisy place, with the great smells of hot pancakes, sausage, eggs, bacon, fresh baked goods, and other pleasant

food smells.

Once people realized Dickie V was in the restaurant, things got even noisier. You could tell he knew everybody, and everybody liked him a lot.

A nice, pretty, young lady wearing a name tag that said *Betty Boop* came over, gave Dickie V a kiss on the cheek, and said, "Looks like you've got some friends with you today, Dickie V."

Bob, the owner, came over and joined them. Dickie V said, "I've got three awesome new friends with me who I just met out front! They all just moved here to Sarasota–KT, Chad, and Prez!"

Bob smiled, then he got an inquisitive look on his face. "Prez?" he said.

"It's a name I got in second grade because I've wanted to be President of the United States since then," Prez explained. Prez looked at Betty Boop, "I'm really curious how you got the name Betty Boop."

Betty Boop smiled. "Oh, one of my customers thought I had the look and other qualities of Betty Boop, the famous cartoon character. He started calling me *Betty Boop*–and it caught on. Now, follow me. I always save Dickie V's table for him whenever he's in town."

When they sat down at their table, KT sat next to Dickie V. Chad and Prez sat across from them, with Chad facing Dickie V and Prez facing KT.

Betty Boop handed them each a large, egg-shaped menu with a crack down the middle, and she said, "I'll be back in a jiffy to take your orders. Don't forget to look at our specials on the board over there." Betty Boop pointed to a big marker board on the wall near the entrance to the kitchen.

Dickie V opened his menu, and said, "Take a look at all the great things on the menu. If you have any questions, I can probably help–heck, I've eaten practically everything on this menu!"

KT, Chad, and Prez opened their menus and were surprised to see all the new items they'd never seen on a menu before.

"Coconut pancakes," KT noted. "You'll never see that on a menu in Fergus Falls, Minnesota."

"Are you from Minnesota?" Dickie V asked.

"Yes," KT replied.

"Minnesota!" Dickie V boomed. "Bob, who you just met, went to the University of Minnesota for awhile! In fact, he's still a fan of Gopher hockey and football!"

Chad said, "The All-American center on the University of Minnesota football team, Greg Eslinger, is from Bismarck, North Dakota. Prez and I both went to the same elementary school as Greg."

"That Eslinger is a PT prime time football player!" Dickie V said. He was quiet for a few seconds. "North Dakota? ... I don't know a lot of people from North Dakota ... Is Phil Jackson, the former coach of the Lakers, from North Dakota?"

"He sure is," Chad replied. "Yankee Roger Maris was from North Dakota, too. I'll bet you know Darin Erstad from the Angels and the basketball coach from the University of Arizona, Lute Olson. They're also from North Dakota."

"I sure do!" Dickie V said. "I'll tell you this for sure, Chad! It's flat out too cold up in North Dakota for me! ... Hey, maybe we should think about ordering. What are you three thinking about?"

Chad said, "There's even a Dickie V burger on the menu–ground turkey with lettuce, tomato, and mustard on an onion bagel. That sounds perfect to me, but it's on the lunch menu."

"Don't worry, Chad," Dickie V said, "I know the cook. What sounds good to you, KT?"

"Banana nut bread French toast," KT replied.

"How about you, Prez?" Dickie V asked.

"The Siesta Key omelette has crab, Swiss cheese, and tomato. That sounds great."

KT asked, "What are you having, Dickie V?"

"I think I'm going with the Siesta Key omelette today, too."

After Betty Boop had gotten their orders, Dickie V asked, "Where do you all live in Sarasota?"

KT answered, "All three of us live on the north end of Siesta Key Beach on Beach Road."

Dickie V said, "That would be near the Old Fishing Pier and Sunset Beach, right?"

"I guess we didn't even know what you Sarasotans called it, but that's exactly where we live," Chad replied.

"Yeah, the local newspaper even called your part of the beach *Doggy Beach* for awhile because many of the people who lived on the key used to walk their dogs in that area," Dickie V added.

Chad sensed it might be a great time to ask Dickie V the question they'd come to The Broken Egg to ask in the first place. Chad almost whispered, "Dickie V, Prez was doing some reading in the library yesterday about Captain Sarasota who lived on his boat out in the bay. Did you ever meet him?"

Dickie V looked a little stunned. He was quiet for several seconds, and by the time he spoke, his voice had dropped in volume big-time. He spoke so only the three teens could hear him. "That whole Captain Sarasota thing is flat out mind-boggling! Anyway, word has it I was probably one of only a few people around here to ever even talk to Captain Sarasota much ... One day about a year before he disappeared, I got a note in the mail from him saying he would like to take me fishing. If I wanted to go, he'd be waiting in his boat at Marina Jack's at 7:00 A.M. that Saturday. The note said he would wait for only 15 minutes, and then he'd leave if I didn't show up.

"Well, I couldn't resist. Captain Sarasota had been a legend in the Sarasota area for years, yet no one seemed to know much of anything about him, so I showed up before 7:00 that morning, and Captain Sarasota was waiting there, just as he said he would be."

Dickie V already had KT, Chad, and Prez at the edge of their seats. KT couldn't keep her mouth closed any longer. "What was he like? What did he say?"

"He was as kind as all the rumors I'd heard over the years. He did very little talking on our excursion, though–I did most of the talking, I guess."

"I can't imagine *that*," Chad said, and everyone, including Dickie V, laughed.

Prez asked, "Do you remember anything Captain Sarasota said?"

"Keep in mind, it's been a long time since this happened, but I remember he asked quite a few questions about sports. I'm sure that's one of the main reasons he asked me to go fishing with him in the first place. He seemed to have a fascination with sports, and he knew that's a huge part of my life."

"Do you remember what sports he was most interested in?" Chad asked.

"Football, without question. He had a big-time interest in football–Tampa Bay Buccaneers football along with Sarasota Sailors high school football especially, I think. Those seemed to be his favorite teams."

With his huge fascination with names, Chad couldn't help getting off the subject and asking Dickie V, "Do you know how the Buccaneers and Sailors got their nicknames?"

"I've heard two explanations for the Sailors' nickname. The first one says the Sailors got their name 'cause their teams actually used to take a boat to Tampa to play the high school teams there before a bridge was built. The second one says many Sarasota High students used to take boats to high school from Longboat Key, and when the students approached the shore near the school, other students used to say, 'Here come the sailors!'"

"Cool," Chad said.

"As far as the Buccaneers go," Dickie V continued, "a Tampa radio station, WFLA, had a naming contest and Buccaneers won ... probably because one of the biggest festivals around here, the Gasparilla, is named after a pirate named Jose Gaspar, who supposedly dropped anchor in Tampa Bay a long time ago. By the way, it's pretty interesting that out of the hundreds of nicknames suggested for the NFL football team in Tampa Bay that eventually became the Buccaneers, you'll never guess what took second."

"What?" Chad asked.

"*Sailors* actually took second," replied Dickie V.

Betty Boop brought their drinks and left right away, obviously very busy.

KT got back on the subject of Captain Sarasota. "How did Captain Sarasota know so much about football if he spent so much time out on his boat?"

Dickie V said, "I have a feeling he listened to a lot of radio. In fact, he even mentioned hearing me on the radio all the time. I remember seeing some newspapers around on his boat, too, so he obviously kept up with what was going on."

Chad asked, "How old do you think he was?"

"I don't have a clue," Dickie V replied. "Word around here is he may have been 80 or even older when he disappeared–but I can tell you this. He was in fine physical shape for a man of *any* age. That dark, tanned face and wiry, muscular physique made him look like an older movie star. Why, he was even more handsome than me, and he certainly had more hair!"

They all had another good laugh.

"Did he look like anyone we might know?" KT asked.

Dickie V thought about that for a short time. "Now that I think about it, he looked quite a bit like that Ricardo Montalban guy from that old *Fantasy Island* TV show, but that might be too old for you to remember."

"No, it's on cable all the time," Prez said. "Ricardo Montalban also played Khan in several *Star Trek* movies, and he was the grandpa in the *Spy Kids* movies, too."

KT asked, "Dickie V, did Captain Sarasota talk about anything besides sports?"

"Yes, the circus. You probably already know, but The

Ringling Brothers and Barnum & Bailey Circus performers used to spend the winters here, and John and Mable
Ringling did a lot of stuff here in Sarasota. Captain Sarasota
seemed to have a fascination with all that. He even showed
me an old circus program he had from the 1920's."

"Anything else you remember?" Chad inquired.

"This is something I'll never forget. Jokingly, I asked him
if he'd ever discovered any pirate treasure in all his years out
on the water. After I asked him about that, he said something flat out amazing! He just gave me a mischievous smile,
winked, and said, 'Dickie V, hundreds of boats have gone
down in these waters since the 16th century–many of them
loaded down with gems, silver, and gold. More than a tril-
lion dollars in treasure is out there somewhere.' Then
Captain Sarasota changed the subject."

At this point Betty Boop brought their food. She said,
"Dickie V, you've never been this quiet as long as I've known
you. The cooks say they can't even hear you back in the
kitchen like they usually can. Are you all right?"

"I'm having a blast! I'm awesome, baby!"

"That's better," Betty Boop said, as she ran off again.

Everyone started eating their delicious food.

Dickie V said, "Let's exchange cell phone numbers. I'm
going to give you a call if I think of anything more about
what we were just talking about. You can give me a call anytime, too, and let's have breakfast again real soon."

"Only if we can buy next time," Prez said.

"Free breakfast with three great young people! Awesome,
baby! ... Hey, how about a little sports trivia with our breakfast?"

KT, Chad, and Prez each tried to hold back a big grin.

Dickie V had no idea who he was asking sports trivia questions!

"Here's what I'm going to do," Dickie V explained. "I'll give each of you one of my little autographed basketballs if you can answer this trivia question. It's a tough, three-part question, and you have to answer all three parts correctly to win."

"Go ahead," Chad said.

"OK. Part one. Who was the most valuable player in Super Bowl XXXVII, the Bucs first Super Bowl?"

"Dexter Jackson," Chad said calmly, almost before Dickie V had finished asking the question. "I think he went to the Cardinals the next year."

Dickie V was impressed. "Wow! Flat out awesome! Question two. How many interceptions did the Buccaneers have in Super Bowl XXXVII?"

"Five!" Chad said immediately.

Dickie V couldn't believe it. "You're amazing, Chad!" he said. "For the mini-basketballs, who was the Oakland Raiders quarterback who threw those five interceptions back in 2003?"

Prez surprised KT and Chad when he quickly said, "Rich Gannon!"

When KT and Chad gave him a strange look, Prez said, "What? I read it on a place mat at a restaurant here."

They all laughed.

"Did you color the place mat, too?" Chad asked, still giggling.

"As a matter of fact, I did," Prez replied, trying to sound serious.

"You three are flat out amazing!" Dickie V exclaimed.

"Hey, are all kids from Minnesota and North Dakota as smart as you are?"

"Probably not," Prez answered. They all laughed again.

Dickie V was reminded of another story. "By the way, you three ever hear why the Buccaneers took so long to win their first Super Bowl?"

"I heard it was because of pathetic ownership," Chad remarked.

"That sure might have been part of it," Dickie V said. "But I heard another explanation from a sea captain out on Sarasota Bay. Did you ever hear about the buccaneers' curse?"

KT, Chad, and Prez shook their heads, indicating that they hadn't.

"Well, the buccaneers were some really nasty dudes. They'd steal anything and have lots of fun doing it. When they couldn't steal stuff from Spanish treasure ships around here, they took everything they could from the Tocabaga Indians who once lived along the Gulf Coast of Florida. They even took many Tocabagas and sold them as slaves.

"Finally, the Tocabagas' spiritual leaders, I think they called them shamans, put a curse on the buccaneers. It's believed by some that the shamans' curse on the buccaneers carried over to the Buccaneers football team until it was broken the only way it could be broken."

"How's that?" KT asked.

Dickie V explained, "By beating another NFL football team with a pirate-type nickname in the Super Bowl–the Oakland Raiders."

"Do you think anyone ever put a curse on the Arizona Cardinals?" Chad asked, and everyone laughed.

6

When they got done with breakfast, KT, Chad, and Prez got on their bikes and rode back home.

On their way, KT asked, "So, what do you guys think?"

Chad did his best imitation of Dickie V. "Dickie V is awesome, baby!"

KT giggled, and said, "I agree—but actually, I wondered what you think about this whole Captain Sarasota thing."

"Oh," said Chad. "I think this is getting more interesting by the minute."

"I totally agree," Prez said. "It might be a dead end—but there's no way we can pass up a mystery like this."

"What should we do next?" KT asked.

Prez suggested, "How about we stop at home for a bottle of water and then head to Point of Rocks and talk over strategy. I get some of my best thinking done there. Besides, I want to see how Jack Lambert's doing."

"Who's Jack Lambert?" KT inquired.

Prez smiled playfully, and said, "He's a special friend of ours who spends a lot of time near Point of Rocks. You'll like him."

Chad bit his lower lip to keep from laughing. "KT, I have a feeling Jack Lambert is going to become a special friend of yours, too."

"I have a strange feeling about this," KT said with a suspicious grin.

After a brief stop at their homes, the three were soon riding their bikes to Point of Rocks, each with a small backpack.

Point of Rocks was located on the southernmost tip of Siesta Key Beach, over three miles from where they lived on the northernmost tip.

As they rode their bikes along the beach, Chad said, "I wonder who gave Point of Rocks its name?"

Prez observed, "Point of Rocks is one of those place names that makes total sense. Point of Rocks is a *point of rocks*. It's a conspicuous landmark with a common sense name."

"Like The Great Barrier Reef in Australia is really a *great barrier reef*," KT added.

"You are so quick, KT," Prez said.

"Well, thanks, Prez," KT replied with a big smile.

Chad offered, "Is that like–Lake in the Woods in Minnesota is really *a lake in the woods in Minnesota*?"

"I think it's Lake *of* the Woods, but that's a great example," KT said.

Prez thought of another example. "Or like the Little Muddy River in western North Dakota is really a *little muddy river*."

"How about Valley City, North Dakota, is really a *city in the valley in North Dakota*?" Chad suggested.

KT said, "It's too bad all place names couldn't make such good sense ... I wonder if there's really clear water in

Clearwater, Florida?"

"I certainly hope so," Prez said, with a giggle.

Chad noted, "When we were in the library, I noticed a town in Florida named *Needhelp*. I wonder if the people there really do need help?"

They all laughed,

Chad said, "Prez, remember when that visitor to our classroom in sixth grade told us about Enderlin, North Dakota, being the end of the railroad line? *End of the line* became *Enderlin*."

"Impressive memory, Chad," said Prez.

"I know," Chad said with a grin.

When they got to Point of Rocks, they parked their bikes next to a catamaran and put their backpacks down on the boat's deck. Chad got a small, deflated beach ball out of his backpack and started blowing air into it as they walked toward the water.

"I sure hope Jack Lambert's around today," Prez said.

KT followed them a little hesitantly.

The three walked on the sea wall near shore, then they stepped off the wall and onto one of the huge, flat rocks that formed the Point of Rocks. After that, they stepped off the rock into knee-deep water.

Prez started splashing and yelling, "Jack Lambert! Come here, Jack Lambert!"

Chad threw the beach ball as far out in the water as he could.

Less than 30 seconds later, a beautiful bottlenose dolphin came to the surface about a 100 yards out in the water from where they were standing and did some spectacular jumps into the air and back into the ocean!

"Wow! That's Jack Lambert, I'll bet!" KT exclaimed.

"Sure is!" Prez replied.

"How did you ever find *him*?" KT inquired.

"Actually, I think he's the one who found us," said Prez. "Chad and I were scouting around here shortly after we moved to Sarasota, and Jack Lambert was swimming in the area. The next time we came here, he showed up again, and we started talking to him."

"I'll bet you talked about sports," KT said with a smile.

"We talked about lots of things," Chad said. "Prez even talked politics. I think Jack Lambert understood what we were saying, too. When he got to know us and trust us, he even started putting on some pretty amazing swimming and jumping shows for us. I've seen some great dolphins in movies and at Sea World, but Jack Lambert is smarter and more talented than any of them–by far. He's like the Olympic champion of all the dolphins!"

"Why did you give him the name Jack Lambert?" KT asked.

Prez explained, "When he gets close enough, you'll notice an L-shaped scar on his dorsal fin. As soon as Chad and I saw that, we thought of the toughest Steelers football player *ever*–Jack Lambert, so we started calling him that."

"He seems to like the name," Chad added, "but then who wouldn't like to be named after the greatest football player in history?"

KT asked, "Do you guys work sports into everything?"

"We try," Chad replied, with a giggle.

Suddenly, Jack Lambert popped out of the water where Chad had thrown the beach ball–with the ball balanced on the end of his beak! With a quick flick of his head, he

smacked the ball through the air, where it landed in the water–right in front of KT! Jack Lambert stuck his head out of the water and started making some happy dolphin sounds.

"I think he likes you, KT," Chad said. "Throw the ball back to him."

KT threw the beach ball as far out toward Jack Lambert as she could, and the amazing dolphin rose out of the water and caught the ball with his flippers! Then, he released the ball and smacked it back to KT with his tail!

"Oh, my gosh!" KT exclaimed. "I've never seen anything like that!"

Jack Lambert swam within 10 yards of the three teens. Then he stuck his head out of the water, took a good look, and started making more happy dolphin sounds.

"Watch this!" Chad said loudly.

Chad reached into his pocket and pulled out a nickel. He threw it as far out in the water as he could. Jack Lambert disappeared for a few seconds, then, suddenly, his head popped out of the water with the nickel in his mouth! With a quick motion of his head, Jack Lambert flipped the nickel into the air, and it landed in the water in front of KT's feet!

"It's your turn, KT!" Chad said. "Throw it to him!"

KT picked the nickel up and threw it as far out into the water as she could. This time Jack Lambert disappeared for a lot longer than before.

When he finally appeared, he had a much larger object in his mouth, and he flicked it over near KT's feet. KT picked it up, and she got a huge surprise!

"It's a Sakakawea dollar coin!" KT exclaimed. She showed it to Chad and Prez.

"Unbelievable!" Chad said. "Why don't you throw that in and see what he brings back *next*. Maybe a gold necklace or something!"

"I'm not going to get greedy," KT said. "Thanks, Jack Lambert!"

Jack Lambert stuck his head out of the water and made lots of happy dolphin sounds before he swam out into the Gulf.

As the three teens were walking back to the catamaran, they turned around and yelled, "Bye, Jack Lambert!" The dolphin performed a few spectacular jumps as he swam further out into the Gulf of Mexico.

Chad reached his hand out toward KT. "Let me see that coin again, KT."

KT handed the coin to Chad. After examining it briefly, Chad said, "Do you say *Sacagawea*, *Sakakawea*, or *Sakajawea*?"

"It's a language thing," Prez explained. " They're all correct, really. When you find out Sakakawea was Shoshone, but she lived with the Hidatsu for many years, and she was married to a Frenchman–and she also helped Americans named Lewis and Clark–you know there are going to be some spelling and pronunciation problems after 200 years."

"That's for sure," Chad said. "Is it really true there are more statues of Sakakawea in America than any other woman?"

"It sure is," Prez replied.

KT asked, "Prez, how many dolphins are around Sarasota?"

"My mom says there are about 130 who hang around Sarasota all year," said Prez. "The people at Mote Marine have been studying them since the 1970's."

"Does your mom know anything about Jack Lambert?" KT asked.

"I haven't mentioned Jack Lambert to her yet–she's mostly into shark research at Mote, anyway–but Chad and I sort of decided to keep Jack Lambert our own little secret. Now you're part of that secret."

"All right," KT said. "I sure would like to know more about him, though. He must have an interesting history. How do they tell all the dolphins around here apart, anyway?" she asked.

Prez explained, "You know how a lot of the time about all you can see of a dolphin is its dorsal fin popping out of the water?"

"Right," KT replied.

"Well, a dolphin's dorsal fin is a little like a fingerprint. Each dolphin's markings are unique. Researchers take photos of the dorsal fins and assign them names or numbers based on those markings."

When they got to the catamaran, each of them took out the bottle of water in their backpack. After Prez took a swallow, he said, "So, here's how I see it. We've got a big mystery of a disappearing sea captain named Captain Sarasota. We've got the numbers 487699 carved on his boat's steering wheel, and thanks to Dickie V, we at least know a little about Captain Sarasota."

KT noted, "Captain Sarasota liked sports–especially Sarasota Sailors and Tampa Bay Buccaneers football."

"And he liked the Ringling Brothers and Barnum & Bailey Circus," Chad added.

Prez continued, "And he probably listened to the radio

quite a bit when he was out on the boat."

Chad suggested, "Prez, I think it might be time to share everything we know with our friends back in Bismarck. If all our brains put together can't figure out what happened to Captain Sarasota, no one can."

KT said, "Finally, I might get a chance to meet your friends. Tell me a little about each of them."

Prez smiled. "I guess they're all typical teenagers, just like us."

"Like–you're *typical*," KT giggled. "You two don't *talk* like typical teenagers. You don't *act* like typical teenagers. I can only imagine what your friends are like! Now, please tell me a little about each of them."

"We can do that," Chad said. "Let's start with the girls, Prez."

"All right," Prez began. "Jan Jones. We call her *Doc* sometimes because she wants to be a medical doctor someday, and she even carries a medical book around with her a lot. She's super-smart."

"Somehow, I expected that. Sounds like a *typical* teenager to me," KT said with exaggerated sarcasm. "What does she look like?"

Prez said, "You'll see all their faces soon enough. Jan's about your height, I guess, maybe a little shorter, with long brown hair."

Chad continued. "Kari Wise. Tall soccer player and ice skater. She's an amazing organizer. Long brown hair."

Prez spoke next. "Jessie Angel. Her last name applies, or at least she has a guardian angel or something, because Jessie and her mom were driving a car over a bridge near their house south of Bismarck and the bridge collapsed. The car they were in fell down into the river below, but they got out without even a scratch. Everyone thought it was a miracle."

"Unbelievable!" KT exclaimed.

Chad added, "She has very light blonde hair–a lot like yours, KT, and she's artistic and really funny–and a very good competitive swimmer."

Chad said, "Now for the boys. Mike Schafer. He's got straight black hair like mine, only his is a little longer. He's an Elvis impersonator."

"What?" KT asked, with a voice much louder than normal.

Prez and Chad were both laughing. "He looks like a young Elvis Presley and even talks and sings like Elvis," Prez said.

"You're not kidding, are you?" KT asked.

"Sometimes we wish we were," Chad replied with a giggle.

"I can't wait to meet *him*," KT said. "Just another typical teenager."

"Nick Hillman," Chad continued. "Asks tons of questions. NASCAR fanatic. University of Minnesota hockey fan. About my height, with short brown hair. He's very strong–a little gullible, too."

"What do you mean?" KT inquired.

"For now, let's just say he still thinks pro wrestling is real," Prez answered.

"I understand," KT giggled.

Prez said, "Kevin Feeney. Short but tough. He has short, black, straight hair. Kevin wants to be the Nebraska Cornhuskers' quarterback someday. He may be the biggest sports fanatic of all of us."

WHEN IT SNOWS IN SARASOTA

"That's hard to imagine," KT said. "I hope I get a chance to meet all those *average* teen-age friends of yours soon." She giggled.

Prez reached into his backpack, took out his cell phone, and said, "You can meet one of them right now. Let's give Kari a call. She can organize the whole crew in Bismarck, and we can take it from there."

Prez pushed one number, and within a few seconds, Kari's face appeared on the small screen of the cell phone.

"Hey, Kari, this is Prez. I'm here on the beach with a new friend, KT—and Chad. We've got a story you won't believe..."

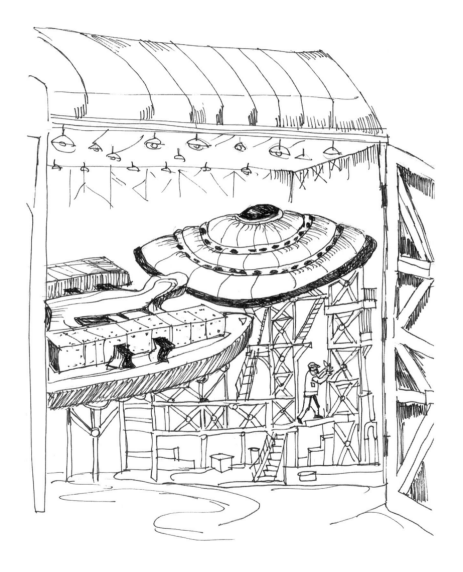

7

The next week involved a massive amount of research activity. The nine teens in Bismarck and Sarasota were on a mission to try to solve the Captain Sarasota mystery. Vast amounts of information were studied and subsequently shared between Florida and North Dakota, mostly via e-mail and cell phone.

On Friday morning, KT, Prez, and Chad rode their bikes six blocks from Sunset Beach to Higel Avenue to a large, four-stall garage Prez and his dad shared and used as their Siesta Key workshop. It was there that Prez and Chad were working on *The Starship Exercise*, the boat they intended to get ready for the Suncoast Offshore Boat Festival.

When they got to the garage, Prez unlocked the front door and flipped three switches to turn on the lights and ceiling fans inside. As soon as KT entered and saw the unfinished boat near the door, she quickly walked right up to it and said, "Wow! That's beautiful! I guess I shouldn't ask anymore, but how could you guys have possibly done all that in the month you've lived here?"

"Actually, we didn't, KT," Prez explained. "My dad had the flying version of *The Starship Exercise* trucked here from North Dakota, and we were able to use much of its structure in building this boat."

Prez and Chad showed KT almost every detail of the 27-foot boat. It was amazing how much it looked like the Starship *Enterprise* from the *Star Trek* movies.

"How many will be able to ride on the boat when it's finished?" KT asked.

"Up to six passengers," Prez replied.

"I sure would like to ride in this with you guys in the parade if there's room," KT said.

Prez smiled. "I think that can be arranged."

Prez looked at the Pittsburgh Steelers helmet clock on the wall and said, "We're going to call the whole group in Bismarck in five minutes. Maybe we should get ready."

On the other side of the large garage, Prez had a huge, wall-sized, plasma screen rigged up for conference calls. Prez pointed out, "Kari has a setup like this in her basement in Bismarck so we'll be able to talk to everyone there and almost feel like they're in the same room, and they'll be able to do the same."

Chad said, "It's almost exactly 11:00. Let's call."

This was especially exciting for KT, since it would be the first time she'd have a chance to see all the faces of Chad and Prez's Bismarck friends. Prez punched a few numbers on a control panel on the TV, and soon, six smiling faces from Bismarck appeared on the screen, sitting on a sofa and the nearby floor in Kari's basement.

"Hi KT, Prez, and Chad!" Kari said.

There were many friendly greetings and all sorts of nonsense exchanged during the next several minutes. It didn't take long for KT to realize what a great time it was to be around this group.

Finally, Prez decided it was time to get a little more serious, and he asked, "So, how's the research work going for everyone back in Bismarck?"

"We were just talking about that," said Kari. "The hardest thing for us is not getting distracted by all the interesting Florida stuff we've been reading about."

"Like what?" Prez inquired.

Kari offered, "Like yesterday, I was reading about the world's smallest police station in Carrabelle, Florida. It was just a phone booth! I don't think it's still being used, but a policeman used to park by it when he wasn't patrolling. College students even tried to steal the whole thing sometimes as a prank."

"I hope the policeman didn't use it as the jail, too," Jessie added, and everyone laughed.

KT, Chad, and Prez could see everyone in Bismarck was holding notebooks or minicomputers, and they were scanning through some of their notes. It looked like they were each looking for something interesting to share.

Nick said, "How about the Bardin Booger, Florida's Bigfoot?"

Everyone laughed just hearing Nick say *Bardin Booger*.

Prez asked, "What's the deal with the Bardin Booger, Nick?"

"Well, Bardin's a town up near Gainesville someplace, and a bunch of people there used to catch the Booger doing stuff like watching TV through someone's window or looking for a tasty snack in someone's refrigerator–harmless stuff like that. He was a pretty friendly Booger. Anyway, about 40 years ago, the Booger disappeared from Bardin."

"And what happened to the Booger, Nick?" Chad asked.

"I could make a joke about Kleenex here, but I won't. They figure he might have moved to a town close by. The legend of the Bardin Booger still lives on, though. A lady named Lena still dresses up like the Booger in Bardin sometimes. They've even got a couple of Booger songs. One's called *The Bardin Booger's Christmas Wish*."

"How touching," Chad said, laughing. "Nothing says Christmas like the Bardin Booger."

"Nick, do you have the lyrics to either of the Booger songs?" Jan asked.

"No, but I'll see if I can get them. Then, maybe Elvis can sing them to us."

In his best Elvis voice, Mike said, "I'll be happy to sing Booger songs whenever the lyrics are made available to me. Thank you. Thank you very much."

KT said, "Mike, this might be a good time to send you my little Elvis surprise."

"Huh?" said Mike.

KT instantly sent a picture via minicomputer that soon appeared on everyone's computer monitor screen. It was Elvis with a bunch of beautiful mermaids in Florida!

"Where did you find *that*?" Mike asked.

"It's from a place about 100 miles north of Sarasota called Weeki Wachee Springs," KT replied. "Elvis visited there in 1961 to watch all the mermaids doing their underwater mermaid shows."

"Do they still have mermaid shows there?" Mike asked.

"I think so," KT answered, "but I'll try to find out for sure."

"Thank you. Thank you very much," Mike said in his Elvis voice.

"Did you know there was once a town in Polk County in Florida called Fargo?" Kevin said. "Turns out some people from Fargo, North Dakota, bought some land in Florida and named their town after their old one. But Fargo, Florida, got confused with nearby Largo, Florida– especially by the people at the post office, so they changed the name to Chubb. It's now called Lake Alfred, but it also had the names Wahneta and Bartown Junction at one time."

"When you hear stuff like that, North Dakota doesn't seem so far from Florida," Jan said.

Chad added, "That's also a good example of a town changing its name several times."

"You've got a town named *Christmas* in Florida, east of Orlando," Mike noted.

"I wonder if it ever snowed on Christmas in Christmas," Nick said. Everyone laughed, except Prez, who was giving Nick's question some serious thought.

"Do you know how it got that name?" Chad asked.

"Sure do," Mike answered. "A fort was built there starting on Christmas Day during the Second Seminole War."

"Speaking of *Seminoles*," said Kari, "Chad's been researching them quite a bit. What have you found out so far, Chad?"

"Too much to share it all right now," Chad said, referring to his notes, "but it's really interesting stuff. Seminoles were Indians who the Spanish called *cimarrones*, meaning *wild ones* or *runaways*. *Cimarrones* eventually became *Seminoles*."

"Why?" Nick asked.

"Sometimes English speaking people tend to mispronounce Spanish words enough times that they end up forming a new word, I guess," Prez explained.

"Oh," Nick said.

"Anyway, the Seminoles weren't native Florida Indians," Chad continued. "They moved into Florida mostly from Alabama and Georgia after the Spanish gave Florida to the British back in 1763."

"Didn't that bother the Florida Indians already living there?" Nick asked.

"Well, they were mostly wiped out by then," Chad replied. "They'd either been killed, died from some disease, or were taken to Cuba as slaves during about 200 years of Spanish rule."

"Sounds like the Spanish weren't nice at all to the Florida Indians," Nick observed.

"That's a huge understatement," said Chad. "Anyway, then the United States got Florida and decided they wanted to kick the Seminoles off their land and force them to move west, into Oklahoma, which was considered back then to be worthless land. Many Seminoles were paid to move to Oklahoma, but a few thousand Seminoles put up a tremendous fight against a huge United States Army from 1817 to 1858. Three Seminole Wars were fought during those years, and you know what?"

"What?" Nick asked.

"The Seminoles never signed a peace treaty, and some of the fighting even took place around Sarasota," said Chad. "For one year, 1840 until 1841, there was even a fort located at Sarasota Bay near Indian Beach called Fort Armistead. An Army captain named Seth Eastman drew some great sketches of the fort while he was stationed there."

"Was it too early for snapshots?" Nick inquired.

Prez said, "Too soon for photos, Nick. A guy with the same last name as Seth–George Eastman, invented the camera in 1888. Edison invented the motion picture in 1891."

"Oh."

"Did you find out why Fort Armistead only lasted for one year?" Jan asked.

"Everyone was getting sick," Chad answered. "Anyhow, Prez will like this. You'll never guess who was head of the First Infantry that was headquartered at Fort Armistead."

"Who?" asked Prez.

"A future President of the United States, Zachary Taylor."

"I had no idea," Prez said. "Zachary Taylor was our twelfth President, and he died after only about a year in office. I think he ate a bunch of bad fruit."

"Killed by fruit?" Jessie said, and everyone laughed.

Kevin asked, "Do you know how many people died in Sarasota during the three Seminole wars?"

"No," Chad replied, "but I'll look into it some more later. Eventually, though, all but 300 Seminoles were forced to move west. The remaining 300 hid in the swamps, and there are about 2,000 of their descendants still living in Florida."

"That's interesting stuff, Chad," Kari said.

"Yeah, Chad," Nick added.

"Thanks, there's a lot more," said Chad, "but I'll save it for another time. There's a great Seminole leader named Osceola I'm reading about right now."

"Osceola–that's the Florida State Seminoles' mascot," Kevin pointed out.

"That's right," Chad said. "I've seen him on his horse during FSU football games tons of times."

Jan asked, "Prez, have you found any Christmas snow days in Sarasota yet?"

"I've been working so hard on this Captain Sarasota number thing the past few days, I haven't had a chance to explore that anymore," Prez answered. "We found out about that 1989 snow on December 23, but that's it so far."

KT hesitated a little, but then she said, "Uh ... when my mom and I were downtown eating yesterday ... we made a little trip to the library, and I couldn't help myself. I tried to find out a little more about snow in Sarasota."

"Cool, KT," Kari said. "Please tell us what you found."

"Well," KT began, "it snowed here in Sarasota in 1977, but it wasn't on Christmas. It was on January 19. Not only did it snow in Sarasota then, but it even snowed in Miami and the Bahamas, two places where it might have never ever snowed in history before."

"Wow!" Prez said. "What else did you find out about that snow event?"

"Quite a bit," KT said. "Women in the luxury hotels on Miami Beach even wore their fur coats to bed because it was so cold there. There was about an inch of snow in Tampa, but not as much in Sarasota. The water got so cold around here that many of the fish died. Some fish stayed alive, but they became stunned by the cold and could be grabbed right out of the water. As you can imagine, citrus and vegetable crops were destroyed. There was lots of ice on the highways around here and tons of traffic accidents."

"What was it like around the rest of the country?" Kevin asked.

KT responded, "In one article I read, they mentioned Minnesota was so cold for such a long time that they were having a home fuel shortage. North Dakota was way below zero. Prez, you might like this. January 19, 1977, just happened to be the same day President Jimmy Carter was inaugurated, and he insisted on walking in his inaugural parade from Pennsylvania Avenue to the White House. It was freezing cold!"

Prez said, "That reminds me of our ninth President, William Henry Harrison. Back in 1841, he was giving his inaugural address outside without a good coat on, and then he decided to give a long speech–over 100 minutes. After that, he got caught in heavy rain during a walk. He ended up getting pneumonia and he died just a month after taking office."

Nick said, "Bad fruit gets one President. Pneumonia gets another. I'm not sure being President is good for your health, Prez."

"Nick, when I become President, I'll hire you to worry about my health," said Prez, giggling. "Uh, KT, did you find anything else about snow down here?"

"A few general Florida snow facts you might like. The largest snowfall in Florida *ever* was four inches."

"Four inches! I've seen pictures of snow drifts higher than the telephone poles during the Blizzard of 1966 in North Dakota," Kevin noted.

Mike added, "Remember that Bismarck High School football game we went to a few years ago, where there were about 10 inches of snow on the ground, and it was still snowing? People were building snow forts on the sidelines."

"Sure do," Chad replied. "Those snow games are the *best* ... Uh–sorry, KT. Did you have any more snow facts?"

"Just a couple more. The earliest in the year it ever

snowed in Florida was on November 28. My mom told me she knows it's snowed as early as August in International Falls, Minnesota. Florida's coldest temperature *ever* is two below zero–by the way, the hottest it's ever been in Florida was 109 ... that's all I've got for now."

"Good stuff, KT," Prez said.

"Yeah, very interesting," Nick added.

Jan said, "I've got a weird high school nickname for you. There's a town not too far from you guys called Tarpon Springs where the high school nickname is *The Spongers.*"

"Where in the heck did that come from?" Mike asked.

Jan explained, "Turns out, a Greek community started around there, and many people made a living by diving for natural sponges from the ocean. Tarpon Springs was once known as the Sponge Capital of the World, in fact."

"Speaking of cool names," Jessie offered. "How about *Tamiami Trail*, the highway from Tampa to Miami? The first three letters from Tampa and the last four from Miami make the word *Tamiami*. They often call it *The Trail* or *41*–short for U.S. Highway 41."

"That's one we needed for the map KT's working on," Prez pointed out. "KT's made a big wall-sized map of the Tampa Bay and Sarasota Bay regions, and she's marked a bunch of the prominent names on there. When we find out how each place got its name, she's going to write the explanation briefly on the map. Who knows, it might even help us solve the Captain Sarasota mystery."

"Great idea, KT," Kari said.

"Thanks. I'll e-mail a reduced copy of the map to Bismarck if you'd like," KT offered.

"Thanks," said Kari. "We can make a wall-sized map for

my basement, too, then."

Kevin said, "I'll bet this is another place name on KT's map. There's a town a little south of you guys called Nokomis. I found out the name came from a poem written by this guy named Longfellow. *Nokomis* is an Ojibway Indian word that means *grandmother*."

KT said, "That *was* one of the names on the map. Thanks, Kevin."

"You're so welcome, KT."

Prez explained, "I've been looking into the name *Florida*, and why Ponce de Leon came up with that name, and it turns out there are some conflicting stories."

"What do you mean?" Nick asked.

"Well, some people think he named his discovery *La Florida* because he saw many flowers on that day, and that's what Florida means in Spanish. But most historians think he was still on his boat on the day he came up with the name, and it's a huge stretch to think he could see any flowers from a boat way out on the water someplace."

"Why do most people think he called it *La Florida*, then?" Nick wanted to know.

"Well, he probably sighted Florida close to Spain's Easter time which they called the Feast of Flowers or *Pascua Florida*," said Prez.

"Cool," Nick said.

"Whatever happened to Ponce de Leon?" asked Mike.

"He was wounded by the Indians south of here in Charlotte Harbor in 1521," Prez replied, "and he died from those wounds in Cuba shortly after that."

"Those Spanish doctors again, I'll bet," Chad said to KT.

"Huh?" Nick asked.

"I'll explain later," said Chad.

Jessie suddenly had an idea. "Hey, speaking of names and everything, I think it would be fun if we come up with a name for our group of Captain Sarasota researchers."

Everyone seemed to be excited about Jessie's idea, and KT felt honored that she would be part of such a great group of friends.

Many suggestions were batted around until Kari said, "How about we take the *Sara* from Sarasota, the *Bis* from Bismarck, the *k* from North Dakota, and the *ota* from Sarasota, Minnesota, and North Dakota–put it all together and get *Sarabiskota!*"

Nick giggled. "Sounds like something you'd eat in our school cafeteria, but I like it!"

"So do I!" Chad agreed.

Everyone was happy with the name.

"That's settled," said Jessie. "We're *Sarabiskota*. If you boys don't mind–KT, Jan, Kari, and I will start working on a possible T-shirt logo, but we promise not to take too much time away from Captain Sarasota research."

"Great!" Prez said. "Speaking of Captain Sarasota, maybe we should get down to business."

Mike began, "As you know, Prez, we've looked at every possible use of numbers we can think of."

Jan added, "So far, we've explored about 20 categories of numbers–from numbers on boats, to football players' numbers, to special dates in Sarasota history, to license plate numbers–no connection to 487699 yet."

Kevin continued, "We've made a special computer program to help us out. We'll solve it eventually–if there's anything to figure out in the first place."

"Fantastic!" Prez said. "Today, KT, Chad, and I are going to focus some more on the numbers and their connection to the circus and to Sarasota High School football and Tampa Bay Buccaneers football. We'll send you any further information we come up with."

Just after five o'clock on Monday morning, while Prez was still in bed dreaming, his watch phone started beeping! Kari was calling from Bismarck!

"What's up? What time is it?" Prez said, dazed, just barely awake.

"It's me, Prez," said Kari excitedly, speaking much more quickly than usual. "I'm sorry–it's really early! Jessie, Jan, and I are having a sleepover at my house, and we think we've hit the jackpot! We were playing around with some of the football information you sent us. It turns out 48, 76, and 99 were the jersey numbers of three top Sarasota Sailors football players in the 1950's–their last names were *Web*, *Middon*, and *Hammer!* We're not sure, but we think Captain Sarasota is leading us to a location not too far from where you live!"

Prez had a rush of adrenaline run through his body, and he was now totally awake, standing on the floor by his bed. "Explain!" he said.

"Well, the spellings are not exactly the same, but a pioneer family named *Webb* came to Sarasota in the 1860's and settled near some *middens* at a place called Spanish Point, not too far south of you."

"I've heard of it," said Prez. "How does the word *ham-*

mer fit in?"

"We haven't figured that out yet," Kari replied. "But we think a trip to Spanish Point might be the key to figuring out that part of the clue."

"You girls are brilliant!" Prez said.

"We know!" they said, giggling.

KT, Chad, and Prez were in the *Rough Rider* shortly after 8:15 in the morning, and Prez launched the boat using his new invention. Everything went smoothly until it got to the part where Prez used the joystick to lower the boat slowly to the surface of the water.

"Oops, sorry," Prez said, as the boat plopped into the water a little rougher than he intended it to. "I guess I must be a little tired."

Despite the less than perfect landing, they were on their way to Spanish Point, anxious to get there before it opened at nine o'clock.

All of Sarabiskota back in Bismarck were in contact with the boat from Kari's basement. They wanted to know what was going on at all times. Along with two-way audio communication, Prez had rigged it so he could send high quality video images back to Bismarck from the boat using the small hand-held video camera Chad was operating.

"Please go slow and give us some shots of the scenery along the way," Kari requested. "Also, let us know where you are so we can follow you on the map KT sent us."

"Aye aye, Kari!" Chad said, as he gave his best naval salute, picked up the camera, and began sending some video of them moving further away from the Old Fishing Pier and heading south toward Spanish Point.

Suddenly, KT spotted their dolphin friend, Jack Lambert, jumping in the water ahead of the boat! "There's Jack Lambert!" KT exclaimed. "Chad, are you getting him on camera?"

"Now I am, KT," Chad said. "Looks like Jack Lambert wants to be our scout on this morning's trip."

"Pretty amazing," Prez said. "It's the first time Jack Lambert's met up with us away from Point of Rocks."

Jessie added, "You guys have your own dolphin escort to Spanish Point. It can't get much better than that!"

Prez pointed out, "It will get even better if we find what we're looking for when we get there ... although I don't have a clue *what* we're even looking for."

"Don't worry, Prez," Kevin said. "You'll know when you find it."

"Hey, Chad," Jan said, as Prez continued to drive the boat south at a moderate speed in the Gulf of Mexico. "Here's another thing we found out during our sleepover last night. Do you know how Siesta Key got its name? Jessie, Kari, and I do."

"Well, no," Chad replied, a little embarrassed he didn't even know how the place he lived got its name. "I'm not really even sure what a *key* is, but I think *siesta* is a Spanish word for *nap*, isn't it?"

"You're right about what *siesta* means, but there's a lot more to how Siesta Key got its name," Jan observed.

"Would you three girls like to enlighten me?" Chad asked.

"Sure," Jan began. "First, you should know the word *key* is an English version of the Spanish word *cayo* meaning small island."

"That makes sense. So, how did Siesta Key get its name?" Chad asked.

"Well, first you should know it was called Clam Island, Little Sarasota Key, and Sarasota Key before it was even called Siesta Key," Kari explained.

"That's cool. Now, who gave it the name Siesta Key?" Chad asked, acting impatient, but he really wasn't.

"It was Harry Higel, a guy who helped develop Siesta Key into a great place to live and also changed its name from Sarasota Key to Siesta Key in 1907–although it didn't really become official until much later," Jessie said.

"Hey, Harry Higel must be the same guy Higel Avenue is named after," Chad noted.

"That's a sure bet," Prez said. "Land developers have a way of naming at least one street after themselves."

"Harry Higel was more than a developer, too," Jan explained.

"What do you mean?" Chad asked.

"He was a mayor of Sarasota three times and did lots of other stuff for Sarasota until he was murdered in 1921," Jan replied.

"What?" Chad said, getting more interested by the moment.

"That's right," Jessie said. "Some people found him by a road on Siesta Key. At first, they didn't know who was lying there, but then they saw his ring with a big *HH* on it. Harry Higel died on the way to the Tampa Hospital."

"Did they ever figure out who did it?" Nick asked.

"Not really," Jessie said. "They thought it was a guy named Rube Allyn. Someone even said they saw Rube hiding near the murder scene about the time it happened, but they were never able to prove it."

"Why would Rube want to kill Harry Higel?" Chad inquired.

"I guess they didn't get along since some old election business," Jessie replied.

"Whatever happened to Rube?" Chad asked.

"He moved to a little town called Ruskin, near Tampa, and he became a hermit," Kari explained.

"What's a hermit?" Nick inquired.

"It's a recluse," Prez answered.

"What's a recluse?" Nick asked.

"The guy basically wanted to live by himself, away from everyone else," KT said.

"Oh," Nick said.

"Prez, maybe we could try to solve the Harry Higel murder," Chad said.

"One thing at a time, Chad," said Prez. "Let's see if we can find out what happened to Captain Sarasota first. Speaking of that, what do you other Sarabiskota know about Spanish Point right now?"

Kevin said, "It's 30 acres of beautiful land right along Little Sarasota Bay."

"How big is an acre?" Nick wanted to know.

"Let me put it this way," Prez began. "Take a football field and remove the end zones. Then remove 10 more yards of the field. You're left with a 90-yard football field with no end zones–that's pretty much an acre."

"Oh," Nick said. "Good explanation, Prez."

"Thanks, Nick," Prez said with smile. "Let's get back to Spanish Point. What else do you all know about it right now?"

Kevin referred to his minicomputer. "Three different groups of people lived there at three different times, starting with the Indians over 4,000 years ago. For some unknown reason, the Indians left about a thousand years ago."

Nick giggled. "Everyone needs a change of scenery after several thousand years."

KT asked, "How do we know the Indians ever lived at Spanish Point?"

Jan said, "That's where the word *middens* comes in."

"*Middens*–that's one of Captain Sarasota's clues," said Nick. "What are they?"

"The Indians had huge mounds of their garbage called middens," Jan explained. "Apparently, there are still several middens at Spanish Point."

"What kind of garbage?" Nick asked.

"No candy bar wrappers, Nick," said Mike. "Mostly the shells and bones left from all the seafood they ate from Little Sarasota Bay."

Kevin continued, "Hundreds of years after the Indians left, the Webb family came to Spanish Point–John, Eliza, and their five children. They were around there starting in 1867."

"That would mean they came there a little after the Civil War was over, right?" Nick guessed.

"Pretty close," Prez said. "The Civil War was officially over on April 9, 1865, when Lee surrendered to Grant."

"When was Lincoln shot?" Nick asked.

"On April 13, 1865," Prez replied.

"Oh, very interesting," Nick said.

"Why did the Webbs come to Florida anyway?" asked

Mike.

Jessie explained, "Partly because Eliza, the mom, had asthma, and her doctor thought she should move to a warmer climate than where they lived in New York. Partly because the Congress of the United States had passed a law called the Congressional Homestead Act of 1862 that gave free land to settlers. Partly because John Webb had read some interesting stuff about the area written by a guy named Robert Gamble, who lived north of Sarasota on the Manatee River."

"And *Webb* was one of Captain Sarasota's clues, too," Nick noted. "What about his third clue, *hammer*?"

"No idea yet," Prez said. "Hopefully, this trip to Spanish Point will put all three of the clues together for us."

"Look in back of the boat everybody!" KT exclaimed. "Chad, get this on camera! Jack Lambert is playing in our boat's wake!"

Chad turned around to capture the scene on camera, and everyone watched with excitement as Jack Lambert did his own version of body surfing on the waves created by the boat.

"Talk about fun! I'd like to join him sometime," Chad said.

"No doubt," KT agreed.

"I'm glad to see he's staying with us so far," said Prez. "I wonder if he'll go all the way to Spanish Point."

"I hope he does," Jan said.

Kari said, "While we're watching Jack Lambert, I want to tell you about the person who came to Spanish Point after the Webbs. She was an amazing lady by the name of Bertha Matilde Honore Palmer."

"How amazing was she?" Chad asked.

"I've been reading about her, and she was *amazingly* amazing," Kari replied. "Just think, her husband had been dead for eight years. She was aleady 61 years of age, and she comes to Sarasota. In just eight years there, she accomplishes tons. She really got Sarasota moving."

KT asked, "What do you mean by that?"

"Well," Kari said, "when Mrs. Palmer came to Sarasota, it was just a little fishing village with only about 900 people living there. After she arrived, she bought about 90,000 acres of land and put hundreds of people to work on it. She studied farming and grew different crops like citrus and vegetables. She bought three large ranches and started a big cattle industry. Because Mrs. Palmer was rich and famous, she got tons of good publicity for Sarasota, and that brought even more people to the area."

"Do you know why Mrs. Palmer came to Spanish Point in the first place?" Mike asked.

"Yes," Kari replied, "after her husband died, she was getting a little tired of her pampered life, living in Chicago in her huge castle with servants and everything. One day, she was reading an ad in the *Chicago Tribune* about Sarasota, and it got her interested. She ended up visiting Sarasota a few weeks later and that was it."

Chad asked, "Did Mrs. Palmer name Spanish Point?"

No one knew.

"We'll ask someone when we get there," Prez said.

"Hey, we're now going past Turtle Beach and Midnight Pass," KT observed. "I read where Turtle Beach got its name from all the turtle nests and little hatching sea turtles around there."

Prez noted, "Midnight Pass was once a way for boats to go from Little Sarasota Bay to the Gulf of Mexico, but it's not really much of a pass anymore because it's been filled in with sand."

"What caused that?" Kevin asked.

"I'm guessing another hurricane or storm, but I'm not sure," Prez said. "Sometimes nature just fills passes in gradually over time."

"How did it get its name?" Chad inquired.

"I thought I read somewhere that some settler in the 1920's saw a hurricane open the pass at about midnight," Kevin answered. "I'll check my notes later to see if I can find it."

A short time later, Prez pointed out, "Casey Key's over there on our left now. Stephen Queen's house is somewhere in that area."

"Do you mean Stephen Queen, the scary movie guy?" Nick asked.

"Actually, Nick, he wrote scary books first, then they were made into scary movies," Mike explained.

"Did you ever see the Stephen Queen movie where that huge deer with the big antlers starts hunting the deer hunters?" asked Nick. "As a deer hunter myself, that totally freaked me out."

"Yeah," Chad said. "I liked the Stephen Queen movie where all of a sudden, everything quit floating all around the world. That *really* freaked me out!"

"Can you get a better close-up of those houses, Chad?" Kari requested.

"I'll do my best," Chad replied.

Chad stood in the boat holding the video camera as steady

as possible while he adjusted the telephoto lens to get a close-up view of one particularly spooky looking house. He zoomed in closer ... closer ... closer ...

"AAAAAAAAAAAAAAH!" A loud scream came from some of Bismarck Sarabiskota and KT!

Chad was startled both by the scream and by what he'd just seen through the video camera's viewfinder. He lost his balance a little and corrected himself, but the breeze created by the moving boat hit his Pittsburgh Steelers cap just right. Chad knew he either had to drop the camera to catch his cap, or hold onto the camera and have his cap blow off and probably go into the water.

He chose to hold onto the camera. Meanwhile, his beloved cap blew off and went into the water. Immediately Chad yelled, "We've got to go back for my Steelers cap!" He pointed to where the cap was floating 30 yards behind the boat, moving further away every second.

Prez glanced back, spotted the cap, and said, "We'll get it." He slowed the boat down and started turning it around.

KT and Prez looked at the cap, still floating on the surface, and Chad pointed the camera toward it. A few seconds later, they got a huge surprise! Jack Lambert suddenly popped out of the water near the cap, picked it up in his mouth, and swam over to the edge of the boat. Then he flipped the cap into the boat near where Chad was standing.

Everyone was amazed at what they'd witnessed, and Chad did his best to capture it all on camera as he thanked Jack Lambert many times! After that, Jack Lambert swam away from the boat–in reverse, seemingly standing on his tail fin, with almost his entire body out of the water. As he did this, he moved his head up and down, making some more happy dolphin sounds.

"Unbelievable!" Kevin exclaimed.

"You've got a great friend there," Kari added.

"Definitely not your average dolphin," Jan said excitedly.

"He's got to be the best, smartest dolphin in the whole world!" Nick said.

Jack Lambert swam toward the front of the boat, putting on a jumping show for everyone.

"What made you all scream back there?" Prez asked.

"Didn't you see it?" Mike asked.

"See *what*?" Prez wanted to know.

Jan replied excitedly, "I'm not sure, but I think Stephen Queen was looking through one of the second story windows with his binoculars–at your boat–at YOU!"

"I saw him, too!" Chad said loudly.

"Me, too!" KT exclaimed. "First, I saw Stephen Queen with his binoculars. Then I think he saw Chad pointing that camera at him, and he moved the binoculars away from his face before he got away from the window."

"I saw him, too," Nick said. "I've seen him before at several Boston Red Sox games on TV. I'd know those thick black-rimmed glasses anywhere!"

"Wow!" Prez exclaimed. "Chad, did you have the camera in record mode? I'd like to see this for myself."

"No, darn it. I didn't."

After their little incident, they continued traveling south in the Gulf of Mexico just off Casey Key. Once in awhile, they'd see Jack Lambert's dorsal fin pop out of the water as he continued to lead them to Spanish Point.

Chad asked, "Does anyone know how Casey Key got its

name?"

"I do, " KT answered. "It's named after a U.S. Army officer who helped survey this area in the late 1840's and 1850's. He was also Commissioner for the Removal of the Seminoles during Seminole War times. Casey must have been a really good guy. I read that the Indians trusted Casey, and he also trusted the Indians."

Kevin asked, "Do you know what happened to him?"

"He died of tuberculosis down here–get this, on Christmas Day in 1856," KT replied.

Prez said, "I don't imagine it snowed that day."

"Sorry, Prez. I don't think so," KT answered.

"What's tuberculosis?" Nick inquired.

Jan explained, "It's an ugly disease, often called TB, caused by a special type of bacteria–called mycobacteria. It usually attacks the lungs, but it can also attack any part of the body."

"That's all I need to know, Doc," Nick said, cringing.

Pretty soon, they entered the inlet to Little Sarasota Bay, and Prez commented, "This is the Venice Inlet–and by the way, an inlet is a narrow water passage–this one's about 100 feet wide, 660 feet long, and about eight feet deep. The rock structures along the edges keep the passage from filling up with sand, and they're called jetties. These are the Venice Jetties."

"I'm finding this all extremely interesting," Nick said.

Chad asked, "Where did the name *Venice* come from?"

Prez explained, "There are lots of Italian place names around here because the area reminded many early residents of Italy, a country many of them had visited. The town of Venice is just south of here."

"Do you know who gave the town Venice its name, Prez?" Chad inquired.

"Yes, it used to be called *Horse and Chaise. Chaise* is a two-horse carriage ... As I was saying, it used to be called Horse and Chaise because there was a clump of trees nearby that looked like a horse and buggy from out on the water. In 1888, Darwin Curry established a post office for the 20 houses in the area back then. Curry wrote *Guava* down on the post office application, but then crossed it out and wrote *Venice*–with fancy penmanship and he even added some quotation marks."

Jessie giggled. "He must have been excited about coming up with a better name than *Guava*."

"What's guava?" Nick asked.

"It's a yellow-skinned fruit–used to make jelly and other things," Prez answered. "They grow guavas down here. I'll e-mail you a picture."

"Thanks," Nick said.

Soon, they were approaching Spanish Point. Jack Lambert was still leading the way.

As soon as they arrived at Spanish Point, they docked the boat near a building called White Cottage. When they got out of the boat, Jack Lambert popped his head out of the water near them.

KT told him, "We'll be right back."

Jack Lambert seemed to understand. He moved his head up and down, made some happy dolphin sounds, then swam further away from the dock.

After that, they walked to the Visitors Center, nearly a mile away. When they got there and walked inside, they were greeted by a friendly, gray-haired lady named Dot, who smiled and said, "I just had a group from Michigan call me and cancel their guided tour of Spanish Point. Are you three interested in a free 90-minute tour?"

"Sure!" was the response from Bismarck over Prez's cell phone before KT, Chad, and Prez could say a word.

"It sounds like you have some friends someplace who are interested in Spanish Point, too," said Dot.

Prez held the cell phone up close to Dot so she could see some of Sarabiskota in Bismarck on the phone's small screen. "Where are you kids from?" Dot asked.

"Bismarck!" they all replied.

"Bismarck, North Dakota?" Dot inquired.

"Yes!" they all responded.

Dot said, "Isn't it cold up there in the winter?"

Sarabiskota laughed because they'd recently talked about the fact that the first thing people think of when *North Dakota* or *Bismarck* is mentioned is COLD. Prez explained to Dot the reason for all the laughter.

"Oh, I wondered what was going on," Dot said. "Now, let's get started. We can talk much more on the tour."

Parked out in front of the Visitors Center was a golf cart-type vehicle, just as wide as a normal golf cart but more than twice the length. There was room for seven passengers on board.

When they got into the vehicle, KT sat in front with Dot, and Chad and Prez got in the seat behind them. As KT held the cell phone with the screen facing Dot, Bismarck Sarabiskota introduced themselves, and then they even introduced KT, Chad, and Prez.

"*Prez?*" Dot repeated, not sure if that was what she'd heard.

Prez explained briefly.

Dot said, "If I'm still on this earth when you run for President, you get my vote, Prez."

"Thanks, Dot," Prez said with a smile.

Before Dot started the vehicle, she talked briefly about the three groups of people who lived at Spanish Point. Then she started the engine and reminded everyone to ask any questions they had during the tour.

They were on their way to their first stop on the narrow, sandy, shell-covered path that meandered throughout Spanish Point. Sarabiskota was thinking about the three words *middens*, *webb*, and *hammer*, and how they might fit together. What would they find when all three clues came together here at Spanish Point–if they ever did? It was beyond exciting!

They drove to the Webb Packing House, built right on the shore of Little Sarasota Bay. Dot explained, "This was where the Webbs washed and sorted the oranges and other citrus fruit they grew here. Then they put it in crates before it was shipped to Key West or Cedar Key."

"Did oranges always grow in Florida?" KT asked.

"Good question," Dot said. "The answer is *no*. The Spanish explorers first brought oranges and other citrus fruit here in the 1500's because they found eating the fruit prevented them from getting a disease called scurvy on their long journeys."

"What's scurvy?" Nick asked.

Dot replied, "It's a disease you get when you don't get enough Vitamin C."

"What happens when you get scurvy?" Nick wanted to know.

"I'm not sure," said Dot.

"I know," Jan said from back in Bismarck. "It's really a disease of the connective tissue, which is found all over the body. You get raised red spots on the skin and around the hair follicles of the legs, arms, and back. Your gums can get weak and spongy–your teeth can loosen–it's not good."

"Thanks, Doc," Dot said. "It's good to have a doctor on the phone."

On the way to the next stop, Dot told them the Webbs actually operated a winter resort at Spanish Point, where northerners could come to enjoy the beautiful bay and the

nice climate. It was Sarasota's first winter resort.

After that, they stopped at Mary's Chapel, named for Mary Sherrill, a young lady who came to the winter resort at Spanish Point in 1892. Dot explained that Mary had tuberculosis, and her mother thought the warm rays of the sun might help her get better.

Dot added, "Mary loved walking the paths here at Spanish Point ... going down to the water's edge and looking at the beautiful bay. But, sadly, five weeks after she came here, she died. Because she loved the place so much, Mary's parents and friends planned to have a memorial chapel built here in her honor."

They walked up the steps and entered the beautiful little church.

"Many people helped with Mary's Chapel," Dot continued. "Will Webb did the actual building. By the way, the cost for materials back then was $441."

"Wow, you can't buy a little metal shed for that much anymore," Chad noted.

"That's for sure," said Dot. "Mary's church group back in Louisville sent two stained glass windows here and four more were donated by friends and classmates. The circular window in front there came from Mary's mom.

"On September 25, 1895, a bell arrived from Mary's classmates. On that very same day, a Webb baby was born. Mrs. Sherrill wanted the baby to be called Mary Bell, but she was eventually named May Belle. Unfortunately, as May Belle grew up, some other kids started calling her May *Belly*–which I know none of you would have done, so she insisted on being called Mabel after that. Would you believe–Mabel was eventually married in this church, and the bell that arrived on the day she was born rang out from the belfry."

Dot then rang the same bell that had rung on Mabel's wedding day. Everyone loved the story of Mary Sherrill and Mabel.

While KT, Chad, and Prez had been touring Mary's Chapel, Stephen Queen docked his 32-foot boat, named *Mayhem in Paradise*, near the *Rough Rider*. He boarded the *Rough Rider* and hid two small listening devices, each smaller than a kernel of corn, under the seats in the back of the boat. When he was done, he quickly got off the *Rough Rider* and boarded his own boat.

Jack Lambert watched, sensing danger for his friends. He took action! After Stephen Queen had pushed his boat away from the dock, Jack Lambert swam in a large circle, picking up tremendous speed! Then he jumped high into the air over Stephen Queen's entire boat—over Stephen Queen himself, too—just barely clearing the man's head! Stephen Queen was so astonished, he lost his balance and fell into the water. His thick black-rimmed sunglasses slowly sank to the bottom of the bay. Stephen Queen swam back to his boat, boarded it, and took off as fast as he could!

On the way to their next stop, KT asked, "Did it ever snow while the Webbs lived here?"

"It's incredible you would ask that, KT," Dot replied. "That's an interesting story. On Christmas Day–"

"It snowed here on Christmas Day?" Prez interrupted, something he would rarely do.

"Not quite, Prez," Dot said. "As I was saying, on

Christmas Day in 1868, the temperatures dipped below freezing for two days, but I don't think it snowed. It was very rare for it to freeze here and awful for the Webbs since they raised a lot of crops. Many tropical trees and mangroves were killed, and the Webb's rice crop was destroyed. Luckily, the citrus trees loaded with fruit were saved because they were close to the warmer water of Little Sarasota Bay. They were also able to get some syrup out of their frozen sugar cane stalks."

"What are mangroves?" Nick asked.

"Those large shrubs around here close to the water with dark green and shiny leaves are mangroves," Dot answered. "There are red, black, and white mangroves here at Spanish Point, and I'll point them out to you. Much of the coastland here is nothing more than skeletons of millions of dead sea life that have been trapped by the stilt-like roots of the mangroves. Some people even call this the *Mangrove Coast*."

Chad asked, "So, how did Spanish Point get its name anyway?"

Dot explained, "When the Webb family came to Florida, they spent some time in Key West, and a Spanish trader they met there recommended this place to them. They included the name *Spanish* to honor him. The *point* part comes from the fact that the land extends noticeably into Little Sarasota Bay, like a point."

Next, Dot talked about Mrs. Palmer and showed them some of the wonderful things she did at Spanish Point. Mrs. Palmer had created many beautiful gardens all over Spanish Point, and she had even built an incredible aqueduct to carry water throughout one of her largest gardens.

After that, they took a tour of White Cottage, Sarasota

County's oldest house, which they learned was first used as a dormitory for the Webb Winter Resort and later as a guest house for Mrs. Palmer. As they were walking through the house, KT asked, "Dot, what impressed you the most about Mrs. Palmer?"

"Let's see, that's a tough question," Dot replied. "I guess I'm impressed so much that such a rich lady, considered one of the most elegant women in America, could become so enthusiastic with such a different life she loved so much here in Sarasota–a life of ranches, and cattle, and crops."

"How rich was she?" Prez inquired.

"Very rich. Let me show you a picture of her home in Chicago called *The Castle* when we get back to the Visitors Center. Its main tower was 80 feet tall. Prez, guess who her first prominent guests were to that home?"

"Who?" Prez asked.

"President and Mrs. U.S. Grant," Dot replied.

Prez was impressed!

Dot challenged Prez. "I wonder if you can tell me two interesting things about President Grant I might not already know, Prez."

"Let's see," Prez thought for awhile. "First one ... Grant was a big hero of the Civil War, yet he was so afraid of the sight of animal blood that he always ordered his steaks almost burned. Second one ... he smoked about 20 cigars a day, and he eventually got throat cancer, in fact."

"You're very smart, Prez," Dot said.

"Thanks, Dot," Prez replied. "You're a bright and amazing person yourself."

"Well ... thanks," Dot said with a huge smile, blushing a little.

When they were on their way again, another question came to Chad. "This is called Spanish Point, right?"

"Very good, Chad," Dot replied, smiling.

"But it's located in the town of Osprey, Florida, right?" Chad inquired.

"That's right," said Dot.

"Dot, why didn't the people who settled around here call their town Spanish Point?" Chad asked.

Dot smiled and said, "That's a great question, Chad, and you're the first person in my 15 years here to ask it. In 1881, Spanish Point was renamed Osprey–after the bird that's around here–because only one word was allowed on the post office application. John Webb was the first postmaster, and he's the one who picked Osprey as the name."

"Do you mean there was a post office right here at Spanish Point?" Chad asked excitedly.

"Yes," Dot replied, "it was located at the house the Webbs built on top of a shell midden when they settled here. We're headed there next."

When they heard the words *Webbs* and *midden* mentioned in the same sentence, Sarabiskota knew they were getting close to whatever Captain Sarasota was leading them to! Now, if they could only figure out how the word *hammer* fit in!

In a few minutes, they were at the site of the Webb house, on top of a shell midden, with a beautiful view of the bay. Although the Webb house was no longer there, a large wooden viewing platform was built at the site of the house.

As they stood there, taking in the fantastic view, Dot said, "This is a special place. Not only is it the high point around here geographically, about 18 feet, but it's also a unique location that represents all three groups of inhabitants of Spanish Point–the Indians, the Webbs, and Mrs. Potter Palmer. The shell midden was left by the Indians, the Webbs built their house here, and Mrs. Palmer later used the Webb House as a tea house, which she called Webb's Tavern–Oh! Look at that!"

"It's Jack Lambert!" KT exclaimed.

Out on the bay, less than 40 yards from where they were standing, Jack Lambert was swimming in circles, doing some spectacular jumps!

"Jack *who*?" Dot asked.

"It's our dolphin friend–Jack Lambert," KT said. "He led us all the way to Spanish Point this morning."

Dot said, "I've watched our dolphins in this area for a long time. I don't think he's one of our regulars. None of them jump like that! When did you start seeing *him*?"

"Shortly after we moved here a month ago," replied Prez.

"Just when I thought I'd seen everything!" Dot exclaimed.

Just then, Jack Lambert swam to the bottom and came up to the surface, holding the pair of sunglasses that had been worn by Stephen Queen.

"Another gift from Jack Lambert," Chad said.

"We'll be back in a little while!" KT yelled to Jack Lambert.

Jack Lambert made some dolphin sounds as if he totally understood KT. Then he swam further out into the bay.

"Unreal," said Dot. "There's nothing like a little halftime entertainment ... Follow me. I think you're going to like what you see next, too!"

How right she was!

From the top of the midden, they descended the slope on a shell-covered path, then went even further down to the base of the midden on some wooden steps built into the path. Just a few yards from there was a special building, built right into the side of the midden, called "Windows to the Past."

Before they entered the building, Dot explained, "A guy named Herman Spang had a winter cottage here in the early 1900's, and he dug a pit into the midden. Later, another guy parked his Model A in the pit. In the 1960's archaeologists carefully excavated the site so they could find out exactly what the Indians left in this midden. Now, a wonderful, air-conditioned building we're about to enter has been built into the pit to show you what the archaeologists did here and what they found."

When they entered the building, the first thing they noticed was one wall was totally glass so viewers could clearly see the layers of shell, bones, and other materials that formed this huge midden. Also inside the building were several exhibits, and Prez was drawn toward one in particular called "Everyday Objects Then and Now." It was designed to demonstrate how the Indians could use shells to make useful tools and items that worked like a knife, a bowl, a fishing net, and—a HAMMER!

When Prez spotted this, he excitedly pushed the button labeled with a picture of a modern-day hammer! When he did, a small compartment in the display case on the wall above him lit up, revealing a tool the Indians used as *their* hammer, thousands of years ago. It consisted of a shell hammerhead and a wooden handle, fastened together with leather straps.

Prez's heart started beating wildly when he noticed a small number on the hammer's wooden handle–19!

"KT and Chad! Come here!" he whispered excitedly.

10

Trying to figure out Captain Sarasota's 19 clue turned out to be a tough challenge for Sarabiskota. Plenty of Tampa Bay Bucs and Sarasota High School Sailors football players had worn the number 19, but trying to associate the players' names with any location in the area led nowhere. Attempts to find a possible connection to the Ringling Circus or anything else also proved fruitless.

Several days passed with no luck. KT, Chad, and Prez stood down by the beach in front of KT's house watching a beautiful sunset. KT said, "Watching the sun go down into the ocean never gets old, does it?"

"It sure doesn't," Prez replied.

"Watching a sunset from Sunset Beach. I like the sound of that," Chad said with a giggle.

When the sun had set completely, Prez said, "Chad, when you think of the number 19 in sports, who do you think of first?"

"Johnny Unitas, of course," Chad answered. "He was unbelievable! Just think, over 40,000 total yards gained passing and running in his career. That's way over seven miles! And that record he has of touchdown passes in 47 consecutive games will probably never be broken!"

"If Captain Sarasota was a huge sports fan, he would have known about Johnny Unitas, right?" Prez asked.

"Without a doubt," Chad replied. "Why?"

"Maybe that's what we need to pursue next," Prez suggested. "Maybe Johnny Unitas had some connection to Sarasota we don't know about."

"It's worth looking into," KT said. "Why don't we call Dickie V and see what he knows."

"Good idea, KT," Prez said. "I'll call him now."

Prez pulled his cell phone out of his pocket and pushed a single button. Seconds later, he said, "Hi, Dickie V. This is Prez. How are you doing?"

"Awesome, Prez! What's going on?"

"KT, Chad, and I were just watching the sunset here on Sunset Beach and we were talking about sports. We have a question for you."

"Flat out awesome! Fire away, Prez!"

"Do you know if Johnny Unitas ever lived in Sarasota or visited here?"

"Johnny U! Some say he was the greatest quarterback of all time! He was awesome, Prez! I know he never lived here, but he did come to town once in awhile to visit friends. I even walked part of Siesta Key Beach with him once. I tell you who might be able to answer more of your questions about Johnny U–and he lives right here in Sarasota!"

"Who's that?"

"NFL Hall of Famer, Otto Graham, former quarterback of the Cleveland Browns! He's getting up in age, but he's as sharp as a tack! If you'd like, I can set you up with a meeting with him tomorrow."

"Where does he live?"

"Right on Forest Lakes Golf Course, not too far east of Siesta Key. I'd love to go along with you, but I have to fly to New York tomorrow."

"That's OK. It would be fabulous if you could set up that meeting, though."

"What time would work for you?"

"Anytime that's convenient for Mr. Graham."

"All right! I'll call you back in a few minutes—oh, are KT and Chad there, too? I'd like to say hi ..."

The next morning, shortly after nine, KT, Chad, and Prez biked to Forest Lakes Golf Course. Sarabiskota in Bismarck was listening in all the time via Prez's cell phone, as they talked about the football career of Otto Graham on the way.

"Chad, I've got to admit I never even heard of Otto Graham before," Prez said.

"Me, either," KT said.

"I knew he was a great quarterback for the Browns a long time ago," Chad explained, "but Kevin and I did some research on the Internet last night. He was really amazing!"

"What did you find out?" KT asked.

"Let's just say he was as good as they get," Chad began, "but he played before TV games and ESPN and all that—in the late 40's and early 50's, so much of his greatness has been forgotten."

"Give us some highlights," Prez requested.

"This was the most amazing thing," Chad said. "Otto Graham was in 10 championship games in 10 years for the Cleveland Browns between 1946 and 1955. No NFL quarterback has even gotten close—not even Terry Bradshaw of the Pittsburgh Steelers."

"That *is* unbelievable," KT said.

Kevin's voice came over Prez's cell phone. "Four of those championship games were in an old professional football league called the All-American Football Conference, or AAFC, and six were in the NFL. Otto Graham won seven titles in those years! Terry Bradshaw had *four* Super Bowl wins in *14* seasons."

"Wow!" Prez said.

When they got to Otto Graham's house, Mr. Graham was standing outside. He had a big, friendly smile on his face. "You must be KT, Prez, and Chad," he said. "Dickie V told me you have some questions for me. Come right on in."

They walked to his den, which was loaded with things like trophies, pictures, autographed footballs, and even a replica of his NFL Hall of Fame bust which was sitting on a mantel. KT, Prez, and Chad were in complete amazement!

After Otto Graham had explained some of his pictures and trophies, Chad said, "You were an incredible athlete!"

"Well, thanks," Otto Graham said, smiling. "Do you want to ask some of those questions you have while you're looking around some more?"

Prez explained, "Mr. Graham, we have some friends back in Bismarck who are on my cell phone right now." Prez held it up and showed Mr. Graham. "Do you mind if they watch and listen?"

"Bismarck, the capital of North Dakota?" Otto asked.

"Yes," Prez replied.

"No, I don't mind at all. Hi, Bismarck!"

"Hi!" was the reply from Sarabiskota in Bismarck.

"What would you say was your best pro game ever, Mr. Graham?" Prez asked.

"Please call me Otto ... Well, during the NFL Championship Game in 1954, we beat the Detroit Lions 56 to 10, and I ran for three touchdowns and passed for three. Is that pretty good?"

"That's incredible!" Prez replied. "I've never even scored a touchdown."

"Don't worry about scoring points," Otto said. "Just have some fun and try your best at whatever you do–academics, athletics, music, or whatever."

KT smiled and said, "Dickie V told me to ask you how much you weighed when you were born."

Otto laughed. "I'll bet he did! I was a state record in Illinois for a baby boy way back then–14 pounds, 11 ounces."

"Wow!" said KT.

"I weighed less than half that when I was born," Chad added.

Kevin's voice came over the cell phone, "Otto, this is Kevin. Is it true what they say about you and the face mask on football helmets?"

"It's pretty incredible you would know about that, Kevin, but it's true. I was the first football player to wear a face mask."

"How did that happen?" KT asked.

"Well, we were playing against the 49ers one time, back in 1953 at old Cleveland Stadium, when a linebacker by the name of Art Michalik threw me out of bounds and smashed my face into the iron leg of a bench on the sidelines. No one wore face masks back then, so my face was ripped open. I had to leave the game, and I went to the locker room and got 15 stitches. After that, I came back in the game."

Jan couldn't believe it! She said, "You went back in after 15 stitches on your face with no face mask?"

"Sure did. I think I completed nine of 10 passes and we won the game 23 to 20, and that's where the face mask comes into the story. After that, Coach Brown wanted someone to come up with a bar or something to put across my face to protect me the next week. Someone came up with a piece of plastic wrapped around my helmet–the first face mask in football."

"That's a great story," said KT.

"I'm glad you think so, KT," Otto said with a smile.

Kevin said, "Otto, could you tell them about your nickname?"

"Automatic Otto," he said. "I guess I got that nickname because I never missed a game during 105 wins and 17 losses–with four ties."

"Talk about an ironman!" Nick exclaimed.

"That's incredible!" said Kevin.

Chad asked, "Do you know how your team, the Cleveland Browns, got their nickname?"

"No one's ever asked me that, but it's a good story. Our owner Art McBride bought the Browns in 1945, and he had a contest to name the team. The winner got a $1,000 war bond. Most people wanted *Browns*, because of our great coach Paul Brown, but Coach Brown didn't want the team named after him, so *Panthers* was selected. Then some guy told Mr. McBride he owned a defunct semi-pro team called the Cleveland Panthers, and he still owned the Panthers name. The guy could have been bought off, but Coach Brown said *no way*. He found out the Cleveland Panthers had been a losing team, anyway, and he didn't want our team to have anything to do with losing. After that, Coach Brown allowed the name *Browns* to be used, but he wanted everyone to know the team wasn't named after him but the great heavyweight fighter, Joe Louis, who was called *The Brown Bomber*. We all knew better, though. No one who'd entered the contest had mentioned Joe Louis at all."

"That's a cool story," said Chad. "I'll bet there aren't a lot of people who know that."

"There aren't," Otto said with a smile. "But now *you* do."

115

"Otto," KT said, "would you mind telling me how much you made back then for playing pro football?"

"Not at all, KT. My last year I made $25,000–and I made more than anyone else in the NFL. Now guys get more than that during warmups before the first game."

"You were definitely grossly underpaid," Prez said.

Otto Graham glanced at Chad and Prez's Pittsburgh Steelers caps and said, "Can I tell you something about the Steelers you might not know?"

"Please do," Chad said.

"Yes, please do," Prez added.

"Well, Johnny U was cut by his first pro team, the Steelers, after the idiot head coach said Johnny Unitas wasn't *smart* enough to play quarterback."

"What?" Chad said. "That's what the Steelers said about Terry Bradshaw for awhile, too, didn't they?"

"That's correct," Otto said. "But at least they gave Bradshaw a chance to win some Super Bowls. They got rid of Johnny U altogether, and the Colts picked him up. By the way, Unitas got $7,000 his first year as quarterback with the Colts, but he was happy because just a few years before that, he was playing for a semi-pro team called the Bloomfield Rams for $3 a game."

"Really?" Chad asked, in amazement.

"Really," Otto replied.

Prez said, "Mr. Graham–I mean Otto–it's incredible you'd mention Johnny Unitas, because we wanted to ask you something about him."

"Go ahead. Johnny and I got to know each other over the years, and I even got to spend some time with him here in Sarasota. What would you like to know?"

"Did Johnny Unitas ever live in Sarasota?" Prez asked.

"No," Otto replied, "but he stayed with friends on Casey Key sometimes."

"Did Johnny Unitas have any other connection to Sarasota you can think of?" KT inquired.

"Well, I guess like any other town, lots of high school players around here chose the number 19 because of Johnny Unitas ... especially in the 60's, 70's, and 80's. One guy here in Sarasota who played quarterback for the Riverview Rams back about 1983 even had the same crew cut haircut and wore those high-top black spikes that Johnny U used to wear. He really looked a lot like Johnny Unitas, too."

"The Riverview Rams?" Chad asked.

"Yes, that's one of our three big public high schools here in town. We've got the Riverview High Rams, the Sarasota High Sailors, and the Booker High Tornados."

KT, Prez, and Chad exchanged excited glances, and KT asked, "Do you happen to remember the name of the quarterback who looked like Johnny Unitas?"

"Sure do," said Otto. "I watched him play several times–he was a pretty good quarterback. Patrick Shaw."

"Bingo!" came an excited voice from Kevin in Bismarck. "Patrick Shaw–Shaw Point!"

"What was that?" Otto asked.

"That was me, Otto," Kevin said, trying to contain his excitement. "You just answered a big question we all had."

"I'm not sure how, but I'm glad I could be of help," Otto said. "Dickie V said I should ask you a trivia question when you were here. Whether you get it or not, I'm going to give you each one of my Pro Football Hall of Fame cards, but you have to promise you'll visit me once in awhile."

"We promise," KT said.

"All right," Otto began. "When football was just getting started in this country, it was really violent, with very few rules. What President almost banned the sport because so many people were getting injured and even dying?"

Prez smiled, and said, "Could it possibly be my favorite President–Teddy Roosevelt?"

"You're so smart," Otto said with a big smile. "It *was* Teddy Roosevelt–back in 1905. They listened to Teddy and made some changes, too, adding rules for unnecessary roughness ..."

Shortly after noon, KT, Chad, and Prez were on their way to Shaw Point in the *Rough Rider*. All of Sarabiskota in Bismarck were again in constant contact with the boat, not wanting to miss a thing.

Kari said, "Prez, if you guys find another clue today, all of us here in Bismarck want to talk to Governor Ed and our parents about flying down to Sarasota."

"Let's see what happens," Prez remarked. "Who knows? Today might be the end of the mystery."

"That would be amazing!" Kari exclaimed.

"Hey, Chad," Jan said, "please give us some more of those great camera shots of the scenery on the way to Shaw Point."

"I live to make you happy," Chad joked.

Jessie added, "Please let us know where you are at all times again, too, so we can follow you on the map."

"Will do," KT said. "Speaking of that, right now you'll notice Big Pass on our right. I hear some people call it Big Sarasota Pass. Has anyone found information on how it got its name?"

There was no response.

"So, this place you're headed to was once called Shaw Point, but now it's De Soto Point," Mike noted. "What's the deal with the name change?"

Kevin referred to his minicomputer and explained, "William Shaw was a settler who lived there in the early 1840's, and after he left, the place was known as Shaw Point or Shaw's Point for a long time. Long after that, though, some people figured out De Soto landed there in 1539, about 300 years before Shaw lived there, and the place became known as De Soto Point. Now, the De Soto National Memorial is there."

"How could anyone possibly figure out De Soto landed there if it was hundreds of years ago?" Jessie asked.

Kevin replied, "Apparently, a group of people studied the journals from De Soto's expedition for four years, and they determined that's where he landed. Some historians still don't believe it, though."

"You'll notice Lido Beach now on our right," Chad pointed out. "When Prez and I first moved here, the lady on the LeBarge tour boat said *Lido* was the Italian word for *beach*, so Lido Beach really is *Beach Beach*, I guess."

"That would make Lido Key–Beach Key," KT said. "I'll put those on the map."

Kevin observed, "Hey, do you realize you're actually following the same path many people think De Soto and his expedition took when they came to that area in 1539?"

"You've done more studying of De Soto than anyone by far, Kevin. Guide us through the journey he took getting here," Prez requested.

"Where do you want me to start?" Kevin asked.

"At the beginning. When Hernando de Soto was still in Spain," Prez replied.

"OK," Kevin began. "First, De Soto had to get permission from King Charles V to make the trip, and then it took him a year to plan everything. He got nine ships ready along with an army of more than 600 men."

"Did King Charles pay for all of that?" Mike inquired.

"No, De Soto did," Kevin replied. "The King gave De Soto some title like *Governor of Florida and Cuba* or something, but De Soto had to pay for the trip. The King also expected a big cut of anything De Soto found while exploring Florida. By the way, Florida *then* really wasn't the Florida we're used to today. *La Florida* to the Spanish was all the land north and east of Mexico, and they really didn't have a clue what a huge amount of land that was."

"Why not?" Nick asked.

"No satellite photos available, Nick," Chad explained. "Also, no European had explored the interior of the United States yet, so their knowledge of the region was zip."

"Oh," Nick said.

Kari asked, "Where did De Soto get all the money for the trip?"

"Apparently, he got rich taking tons of gold and stuff from the Incas," Kevin answered.

"Do you mean the Incas from Peru?" Jessie asked, recalling the one fact she remembered from her study of the Inca Indians.

"That's right," Kevin said. "De Soto went to Peru when he was only 19 and spent about 16 years taking gold and other riches from the Incas. When he got back to Spain, he was really rich—one of the richest men in Spain."

"This is cool," Jessie said. "All I remember learning about De Soto in school was he discovered the Mississippi River. It's fun learning all this other stuff...So, De Soto really didn't

come to Florida from Spain to discover the Mississippi River."

"Not really," said Kevin. "He really went there for more gold and glory, like he got during his years in Peru."

"What gave him the idea there was gold in Florida anyway?" Jessie asked.

"Rumors and wishful thinking," Kevin began. "Some of the men on previous, unsuccessful Spanish expeditions that didn't get very far inland talked about gold when they got back to Spain, and the stories probably got exaggerated. Before you know it, De Soto thinks there's more gold and other riches in Florida than there was in Peru."

"So, middle school girls aren't the only ones who exaggerate their stories, huh?" Mike said with a giggle.

"Careful, Mike," Kari said jokingly.

"Was there really gold there in Florida?" asked Nick.

"Maybe a little—worn by the Indians for decoration, but there certainly wasn't a lot of it," Kevin replied. "What the Indians had, they probably got by trading with some Indians living up where Georgia is now. Anyway, there sure wasn't *much* gold."

Prez said, "Let's get back to the De Soto expedition, Kevin. He had his trip ready to leave Spain. What happened next?"

"They took off from Spain on April 6, 1538, and sailed to Havana, Cuba," Kevin answered.

"Was Sara with him?" KT wanted to know.

"I couldn't find any mention of Sara de Soto," Kevin replied, "but it did say his wife, Isabella, was with him for sure."

"So, what happened next?" Nick was enjoying this story, as was everyone else.

Kevin continued, "While De Soto was in Cuba, making final preparations, De Soto's chief scout named Juan Anasco spent two months during the fall of 1538, right in the area you're boating today–exploring the Gulf Coast, looking for a good landing place for their expedition. In fact, I read a story about Anasco and his scouting party wrecking on Longboat Key, and they lived off stuff like pelicans, seagulls, and fish while they were fixing their boats. Some guy named Whitney actually found part of a wrecked boat in 1941 off Longboat Key, and they think it might have been one of Anasco's boats."

"Seagull and pelican, huh?" said Nick. "I wonder if they taste like chicken."

"Getting hungry, Nick?" Kevin chuckled. "Anyway, Anasco may have been the first European to explore around where the *Rough Rider* is right now. He eventually made repairs, and he found a good landing place at Shaw Point."

Prez said, "So, Anasco scouts for a good landing place, he finds it at Shaw Point, and he goes back to Cuba to tell De Soto about it. De Soto and his crew are making final preparations in Cuba. When did the whole expedition leave Cuba and finally come to Florida?"

"In the spring–specifically on May 18, 1539," Kevin answered. "By the way, Isabella stayed in Cuba–and I still don't have a clue about Sara de Soto. About a week later, De Soto's fleet cruised by where you are right now, and the Indians living there had scouts keeping track of the big ships. They sent warnings by signal fire to their Indian neighbors."

KT asked, "Why were the Indians worried about De Soto's ships?"

"This is where history gets a little ugly," Kevin replied.

"On those other expeditions to Florida before De Soto, the Spanish killed lots of Indians. Not only that, they passed some deadly diseases on to the Indians like smallpox, whooping cough, and measles. So you can see where the Indians wouldn't be too happy to see De Soto's ships coming by."

"Why were the Spaniards so mean to the Indians?" asked Jessie.

"Keep in mind this was back in the 1500's," Kevin replied. "Back then, the Spaniards didn't even consider Indians to be fully developed humans. They wanted gold, and they weren't going to let the Indians stop them from getting it."

Jan said, "Now it makes sense De Soto had 600 soldiers with him. He must have expected he was going to run into Indians that didn't like him, and he was willing to kill any of them who got in the way of him getting his gold."

"That's right," said Kevin. "And besides soldiers, the Spanish had tons of weapons like guns and crossbows–and even war dogs."

"War dogs!" Jessie exclaimed.

"That's right," Kevin said. "I wasn't going to mention it, especially with you girls around–but De Soto had packs of big, mean war dogs."

Kari seemed a little shocked. "Yikes! War dogs! What did they use them for?"

"Let's just say the dogs were killing machines," Kevin explained. "I read someplace that the Indians were more afraid of 10 Spaniards with one war dog than a 100 Spaniards without one."

Prez asked, "Did you read about De Soto's horses, Kevin?"

"I don't remember that much about the horses," Kevin replied. "What's the deal?"

"Well," Prez began, "horses gave the Spanish a huge advantage in fighting the Indians. De Soto knew this from all the years he fought the Incas. That's why he brought about 350 horses here, knowing how important they'd be."

"Prez, I can barely get my dog to ride in our car for an hour," Jessie noted. "How did De Soto get 350 horses to ride in ships for several days?"

"That's a story in itself, Jessie," Prez said. "Winches were used to get the horses aboard the ships and to get them off."

"What's a winch?" Nick asked.

"It's a lifting device with a hand crank, rope, and cylinder–like the thing on the back of your dad's pickup," Prez explained. "Anyway, once the horses were on board the ships, they were suspended in slings below deck. That way, when the ocean got rough, they wouldn't break their legs."

"I can only imagine what it smelled like after several days where all those horses were," Nick said.

"Gross!" Jan and KT said at exactly the same time. Then everyone laughed.

Kevin added, "I'm not going to even mention the hundreds of pigs on board that were brought along for food."

Nick giggled. "I guess history can get a little smelly, too."

Prez said, "So, getting back to the story, De Soto and his nine ships are traveling along where we are now, the southern part of Longboat Key, and the Indians are keeping track of their progress in their canoes. Signal fires are burning all along here. What happened next?"

Kevin continued, "De Soto's pilots couldn't find the landing place Anasco had found earlier, so De Soto lowered a long boat, which was a ship with oars they could lower from the big ship to explore–"

Chad interrupted, "Is that how Longboat Key got its name?"

"Probably," Kevin said. "Anyway, then De Soto took Anasco and his head pilot with him in the long boat to take a look around. They headed for the beach somewhere near where you are right now. By the way, that was probably De Soto's first landing in North America.

"They didn't find any fresh water once they landed there, so De Soto and his men took the long boat north right where you're going now. Then they probably went through Longboat Pass at the north end of Longboat Key, and boated into upper Sarasota Bay and then into Tampa Bay. It was getting dark, so the three men spent the night at Palma Sola Point, up the Manatee River a short distance, in an Indian camp that had just been deserted."

"Sounds like the Indians wanted nothing to do with De Soto," Jessie noted.

"No doubt," said Kevin. "By the way, I checked the name *Palma Sola*, KT, and it means *lone palm*. Apparently there was a small island close to Palma Sola Point that had just one palm tree on it, and that's how it got its name."

"While De Soto and Anasco stayed at Palma Sola Point, where were all the big ships?" Jan asked.

"By this time, the nine big ships were in the Gulf off Anna Maria Island someplace," Kevin answered. "The next morning, Anasco found the Shaw Point landing place he'd scouted out earlier in the fall. After that, one of the big ships picked Anasco and De Soto up. Then they used small boats to guide the big ships near their landing point, constantly checking for depth. It took about four days to get the ships safely off Shaw Point."

"Why so long just to land?" Nick asked.

Kevin explained, "The boats–especially the ones with the animals, water, and feed on board–were loaded down, and the ships could run aground if they weren't careful. They also had to allow for the tides and currents.

"Anyway, on May 30, 1539, the soldiers and the animals finally landed at Shaw Point. Almost all the soldiers and the animals marched from there, while the ships sailed a short distance to the northeast, toward the Indian town of Ucita on Terra Ceia Island."

Mike said, "KT, we found out *Terra Ceia* means *heavenly land*, and it got its name because the Indians had a beautiful temple built there where they worshipped the sun. *Ucita* was the leader of the Timucuan Indians who lived there when De Soto came."

"Thanks," KT said.

Kevin continued, "De Soto went with the ships, and his men took over Ucita, which had been deserted by the Indians by then. The men and animals who'd walked, took about 48 hours to meet up with De Soto at Ucita. Then they all rested at Ucita for about six weeks before they took off on July 15 of 1539. About 100 men stayed behind at a base camp."

Jan asked, "How long did De Soto's expedition last?"

"Four years and about 4,000 miles," Kevin replied. "They covered a huge part of the southeastern United States, but De Soto didn't make it all the way. On March 21, 1542, about three years after landing at Shaw's Point, he died from a fever, and he was buried in the Mississippi River. Half of

De Soto's men were also killed in fights with the Indians before the survivors made it back to safety somewhere in Mexico."

"Do you think any good came out of De Soto's expedition?" KT asked.

"I guess they got a lot of information about the Indians and a huge chunk of land they knew almost nothing about," Kevin said, "but it certainly didn't turn out anything like De Soto expected, did it?"

"That's for sure," said Nick. "No gold–no glory."

Chad added, "I read someplace about another contribution of the De Soto expedition. A bunch of De Soto's pigs got away during their long journey, and their relatives are still running around the southeastern United States."

"That's very interesting, Chad," Mike said.

"Oink, oink, Chad," Nick said with a laugh.

KEVIN KREMER

Once KT, Chad, and Prez got to the mouth of the Manatee River, where it flows into Tampa Bay, they boated a short distance up the river to a dock near the Visitors Center of the De Soto National Monument. After they'd docked, they got off the boat, walked past the Visitors Center and onto a narrow, shell-covered, sandy path that led to Shaw Point. KT was holding a small notebook and pen, Chad had the video camera in hand, and Prez was holding his cell phone so Bismarck Sarabiskota could get in on everything happening.

Once on the path, they picked up the pace, walking as fast as they could. They were so surrounded by thick vegetation, mostly mangroves, it was almost like walking through a tunnel.

Chad said, "Can you even imagine De Soto traveling along paths like this with all those soldiers and animals?"

"The Indians made things a whole lot easier for them," Kevin explained from Bismarck. "Back then, there were many Indian villages, and a lot of the time De Soto and his men could move from village to village on Indian trails. In fact, they were also led by Indian guides, with the Indians doing a lot of the heavy carrying, too. De Soto and his men even ate a lot of food they took from the Indians."

"This path would sure make a great haunted forest at Halloween!" KT exclaimed.

"No doubt," Prez agreed.

"I wouldn't be caught dead here at night," Chad said. "Talk about spooky."

After walking about a 100 yards, they came to a wooden footbridge over some marshy land. The footbridge zig-zagged approximately 150 yards through a tunnel of man-groves.

They stopped in the middle of the footbridge when KT spotted what looked like large, black spiders, but turned out to be three little fiddler crabs. They looked so funny running sideways on their four pairs of legs.

Upon closer look, they could see the fiddler crabs' eyes mounted on long stalks. The male's large claw was poised as though it was playing a fiddle. Chad got a close-up of the creatures, so Bismarck Sarabiskota could get a good look.

After they got over the footbridge, they hurried a short distance further to a clearing near the bank of the Manatee River. As soon as they got there, they all sensed they were getting close to whatever Captain Sarasota had left.

There, in the clearing, were the ruins of the house William Shaw had built for his family. Large chunks of what looked like cement with shells in it made it quite easy to make out the foundation of the small house that had once stood there. Many sea grape and cabbage palms grew around the perimeter of the old home site.

Prez read the inscription on the historical marker near-by out loud, "Tabby House Ruin–William Shaw settled here in the early 1840's and built this house of tabby, a cement-

like mixture of sand, lime, and shell. The Shaw family lived and worked here until a Seminole uprising in 1856 drove them to Key West. Later they returned, salvaged reusable portions of their house, and rafted them 200 miles to Key West."

Immediately, KT, Prez, and Chad fanned out, looking for whatever Captain Sarasota might have left. Chad was holding the video camera, and Prez had the cell phone in hand, so they were still sending both video and audio back to their friends in Bismarck.

The teens in Bismarck were even telling KT, Chad, and Prez where to look next. "Look over there by the historical marker!"

"Over there by the big tree, Chad!"

"Check out those big chunks of tabby!"

It didn't take long before they found what they were looking for. After less than 10 minutes, KT found small, dark seashells deeply embedded into one of the large chunks of tabby.

"Over here you guys!" KT almost screamed.

Chad ran over and focused his camera on the shells. They clearly formed the number 47–followed by the letters JB!

"It's letters and numbers this time–47 JB!" Prez exclaimed.

At that moment, rustling sounds coming from the thick woods nearby got the attention of the three teens!

"I'm just hoping that's a friendly little animal," Chad said nervously, pointing the camera in the direction of the sound. "Or possibly the Bardin Booger."

None of them could see anything, and the sound quickly moved away from them, deeper into the woods.

KT was a little nervous. "That was definitely too big to be a rabbit! I'm sorry I mentioned Halloween before."

"That's all right," Prez said with an edgy giggle. "We need a little more excitement in our lives."

"Prez, the number 47 rings a bell," Jan said anxiously, "but I can't remember where I saw it before. It won't take me long to find it on my computer, though."

"Please get right on it, Jan," Prez said. "We're going to head back now, but I think we'll stop at the Anna Maria City Pier on the way. There's supposed to be an ice cream shop near there I want to try out. I could use a scoop of chocolate chip cookie dough right now."

"Hey, Prez! This clinches it!" Kari said excitedly. "We want to come down to Sarasota as soon as we can make all the arrangements!"

"My parents already said Jan, Kari, and Jessie can stay with me," KT said.

Chad added, "Prez and I have tons of room for Kevin, Mike, and Nick."

"My parents have extra bikes for everyone at the store, too," KT pointed out.

"Let's get the process rolling," Prez said enthusiastically. "We can all talk to our parents today. After that, we can give Governor Ed a call to find out when he might be able to fly the six of you down to Sarasota."

"I'm so excited, I could sing!" Mike said. That's exactly what he did. He proceeded to sing *Bossa Nova Baby*, one of Elvis's big hits from the 1960's.

It took only a few minutes to get to the Anna Maria City Pier. As they approached slowly to within 50 yards of the

pier, they couldn't help but notice the awesome view around them. Behind them was the beautiful Sunshine Skyway Bridge, Egmont Key, and Passage Key, with St. Petersburg in the distance. Directly in front of them was Anna Maria Island.

As they closed in on the long wooden pier, they noticed a small restaurant and a bait shop built at the end of it. Several people of all ages were fishing up and down the entire length of the pier.

Ten yards to the right of their boat, Jack Lambert suddenly leaped 15 feet into the air and dove back into the water!

"I can't believe it! It's Jack Lambert!" KT exclaimed.

Jack Lambert put on a dolphin show that attracted the attention of everyone on the pier! Then he swam slowly on his side, close to the boat, while seemingly staring at KT, Chad, and Prez with one eye.

"Jack Lambert, are you giving us the evil eye?" Chad asked.

Jack Lambert made some dolphin sounds that sounded a little like scolding.

KT said, "I get the feeling Jack Lambert is telling us we should let him know where we're going next time and ask him to come along."

"That's so cute," said Jan.

Jack Lambert swam right next to the boat and popped his whole head out of the water. KT, Chad, and Prez apologized to Jack Lambert, assuring him they'd keep him informed of their boating plans in the future. He seemed to accept their apology, and he made some happy dolphin sounds as he performed several acrobatic jumps that had all the people on the pier watching in amazement!

Then they docked the boat, and KT told Jack Lambert where they were going. Jack Lambert swam further out into Tampa Bay to explore his new surroundings.

KT, Chad, and Prez walked down the pier toward shore, looking for Mama Lo's Ice Cream Shop. It turned out to be located near the end of the pier, across the street in a small shopping center.

As soon as they entered the store, they knew they'd come to the right place. A huge, glass-covered, open cooler revealed many delicious flavors of ice cream in large containers.

KT was drawn to the back of the store, where two large maps hung on the wall–one a world map and one a map of the United States. All over the maps were colored push-pins, and near the maps were instructions for customers to stick a pin in the map to indicate where they'd traveled from to visit Anna Maria Island.

Prez and Chad followed KT back to the maps, and they noted there was already a pin near Fergus Falls, Minnesota. Near Bismarck, however, there were no pins; and in all of North Dakota, there were only five.

As they were standing around the maps, a nice lady behind the counter said, "Where are you kids from?"

"Fergus Falls, Minnesota," KT said.

"Bismarck, North Dakota, but we all just moved to Sarasota," Chad answered.

After Chad introduced the three of them, the lady said, "I'm Mama Lo. You three come from God's country. I've visited the Badlands of North Dakota and several lakes in Minnesota, and I love it in both places. What are you doing

on Anna Maria Island?"

Prez smiled. "We came here just to have ice cream at your shop," he said. "We've heard you've got the best ice cream around."

Mama Lo smiled and said, "Why don't you come on up here and pick out your favorite flavor and we'll talk. Since you're the first people here from Bismarck *ever*, I'm buying today."

"Thanks, Mama Lo!" they all said.

After they'd picked out their ice cream and started eating, Chad asked, "Mama Lo, do you know how Anna Maria Island got its name?"

"No one seems to know for sure," she began, "but I can give you some possibilities. A couple of the stories I've heard credit the Spanish for naming the island. As one story goes, Juan Ponce de Leon, the man who named Florida and supposedly was looking for the Fountain of Youth, landed out there on Egmont Key in 1513. They say an Indian killed one of his men in battle there–the first white man within the boundaries of the United States killed in battle, by the way. Sometime shortly after that, the Spanish supposedly named this place after the mother of Christ–Mary, and Mary's mother–Ann. In Spanish, it's *Anna* and *Maria*, of course.

"There's another simpler explanation that has the Spanish naming the island after two Spanish princesses named Anna and Maria. Besides those two stories, I've heard one more, and I tend to believe it the most. Do you want to hear it?"

"Sure!" they all replied.

"Well, a survey team came through here in the mid-1840's that included a Captain Casey, for which Casey Key is named. Do you know where Casey Key is?"

"Yes," Chad replied.

KT, Chad, and Prez smiled at hearing these familiar names.

Mama Lo continued, "While Captain Casey and the rest of the survey crew were in the area, they stayed with the Scottish mayor of Tampa, a man named Mayor Post. As a way to show his appreciation, the survey crew decided to name one of the islands after the mayor, but the mayor didn't want that. He suggested they name it after his wife. The survey crew liked the idea, but Mrs. Post wanted her sister, who was living with them at the time, to be included, too. Well, the mayor's wife was named *Anna*, and her sister was *Maria*."

Chad said, "That was great! Do you know how Cortez got its name?"

"This is so extraordinary!" Mama Lo said. "You're the first teenagers I've met who are so interested in the local history around here. I can tell you what I know about Cortez ... Back in the 1870's, the land where Cortez is now was inhabited by a small group of fishermen from the Bahamas, and they called their location Hunter's Point. But then, in 1896, someone applied to Washington for a post office, and Hunter's Point was already taken by another place in Florida. I don't know who did it, but someone wrote down *Cortez* on the application. Cortez, of course, was the Spanish *conquistador* who conquered the Aztecs."

Prez's cell phone rang, and Prez said, "Excuse me. I think I'd better answer this." He politely stepped outside to answer it.

"Hey, Prez! This is Jan! We solved the 47 part, and we're working on the JB!"

"That's great! What's the deal with the 47?" Prez asked

excitedly.

"A famous guy who lived in the Sarasota area named Whitaker had 47 as his cattle brand. I think it represented the year he started to raise cattle in Sarasota–1847. We're still working on the JB."

"Fantastic job!" Prez said. "We'll call you on the boat in a few minutes."

"All right!" Jan said.

When Prez got back inside, Chad was just asking Mama Lo, "Did you ever hear of Captain Sarasota?"

Mama Lo seemed a little stunned. "How could you possibly know about Captain Sarasota if you just moved here? He disappeared a long time ago."

"Oh, we were just doing some research at the library, and we read about him," Chad replied.

"Yes, I did know Captain Sarasota," Mama Lo began, sounding sad. "He was often spotted in his boat, the *Ponce de Leon*, out there in the bay doing some fishing. He actually stopped in here once in awhile for ice cream and coffee. The man was extremely handsome and the best listener I've ever known, but he seldom talked about himself at all. I used to even check out books from the library for him, and he always brought them back long before they were overdue."

"Do you remember some of the subjects of the books you checked out for Captain Sarasota?" Prez asked.

"They covered many topics. He seemed to have numerous interests," Mama Lo replied. "I remember some books on advanced aeronautics ... there were lots of mathematics books ... some electronics books ... some novels ... some books on sports ... even some dealing with advanced submarines."

13

After dinner, KT, Chad, and Prez rode their bikes over to Prez's workshop on Higel Avenue. The three teens had just learned that Sarabiskota in Bismarck had figured out the JB part of the clue, and they were anxious to find out all the details.

On the way to the garage, KT said, "Prez, if everyone from Bismarck comes down here to Sarasota, there'll be plenty of people to help get *The Starship Exercise* ready for the Suncoast Offshore Boat Festival."

"You're right, KT," Prez agreed. "I just can't wait to have the whole group together again! They're going to love Sarasota!"

Chad said, "*Sarabiskota on Siesta Key Beach*. It could be the title of a good movie."

"How about *Sarabiskota Solves the Captain Sarasota Mystery*?" Prez suggested. "That's the movie I'd like to see soon."

"No doubt," KT said.

Just then, Prez's cell phone rang.

"Hi, Kari. We're almost at the workshop. We'll call you from there in a few minutes ... Bye."

When they got to the workshop, they hurried inside, walked past *The Starship Exercise*, and sat down in front of the wall-sized screen. Prez pushed some buttons on the control panel, and Bismarck Sarabiskota soon appeared on the screen.

"Hi, everyone!"

"Hi!"

"We've got some fabulous news!" said Kari. "All of us here have already talked to our parents about coming to Sarasota, and they've started calling each other. They plan to call Sarasota tonight to talk to all of your parents. Our goal is to be down there by the weekend, if possible. Prez, maybe you should give Governor Ed a call tomorrow to see what his plans are."

"Fabulous!" Prez said. "I'll call Governor Ed tonight. Right now, I want to know all about this Whitaker guy who had the 47 cattle brand and what you found out about the letters JB."

"No problem," Jan explained. "The Whitaker guy was William H. or Bill Whitaker. Some people call him the Father of Sarasota because he was the first permanent settler to come to the Sarasota Bay area. The JB stands for Judah Benjamin, a guy who visited the Whitaker family in one of the most famous incidents *ever* in Sarasota."

Prez asked, "Would anyone mind if we start out at the beginning? I'd like to know about Whitaker's whole life so I can see how the 47 and JB fit into the big picture."

Kari referred to her minicomputer and said, "No problem. We've been studying this stuff for the last few hours in an old book we found on the Internet called *The Story of Sarasota* by Karl Grismer. It's a really interesting story ... I can start by telling you William Whitaker was born in Savannah, Georgia, on August 1, 1821. He ran away from home when he was just about our age–only 14."

"Why?" Chad asked.

"Apparently his real mom had died a year before, and his father had remarried," Jan explained. "Bill didn't like his new stepmother much, so he took off. His dad actually saw him leave and asked him what he was doing. Bill even admitted he was running away, but his dad didn't try to change his mind. Instead, he gave Bill some money and a big gold watch."

"Fourteen and on his own. That's pretty amazing," Jessie observed.

"That's for sure," Jan said. "His dad wanted him to go to Tallahassee to live with his half-brother named Hamlin Valentine Snell, who was a 25 year-old attorney there. At the time, Tallahassee was the capital of the Florida Territory–Florida wasn't even a state yet."

"That's right," Prez pointed out. "Florida didn't become a state till 1845, and this was 10 years before that."

Chad asked, "Did Bill Whitaker go to live with that Hamlin guy?"

"No," Kevin replied, "he wanted more adventure than that. He went to Savannah, and it took him less than an hour to get a job as a deckhand on a schooner headed to Key West."

"What's a schooner?" Nick inquired.

"It's a sailing ship with two or more masts and sails that run the whole length of the ship," Prez explained.

"Oh."

KT observed, "So Bill was about our age, he's on his own,

and he's on a schooner to Key West? Unbelievable."

"That's for sure," Jessie said. "A year after that, he was a fisherman in St. Marks, Florida."

"Where's St. Marks?" Chad asked.

"It's a town right on the Gulf of Mexico, southeast of Tallahassee," Jessie answered. "One day, Ham Snell saw Bill there and talked him into going to school in Tallahassee. He stayed for two years, mainly because he met a great friend there who he even got to stay with."

"What happened after that?" KT asked.

Mike said, "He fought Indians during the Second Seminole War for four years. When the war was over, he was still only 21 or so, but he was ready to settle down some-place, so he went back to Tallahassee to discuss things with Ham Snell."

"It turned out to be great timing, too," Kevin said. "Now that the Second Seminole War was over, Congress passed the Armed Occupation Act of 1842 that said settlers would get six months' supplies and 160 acres of land if they lived anywhere south of the Gainesville area. All they had to do was live on the land for at least five years and carry arms to defend themselves. If they wanted any more land, they could buy it for the cheap price of only $1.25 an acre."

"So, for the price of a small bottle of water today, you could almost buy a football field back then," Nick noted.

"Great observation, Nick," Kari said. "By then, Florida seemed pretty safe, too, because most of the Seminoles were either in Oklahoma or on reservations down in the Everglades."

"What happened next?" Chad asked, really getting into the story.

Kevin said, "Ham said he'd help Bill buy what he needed, and he'd even go along on the expedition to help Bill find his new place to live. Many of Snell's friends had already moved from Tallahassee to the Manatee River area, so he decided he could visit them and also help Bill out."

Jan continued, "Snell bought a sloop, and they loaded it down with everything they'd need–tools, supplies, food, and stuff. They took off from St. Marks at the end of November in 1842."

"What's a sloop?" Nick asked.

"In this case, it's a small ship with sails on it," Kevin answered.

"Oh."

Kari went on with the story. "They sailed south along the Gulf Coast, looking for a great place to build a home. They didn't find anything by the time they got to the village of Manatee, so they stayed a few days at the Gates House, which was really a hotel built by a man named Gates. Ham got a chance to see some of his old friends there."

"Who was Gates, and where was Manatee?" Chad inquired.

Jessie answered, "Gates was the first white settler south of Tampa, and Manatee was the village that grew up around his homestead. Manatee no longer exists. It's part of the city of Bradenton now."

"The village of Manatee was located in the area around 15th Street East in Bradenton," Prez noted. "Supposedly, some of Manatee's old historical buildings are still there. We'll have to check it out sometime."

Jan went on. "So Whitaker and Snell were talking to some of Ham's friends in Manatee, and they heard about good land south of there in the Sarasota Bay region which hadn't been claimed by anyone yet, so they took off from Manatee to take a look. On December 14, 1842, sometime in the afternoon, they were sailing in Sarasota Bay when they spotted a place with yellow bluffs ... by the way, the bluffs got their yellow color from the sandstone in them. Later, Bill even named the place Yellow Bluffs."

"What are bluffs?" Nick asked.

"They're steep, rocky hills," Prez explained.

"Was that where Bill built his home?" KT inquired.

"That's right," Jan answered. "The more they looked around, the more they liked the location. There was a bayou nearby–bayous are basically what they call some creeks down south. There also was fresh spring water not too far up the bayou from Sarasota Bay. Plenty of fish and game were around, the land was good for growing things, and the view was fantastic."

"It's hard to believe no one had taken the land already," KT observed.

Jessie said, "It sounded like there were so few people around at all then–just some Cuban fishermen out on Longboat Key and a Spanish fisherman named Alzartie a little ways up the coast from Yellow Bluffs."

"So, what happened next?" Chad asked.

"Ham and Bill built two temporary huts mostly from palmetto branches," Kevin said. "They built one to live in for awhile and used the other for storage. When they got done, they started building a log cabin from cedar logs they floated over from Longboat Key. When the log home was done, it was spring already, and Ham had to go back to Tallahassee so Bill was at Yellow Bluffs all by himself."

Prez asked, "Did Ham Snell ever come back?"

"A lot," Kevin replied. "Somewhere I read that during one of those trips, in fact, Ham brought guava seeds from Cuba and planted them at Yellow Bluffs–the first guavas ever grown in Florida."

"What did Bill do after Ham left?" KT inquired.

Jan said, "He sold dried mullet–a small silver fish, and dried roe–fish eggs, to Cuban traders who used to sail along the Gulf Coast."

"This was the part of the story I really liked," Nick said. "It sounded like it was the easiest thing in the world catching fish in the Sarasota area back then. There were huge schools of fish in Sarasota Bay! It's hard to even imagine, but it said the schools were several football fields in size, with zillions of fish in them. Sharks and dolphins would chase the *gazzillion* fish through Big Sarasota Pass, and the fish went bonkers trying to escape! They'd even jump high into the air and make a strange, bizarre noise that sounded like big waves hitting the beach. Would you believe people could hear the sound several miles away!"

"Unreal!" Chad exclaimed. "What did Bill do? Just go out in the bay and let the fish jump into the boat?"

"That's about it," said Nick. "He'd cast his net in, and he'd have his boat filled with fish in no time. Cleaning, salting, and drying them, and then putting them in crates until the Cubans came by in their ships and bought them, was the tough part. But it was well worth it, because the Cubans paid big money for the fish."

"How much?" KT wanted to know.

"One cent for each dried fish," Nick answered. "But don't laugh. Back then, a penny was worth something, and with thousands of dried fish—that's a lot of money. A little later, Bill got a partner—a guy named Joseph Woodruff who lived north of Yellow Bluffs a mile or so. The partnership worked. Bill even saved enough money to start his cattle business."

"That's right," Mike said. "That's where the 47 comes in. By the year 1847, Bill had enough money to buy some cattle, so he rode his horse to Dade City, about 100 miles northeast of Sarasota, and bought 10 cows and some calves. He actually had to create his own road on the way back from Dade City to get the cattle back to Yellow Bluffs. It was the first road through the wilderness south of Tampa, in fact."

KT asked, "How did he build a road back then, Mike?"

"It really wasn't a very fancy road," Mike replied. "It was barely a path. Bill made it by burning trees, cutting away brush, and finding places for the cows and calves and him to cross streams and rivers. The 10 cows and calves he brought back from Dade City were the first ones to ever get the number 47 branded on them."

"Bill also planted the first orange grove in the whole area," Jan added. "He got orange seeds from the Cuban traders. Ten years later, he had an orange grove producing fruit."

"Life sounds pretty good for Bill," said Chad. "Was it happily ever after from that point on?"

"Not really," Kari said.

"Oh, no. What happened?" Chad asked.

Jan said, "Two hurricanes happened–the Hurricane of 1846 and the Hurricane of 1848."

"Didn't the hurricanes have names back then?" asked Chad.

"No," Prez explained, "they actually called them *equinoctials* because they usually hit somewhere around the first day of fall–the *autumnal equinox*. They started naming hurricanes after girls during World War II when the servicemen started naming Pacific storms after their wives and girlfriends. Then, some feminists objected to the storms just being named after women, so now, every other storm has to have a man's name."

"That only seems fair," Jessie commented. "Before we talk about the hurricanes anymore, though, would you mind if we make some popcorn? Hurricane talk makes me hungry."

Everyone laughed.

"Sounds good," Kari said. "I've got tons of microwave popcorn upstairs."

"I've got some microwave popcorn here in the workshop, too," said Prez. "Let's take a snack break, and continue the Whitaker story in a few minutes starting with the Hurricanes of 1846 and 1848."

14

After they'd made some popcorn and had a chance to eat a little, they got back to talking about the hurricanes, while still munching. Prez asked, "Jan, what happened to Bill during the Hurricanes of '46 and '48?"

"His log home must have been built real solid, because he made it through the 1846 hurricane fine," Jan said. "The 1848 hurricane was different, though. Back then, they called it the 'grand daddy of all hurricanes.'"

"What happened?" Jessie asked, her mouth full of popcorn.

"Lots happened," Jan replied. "The storm hit on September 22. The strong winds came from the southwest, so the water of the Gulf was pushed up on the land with tremendous force. All the keys were covered with water and virtually everything was washed away. There were ships out in the Gulf that were washed ashore and totally destroyed by the huge waves! There was even a brand new lighthouse just built on Egmont Key that was knocked down like it was nothing!"

Jessie started eating her popcorn faster, and you could tell she was a little nervous and scared. "What happened to Bill?" she asked.

Jan said, "His cabin was sturdy, but it was facing the bay, so the winds smacked it head-on. Bill didn't think he'd make it through the night; he thought the logs of his home would eventually come crashing down on him!"

"Oh, no! He died, didn't he?" Jessie said, with an agonized expression on her face.

"No, both Bill and his log cabin made it," Jan said. "The roof had some damage, but that was about it."

"Thank goodness," Jessie said with a sigh of relief.

"It wasn't all good news, Jessie," Jan said. "Bill had left many of his valuable fishing nets out on the beach at Longboat Key, and they were long gone ... and so was the whole beach, and a chunk of Longboat Key, too. The hurricane had cut a new pass through the key and Whitaker called it–"

"New Pass!" KT and Prez said at the same time.

"That's right," Jan said. "The name stuck, and now you know ... *the rest of the story.*"

Jan added, "I know there isn't much funny about this whole hurricane thing, but something sorta funny happened that actually helped people like Bill a little bit."

"What?" KT asked.

"Well," Jan explained, "there apparently were quite a few smashed ships along the coast, and many of them were filled with merchandise. Some of the stuff was still usable. Someone even found a set of beautiful mahogany furniture in great condition. It was like a big hurricane sale along the beach–everything free."

"Any NASCAR merchandise or hockey pucks?" Nick asked with a mischievous smile.

Several of Nick's friends gave him funny looks, and then

they laughed. "Hey, just kidding," Nick said.

"Did things get better for Bill after the hurricane?" KT wanted to know.

Kari smiled and said, "After that, something more powerful than any hurricane hit Bill and changed his life forever."

"Bill got hit by a comet?" Nick asked, kidding again.

"No, Nick," Kari said, giggling. "Bill Whitaker fell in love with a cute, short girl with black hair and blue eyes from Manatee by the name of Mary Jane Wyatt."

"What was Mary Jane like?" KT asked.

"Would Sara de Soto and Mary Jane have gotten along?" Chad asked, chuckling.

"Mary was pretty amazing," Kari explained. "And, yes, I think she would have gotten along with Sara de Soto and maybe even *you*, Chad."

"Please tell us about her," Prez requested.

Kari said, "She was born in Tallahassee on April 11, 1831, so she was about 10 years younger than Bill. Her mom was named Mary, too, and her dad was Colonel William Wyatt. Mary was the youngest of three children, and she was pretty much spoiled by her dad and her older brothers, Hance and Wyatt. By the way, Colonel Wyatt was one of the richest and most powerful men in the South at one time. He actually lost the election for governor of the Florida Territory in 1838 by just one vote."

"Whoever said one vote doesn't count?" Prez said.

"I remember all too well," Jan said, making a face at Prez, recalling the time she lost to Prez by one vote.

Kari continued, "The Wyatts moved to Manatee in 1842. Sometime after that, Mary Jane was sent to a private girls' school in Kentucky where she got sick. She went back home and spent the summer recuperating with her brothers on their family ranch near Manatee."

"Did she get better?" Nick asked.

"That's for sure," Kari replied. "Not only did Mary get well, but she also became a real outdoors girl. She learned to ride horse, round up cattle, swim, row a canoe, and even shoot a rifle really well. Her dad used to brag that she could shoot a turkey in the head 100 yards away."

"This sounds like a girl I could love," Nick said. "I'll bet she would've liked NASCAR races and professional wrestling, too."

Nick got a few more funny looks.

Kari went on. "When Mary went back home to Manatee in the fall, she was strong and tan and she got Bill's attention. For the next two years, Bill rode 15 miles through the woods from Yellow Bluffs to Manatee to see Mary. Then Bill asked Mary to marry him, and she said yes. They got married in the Methodist Church in Manatee–it was the first wedding in Manatee County *ever*."

"That's so romantic, I could sing an Elvis love song–but I'll save it for another time," Mike said. "What happened after that?"

Kari said, "Well, then they moved down to Yellow Bluffs, where it was a little lonely for Mary with no neighbors for miles, but they were still very happy. On April 19, 1852, they had their first child–a curly-haired redhead named Nancy Catherine Stuart Whitaker. Nancy was the first white child born in what's now Sarasota County."

"She sure had enough names, didn't she?" Jessie noted.

"That's for sure," Kari replied. "I guess Nancy was given

all those names because her parents didn't expect to have any more children–but they sure did! They had 10 more kids the next 14 years."

"This is interesting," Chad said. "What happened next?"

"After Nancy was born, things went great for the next four years," said Kari. "The cattle herd got bigger. Fishing was great. Their gardens did well, and their orange groves produced lots of good oranges. They owned about a mile of choice coastland along Sarasota Bay."

"Oh, no! I'm sensing something bad is about to happen. What was it?" Nick asked.

Kevin said, "This is a great story! It was the banana patch incident involving Billy Bowlegs."

"The banana patch incident involving Billy Bowlegs? You're kidding, right?" Chad asked.

"No, I'm not," Kevin replied. "Billy Bowlegs was chief of the Seminole Indians that were still living in Florida. Mary Jane Whitaker actually had met Billy Bowlegs that summer she was on her father's ranch, and Billy Bowlegs and Mary got along pretty well. Billy was usually a friendly, peaceful guy, who used to trade with the pioneers around the Sarasota Bay-Tampa Bay area. He even ate with the Wyatts and other settlers once in awhile in Manatee."

"But the banana patch deal changed everything?" Nick guessed.

"It did," Kevin said. "It actually led to the Third Seminole War which some even called The Billy Bowlegs War."

"How?" Chad asked.

"I'll try to explain," Kevin began. "After the Second Seminole War, the small number of Seminoles still in Florida were living on a reservation in Big Cypress Swamp,

down in the Naples area. One week before Christmas in 1855, a group of U.S. Army surveyors were down in Big Cypress Swamp. Billy was well-aware of their presence, since they had been hanging around for about two weeks. Anyway, the surveyors were frustrated about not being home for Christmas and thought it would be fun to wreck Billy's garden just for the fun of it. By the way, Billy had some other stuff growing in his garden besides bananas, too, like pumpkins and potatoes and squash."

"Why was it Billy Bowleg's banana patch and not Billy Bowleg's garden if he had things other than bananas?" Jessie asked.

"That's a great question, Jessie, and I wondered the same thing," Kevin replied. "It turns out the banana trees were Bill Bowleg's prized possession. He had several acres of banana trees, most of them were more than 15 feet high. Billy took a lot of pride in them–he even used to give bananas as gifts to white people and as treats for Seminole children.

"Well, the Army guys basically trashed Billy Bowlegs' whole garden. When Billy returned and saw what had happened, he went to the soldiers' camp and demanded the men pay him cash for all the damage. The man who was in charge of the surveyors, Lieutenant George Hartsoff, wasn't there, but his 10 men admitted to destroying the garden. Instead of paying Billy, though, they laughed, and even tripped Billy and knocked him down.

"This made Billy Bowlegs fighting mad! Billy came back early on Christmas Eve morning with some of his warriors in war paint, and they attacked the Army men in a screaming rage! Four soldiers were shot, while two others quickly got on their horses and escaped. Lieutenant Hartsoff himself got clipped just below the elbow by a shot fired from behind the trees, and then he got hit again in the chest before he could crawl into some trees.

"After that, Billy and the other Seminole braves still left in Florida went on a rampage! They began stealing, shooting people, and burning settlers' property. It was the beginning of the Third Seminole War, and it affected the Sarasota-Manatee region big-time and the Whitaker family, too."

"How?" Mike asked.

Kevin explained, "Many of the settlers in the Sarasota and Manatee regions got together for protection in two places up in the Manatee area that were fortified–Braden Castle and Branch Fort. Mrs. Whitaker, in fact, was at Branch Fort with Nancy and her baby, Louise Antsie, when *another* bad thing happened!"

"Don't tell me one of the Whitakers died!" Jessie said.

"Actually, someone *did* die," said Kevin, "but not any of the Whitakers. While Nancy and the kids were safe at Branch Fort, and Bill was on his way to a military camp with some other volunteers to get help, a band of Seminoles raided the Whitakers' house at Yellow Bluffs and burned it to the ground!"

"Who died?" Jessie asked.

"A guest of theirs named George Owen, who was the first tourist ever in the Sarasota area. He was spending the winter with the Whitakers trying to recover from tuberculosis, and he was working as kind of a handyman. George said he wasn't afraid of the Seminoles, and he refused to leave Yellow Bluffs like the others did. They figure he might have hidden in the storage room during the attack, and the smoke got to him during the fire. George was the only person ever killed by the Seminoles in the Sarasota area."

Prez asked, "How long did the Whitakers and others have to stay together in Manatee?"

"Nine long, hot months in almost unbearable conditions," Kevin said. "With no air conditioning, lots of mosquitoes and bugs, and the close living conditions, it must have been tough. They also had the problem of diseases like measles and whooping cough breaking out and spreading quickly. Would you believe three babies were even born in Branch Fort? Mary Whitaker had the first baby–it was her first son, Furman Chaires."

"When did this Third Seminole War finally end?" KT asked.

"Well," Kevin continued, "by the end of 1856, the Seminoles had pretty much been chased into the Everglades, and the settlers felt safe enough to go back to their homes. They felt even safer sometime in early 1858, when Billy Bowlegs and 139 of his warriors were put on boats headed west."

"Did the Whitakers build another home after that?" asked Chad.

"Yup," Mike replied, "but Mary made Bill build the new home further back from the water. Before, her garden got damaged quite a bit from the winds coming off the bay."

"So, I imagine there's no chance the Whitakers lived happily ever after from then on," Chad guessed.

"You're right, Chad. There's no chance," Nick answered.

"What happened this time?" Chad inquired.

"The Civil War happened," Nick replied, "and the JB or

Judah Benjamin thing happened right after that. In fact, the two are related."

"I read a great Civil War story involving Mary Whitaker," Jessie said. "Florida was on the Confederate side of the Civil War, and Florida people like the Whitakers were supporting the Confederate troops any way they could. Because of this, Union ships were blockading Florida, trying to prevent anything from getting out to support the Confederate side. Also, Union troops were raiding, stealing, and burning many of the settlers' possessions, including livestock, gardens, and the stuff in the settlers' homes.

"One day back in 1863, some Union soldiers stopped at the Whitakers' home. The soldiers took as much of the stuff they could carry from the house, and then they told Mary to give them some matches so they could set the house on fire."

"What did Mary do, Jessie?" KT asked.

"She went into the house, got some matches, handed them to the commanding officer, and said, 'Sir, I want to look into the eyes of a man who can stoop so low as to burn the home of a helpless woman and her family.'"

"Wow, that Mary was a tough lady!" said Nick.

"Did they burn down the house?" Chad asked.

"No," Jessie said, "that would've ruined a good story. The soldiers left after that."

Jan added, "It got pretty tough for the Whitakers during the Civil War, though. Prices for things like shoes got so expensive, Bill had to start making them himself. He got pretty good at making shoes out of soft pine wood and deer hide made to fit the person's foot, and wooden pegs holding everything together. Mary actually liked Bill's shoes better than store shoes."

Nick said, "Union soldiers kept raiding the house at Yellow Bluffs and they took almost everything. Finally, the Whitakers moved to Manatee until the war was over."

"When did the war end again?" Chad asked.

"April 9, 1865–General Lee surrendered to Grant," Nick replied. "I think that's what Prez told me before."

"That's exactly right, Nick," Prez said with a big smile.

"That's about where the JB–Judah Benjamin story comes in, too," Nick explained. "This is really interesting stuff. Judah P. Benjamin was a big shot for the Confederacy, and when the war was over, he was a war criminal, running for his life. There was a $40,000 reward for him–dead or alive."

"What did Benjamin do for the Confederacy?" Prez asked.

"He was called the 'Brains of the Confederacy,'" Nick replied. "He was President Jefferson Davis's attorney general, then his secretary of war, and after that, his secretary of state."

"How did he end up with the Whitakers down on Sarasota Bay?" Jessie inquired.

"Well," Nick began, glancing at his minicomputer, "he was trying to get out of the country, and he thought he might find a boat he could use in Florida. He made it to Tampa dressed like a farmer, and he hid for quite a few days in a home there. Tampa was pretty dangerous for him–it was loaded with Federal troops and sailors at the time. He wasn't able to make arrangements for a boat in Tampa, but the guy he was staying with named James McKay advised him to go to Manatee where he could maybe get help from Captain Archibald McNeil, who was a famous blockade runner."

"What's that?" Chad asked.

"It was a person who was willing to risk his life getting his boat past the Union boats who were blockading Florida," Nick replied.

"Oh," Chad said.

Nick went on. "Benjamin got to the Gamble Mansion on the north banks of the Manatee River where Captain McNeil was living. He hid upstairs in a bedroom where he had a great view of the Manatee River so he could see if soldiers were coming. One time, he almost got caught by a squad of Union soldiers who got close to the house before anyone saw them. Benjamin and McNeil managed to escape just in time, though. The soldiers didn't find a thing when they searched every inch of the mansion, so both of the men returned when the soldiers left.

"After about three weeks at the Gamble Mansion, Benjamin finally got help from a man who lived nearby named Captain Tresca, who was able to buy a 16-foot yawl, which is a sailboat with two masts. Tresca then sailed the boat to Whitaker Bayou and hid it. But Judah Benjamin didn't go by boat. He got to the Whitakers' house another way–this is so cool! He hid in an ox cart! Ask me where he was hiding."

"Where was Benjamin hiding?" Mike asked.

Nick said, "Benjamin was hiding underneath a bunch of fresh beef!"

"Gross!"

"Ewwww!"

"My mom says never play with my food–or hide in it, either," Chad said, laughing.

Everyone laughed.

Nick continued, "After that, Mary Whitaker made Benjamin a great dinner."

"I hope Benjamin bathed before he ate," Jessie said with a giggle.

"I hope they didn't eat the beef that Benjamin was hiding in," KT added, giggling.

"I don't know," Nick said, chuckling, "but after dinner, Benjamin boarded the yawl with Tresca, and the Whitakers stood and watched from Yellow Bluffs as the boat sailed away."

"Did Judah Benjamin make it to safety?" KT asked.

"Yes, with some difficulty," Nick said. "Not too far south of Sarasota, near Charlotte Harbor, they were stopped by a Federal gunboat. Benjamin was disguised as a cook, and he had grease and stuff on his face, so luckily, the sailors didn't recognize him.

"Then, further south at Knight's Key, Tresca bought a bigger boat called the *Blonde*. Eventually, they made it safely to Nassau, the largest city in the Bahamas. After that, Benjamin gave Tresca the *Blonde*, $1,500 in gold, and even bought 10 yards of black silk for Mrs. Whitaker and the ladies of Manatee who had helped him."

"This is a phenomenal story, Nick," Prez said. "Where did Benjamin go after that?"

Nick replied, "He sailed to London where he gave advice to Queen Victoria and became a friend with many of the rich and powerful people of England."

"Nick, could I tell them how Sarasota got purple after that?" Kari asked.

"Sure," Nick said.

"What do you mean?" KT inquired.

"Well," Kari said, "before he left Nassau to go home, Tresca bought a boat load of merchandise, including several large rolls of cloth called bolts. He bought a lot of English calico–a heavy, coarse, cotton cloth with different designs on it–and practically all of it was purple, Tresca's favorite color. Anyway, when he got back to Sarasota, Tresca gave a bunch of the material to Mary Jane Whitaker, and the rest was sold in Manatee. After that, for a long time, all the girls and ladies in the area wore lots of purple dresses. Bill didn't wear any purple dresses, but he did buy the *Blonde*, which he used around Sarasota for a long time."

"I have a feeling there's another clue waiting for us right now in the Yellow Bluffs area," Jan said anxiously. "Do you know if there's still anything left of the Whitakers around there?"

"I'm looking at the area on a Sarasota map right now on my computer screen," Prez replied. "There's a park north of Yellow Bluffs called Whitaker Gateway Park on 14th Street. North of there is Whitaker Bayou. A few blocks southeast of there, near where the Whitaker's second home was probably located, is the Whitaker Pioneer Cemetery. You're right, Jan–that's where we've got to look next. Maybe KT, Chad, and I can go there tomorrow morning. Tonight, though, let's keep working on getting you Bismarck Sarabiskota down here to Sarasota by this weekend. I'll call Governor Ed in a few minutes."

15

The next morning, shortly after sunrise, KT, Chad, and Prez were in the boat and on the way to Point of Rocks to see if Jack Lambert wanted to go to Yellow Bluffs. They were only halfway there when Jack Lambert jumped out of the water 20 yards in front of the boat and then dove back into the water.

Prez said, "Let's turn the boat around and see if he leads the way to Yellow Bluffs."

That's exactly what happened. Prez turned the boat towards the north, and Jack Lambert swam out ahead of the boat about 30 yards, his dorsal fin popping out of the water once in awhile.

Bismarck Sarabiskota was again in contact with the boat, and Chad was sending video to them.

"Jack Lambert is incredible!" Jan exclaimed.

"There's no doubt about it," KT agreed. "Maybe he knows the sound of Prez's boat or something, but it sure is amazing how he finds us so quickly!"

"What did Governor Ed have to say when you talked to him last night, Prez?" Mike asked.

"It was all good news," Prez replied. "Governor Ed can fly all of you down on Saturday morning, spend the afternoon and evening with us here in Sarasota–then he has to fly back on Sunday morning sometime. Do you think all of you can make arrangements by then?"

"Nick is the only one who has to work some things out yet," Kevin said. "The rest of us already got the OK from our parents."

Nick explained, "I have a few hockey camp commitments I've got to get out of, but I should be able to do it by the end of the day."

"Fabulous!" KT said. "This is great!"

"This is the best!" Jessie exclaimed. "We could all be together in just a few days!"

As they approached the beautiful John Ringling Bridge and saw the big purple Van Wezel Performing Arts Center in the distance, KT asked, "Do you think the building's purple color has anything to do with that purple cloth the people around here got from Captain Tresca?"

"I wouldn't doubt it," Prez said.

"What's the plan once we get to Yellow Bluffs?" Chad asked.

Prez said, "I suggest we check the two places we know Judah Benjamin was for sure–Whitaker Bayou and the site of Whitaker's second home, near that cemetery."

"Which one are we going to check first?" Chad asked.

"We'll let KT pick," Prez said.

"Let's go to the cemetery first," KT suggested.

Nick asked, "Do you know what's at the site of the Whitaker's first house at Yellow Bluffs now?"

Jan said, "I read where a mansion called *The Acacias* was built there in 1911."

"*Acacias* is a pretty cool name. Do you have any idea

where it comes from?" Chad asked.

"I looked it up. They're trees and shrubs from the pea family," Jan explained. "A Russian Prince lived there along with his wife–who just happened to be the granddaughter of President Grant and the niece of Mr. Potter Palmer. The mansion was torn down a long time ago. Now there are luxury condominium buildings there called the Sarasota Bay Club."

"What happened to the Whitaker's second house?" Kevin asked.

Prez said, "I found some pictures of the ruins of the house, but I don't think there's anything left of it now. The Whitaker Pioneer Cemetery used to be behind that house."

As they approached Yellow Bluffs, with Jack Lambert now swimming next to the boat, they could see a clump of trees and a damaged sea wall still left from The Acacias. Two high-rise condominum buildings rose prominently in the sky behind the Yellow Bluffs area.

They docked at the Whitaker Gateway Park, just north of Yellow Bluffs, then stood on the dock and took in the fabulous view. It certainly wasn't hard to see why Bill Whitaker had chosen this location way back in 1842.

KT told Jack Lambert what they were going to do, and then KT, Chad, and Prez walked from the dock onto a sidewalk that led through the park. Chad was still carrying the video camera and sending pictures to Bismarck.

They went one block east through the park until they got to Tamiami Trail. After crossing the busy highway, they went two blocks south to 12th Street, then half-a-block east to the Whitaker Pioneer Cemetery.

Prez opened the iron gate at the entrance, and the three

teens entered. They immediately walked over to the most prominent structures in the whole cemetery–the monuments for William Whitaker and Mary Jane Wyatt Whitaker.

They carefully examined the large monuments, looking for Captain Sarasota's clue. After that, they walked all around the small cemetery, reading the inscriptions on the gravestones and inspecting everything carefully.

Finding nothing, they left the cemetery, and walked over to a small house nearby, owned by the Daughters of the American Revolution. Prez said, "This organization must have built their house where the second Whitaker house was once located. The sign over there says they take care of the cemetery now."

KT, Prez, and Chad looked all around the outside of the house but saw nothing. Finally, Prez suggested, "Let's head back to the boat and ride up Whitaker Bayou to see if we can find anything there. We can always come back here later."

They slowly jogged to the boat. When they got back there, Jack Lambert was swimming next to it, acting strangely, making excited dolphin sounds. After that, he swam north toward Whitaker Bayou and then back to the boat.

"He definitely wants us to follow him," said KT.

"Let's do it, then," Prez said.

They got in the *Rough Rider* and followed Jack Lambert as he swam 50 yards to the mouth of Whitaker Bayou. Then he proceeded to swim up the narrow bayou.

The bayou was now lined with houses, but it wasn't hard to imagine what it might have looked like when Judah

Benjamin's boat was hidden there in 1865. When they'd gone approximately 80 yards up the bayou, Jack Lambert stopped, stuck his head out of the water, moved his head up and down rapidly, and made some excited dolphin sounds that indicated this was the place!

Prez guided the boat as close as he could safely get to the sea wall. Jack Lambert, who was slightly below the water's surface, had his beak right up against that wall.

"He wants us to look where he's pointing!" KT said. "I'll put my swim goggles on and take a look."

KT took off the T-shirt she had on over her swimsuit and jumped in next to the boat. Jack Lambert was still pointing to the exact location.

"I'll bet whatever they're looking at would be easier for us to see during low tide," Prez noted.

Within seconds, KT popped up out of the water and almost yelled, "030256!"

"Good job, Jack Lambert! Way to go, KT!" Chad said.

"You're the best!" Prez added.

"Hey, that 56 jumps out at me big-time!" Mike said excitedly.

"It should," Chad said. "It's one of the magic numbers in sports. Yankee Clipper Joe DiMaggio hit safely in 56 consecutive baseball games back in 1941."

"Is he the guy who married Marilyn Monroe?" Nick asked.

"That's right," Chad answered.

"No, you guys," Mike said. "I'm talking about 56, as in 1856, has special significance around Sarasota. Wasn't that the year after the Billy Bowlegs banana patch incident took place?"

"That's right, Mike!" Jessie exclaimed. "So the 03 02–that could mean March 2. What was going on March 2, 1856?"

"I think I know!" Jan cried. "KT sent me an interesting letter written by a girl who was living in Manatee. It's somewhere in my notes ... Oh, here it is! And it's dated March 2, 1856!"

"Who wrote it? What does it say?" Prez asked anxiously.

Jan said, "Remember that Gates family living in Manatee, whose dad was the first white settler south of Tampa? Well, there's a letter dated March 2, 1856, from his 17 year-old daughter, Sarah Gates, in Manatee. She's writing to her 15 year-old sister, Janie Gates, who was visiting someone in Tampa."

"What was so special about that letter?" Jessie asked.

Jan explained, "It vividly describes a huge event that happened a few days before March 2–when some Seminoles attacked Braden Castle."

"What exactly happened?" Mike asked.

"I've got a copy of the letter right here. I'll give you the highlights," Jan began. "It was a moonlit night. Because of the Seminole attacks around the area, Dr. Braden made sure everyone was inside each day at sunset, and the shutters and doors were closed and everything was boarded up. Then the men got their guns and ammunition ready, just in case.

"That evening, Dr. Joseph and Virginia Braden had two guests from Tallahassee for dinner–Furman Chaires and Reverend Sealey. The Braden children were there–Amy was 16, Robert was 14, Mary Virginia was 11, and there was a baby upstairs with a slave girl. A servant girl was in the kitchen.

"The servant girl saw someone on the *piazza*, which is

like the porch, and she thought it was just somebody who wanted to talk to Dr. Braden. About the same time, the girl who was upstairs with the baby came running down, saying there were Indians outside! Dr. Braden blew out the lights, and he told his family to get upstairs. Later, Mr. Chaires and Robert went upstairs with Dr. Braden.

"I guess one of Dr. Braden's guns was pretty advanced for the time. He'd gotten it from Mr. Gamble across the river. Anyway, with this gun, you could get nine shots off really fast. Dr. Braden stood by the second story window, holding that gun. Suddenly, he saw two Indians out there! He could have killed them, but he thought it was just his neighbors playing a prank–trying to scare him a little. Dr. Braden yelled at the two, and no one answered–then the Indians fired up at the window where Dr. Braden was yelling! Fortunately, they only hit the house near the window!

"Since Gamble's rapid-fire rifle made it seem like more men were shooting than actually were, the Indians retreated from near the house, stopping and shooting back at the house occasionally. Eventually, they retreated to a pond and escaped.

"After that, the Indians went to the Braden plantation nearby, where the slave quarters were located, and they took several slaves including some children. They also stole three of the doctor's best mules and a bunch of blankets and other things."

"Did they ever get the people back?" Nick asked.

"Yes, they did," Jan said. "Bill Whitaker left his family at Branch Fort and rode four days through the wilderness to the nearest military fort to tell them about the attack. Several volunteers took off from Manatee after the Indians, too. Eventually, they caught up with the seven Indians at a place called Joshua Creek, where there was a shootout lasting about 30 minutes. Four Indians were killed and three were wounded, but all the captured slaves were OK. I guess they had some really scary stories to tell, too. The whole thing was big news around the area."

KT said, "It looks like Braden Castle is our next stop, but we should find out more about it before we go."

Kari asked, "Would you Sarasota Sarabiskota mind waiting until this weekend to go to Braden Castle so we can go along with you? ... Please? I don't want to miss that."

"I don't either," Nick said.

"Me, either," Jessie added.

"We can wait a few days," Prez said. "That will give us a few days to help our parents get ready for your visit."

"And we can do some work on *The Starship Exercise*, too," said KT.

Stephen Queen sat on his boat, anchored in a small, secluded bay north of Whitaker Bayou. The listening devices he'd planted on the *Rough Rider* were working great! He could easily hear conversations on board the boat.

Stephen Queen smiled. "It looks like I'm going to get to Braden Castle before these kids do," he said out loud to himself.

16

The next few days were exciting ones, as Bismarck Sarabiskota prepared for their trip to Florida, and Sarasota Sarabiskota made preparations for their friends' visit. KT, Prez, and Chad also got some quality work time in on *The Starship Exercise*.

The Bismarck girls called KT several times, especially concerned about packing the right clothes for Florida. KT told them they could go shopping when they got to Sarasota if they needed any new beach clothes.

KT and her parents turned their family room into a comfortable place for the four girls to sleep and hang out. Prez and Chad worked hard making Prez's bedroom and adjoining guest room into a comfortable sleeping and living area for the five boys.

Saturday morning and early afternoon, KT, Chad, and Prez got several calls from their friends on board Governor Ed's jet, as they wanted to share what they were seeing and talking about on their exciting flight from Bismarck to Sarasota.

At about 2:00 P.M., Prez got yet another call on his cell phone from Governor Ed's jet. "We're getting close, Prez," Kari said. "Governor Ed said we're about to fly over the

Capitol in Tallahassee, and after that, we're going to fly right down the Gulf Coast to Sarasota. We should be on the ground in about an hour."

"Kari, we'll leave for the airport in a few minutes. Did you talk to Governor Ed about what he wants to do during his brief time in Sarasota?"

"We've given him lots of suggestions," Kari replied, "and I think a trip to Mote Marine Laboratory to see the manatees and going out for some great seafood are two things he might want to do with us down there."

Prez said, "I'll bet my mom can arrange the VIP tour at Mote for us, especially when they find out the Governor is visiting. She's even working at Mote right now–I'll give her a call. As far as seafood goes, there's supposed to be an excellent seafood place right on Phillippi Creek–the place with the huge Great White Shark hanging in front of it."

Kari giggled. "As long as the shark is dead, I have no problem."

Nick was next to get the phone up in the jet. "Prez, this has already been one of the coolest trips I've ever taken. It's beautiful up here."

"Enjoy the rest of your flight, Nick. We're on our way to the airport to pick you up right now."

After that, Mike was handed the phone. "Now I know how Elvis must have felt flying around in his own plane. It's a great life, Prez."

"I'm glad you're enjoying it," Prez said. "I'll see you in a few minutes."

Jessie was next to talk. "Prez, please give the phone to KT. I want to talk to her ..."

Prez's dad drove their RV to the Sarasota-Bradenton International Airport to pick everyone up. KT, Chad, and Prez sat in the back of the RV.

Prez called his mom to see if a tour of Mote Marine Laboratory could be arranged, and she said it was no problem. They'd be honored to take the governor of North Dakota and Prez's friends on a special tour anytime they got out there.

Chad said, "It's going to be so awesome having everyone together down here."

"I'm so excited I can hardly stand it!" KT added.

Prez whispered, "We can use all their help, too. I have a feeling this is going to be a time we'll never forget."

KT smiled. "Since I started hanging out with you North Dakota boys, my life has been pretty wild—but I've enjoyed every minute of it," she said.

"Well, thanks, KT," Prez said. "You've made everything more fun for us, too."

"That's for sure," Chad added.

Watching Governor Ed's jet land at the airport was awesome, but the excitement after they landed and everyone got off the jet and into the terminal was even better! There were tons of hugs and greetings, and everyone was so happy to see each other.

After awhile, Prez said, "Governor Ed, if you want, we can go right to Mote Marine before we go to Siesta Key. It's not too far from here, and my mom says they want to give us a special VIP tour."

"That would be great—if the rest of you want to," Governor Ed said.

"That'd be fabulous!" Kevin said.

Everyone else agreed.

On the way to Mote Marine Laboratory, Governor Ed sat in back of the RV with Sarabiskota.

"Prez and Chad, Bismarck is just not the same without you two," Governor Ed said with a smile.

"We miss North Dakota a lot, too," said Prez. "We promise to visit you guys as often as we can. I hope you can come visit us down here sometimes, too."

"How's First Lady Nancy doing, Governor Ed?" Chad asked.

"She's doing great, and she wanted me to say *hi* to all of you. She hopes to fly down here to Sarasota with me when some of you have to return to Bismarck, and then we can both maybe stay for a few days before we fly back."

"That would be awesome, Governor Ed," Prez said.

The tour of Mote Marine Laboratory was fantastic! They got the VIP treatment from the time they arrived–when Prez's mom met them at the Sea Turtle Center.

There, they watched the huge sea turtles swim in their large pools. They found out most of the turtles were recovering from injuries. One turtle they saw was blind and would have had no chance surviving out in the ocean.

When they got to the large manatee tank, Governor Ed wanted his picture taken with Sarabiskota, along with Hugh and Buffett, the two teen-age manatees, who were in the large tank behind them. Governor Ed said, "Before I left North Dakota, First Lady Nancy asked for a postcard with manatees on it. This will be much better. These manatees are unbelievable animals!"

Next, everyone walked over to another building, where many aquarium exhibits were housed, including a huge shark aquarium. After browsing through all the interesting exhibits, they all enjoyed petting the manta rays in a pool of water. They were so surprised how silky soft the manta rays were, and how they swam right up to their hands as if they were the most friendly creatures in the world. The Mote volunteer standing there told them the rays' stingers had been removed.

After that, Prez's mom took them to some areas of Mote that most of the public never saw, including the shark research lab, part of the largest shark research organization in the world. There they watched a short video of Mote scientists swimming with the largest fish in the sea, the huge 40-foot whale sharks living off the coast of Mexico.

While they were watching this interesting video, Jan glanced over to an area nearby, where some scientists were studying pictures of a particular dolphin on their computer screen. Being the curious person she was, Jan slowly wandered closer to get a good peek.

As she got within 15 feet of the large computer monitor, Jan realized the dolphin they were studying was Jack Lambert! She'd seen him enough times to know that for sure!

When one of the scientists glanced back and saw Jan standing there, Jan asked her, "Is that a special dolphin you're studying?"

The lady answered, "That's a *very* special dolphin they call *Admiral Flip*–the Navy's most gifted bottlenose dolphin. The Navy apparently retired him recently and released him near Miami, but they've lost track of his whereabouts. They want us to be on the lookout."

"Do you know what Admiral Flip did in the Navy?" Jan inquired.

"It's likely he did things like finding dangerous mines in deep water and taking tools deep into the water where Navy divers might be working. They might even have attached a small camera to him to get a close view of something they wanted to see below the surface somewhere. If this was the Navy's best dolphin, who knows what else he was capable of?"

"Thanks," Jan said, as she made her way back over to the rest of the group, anxious to tell them what she'd learned. They were all busy watching scientists working with small sharks on various research projects, including the study of sharks' immune systems.

Before they left Mote Marine Laboratory, they thanked all the people who gave them the close-up look at the large facility. On the way to the RV, Jan was able to quickly whisper most of what she'd found out about Jack Lambert to the rest of Sarabiskota. They couldn't believe it!

Since everyone seemed to be really hungry, they drove right to Phillippi Creek Oyster Bar for dinner. Before they entered the restaurant, they gathered around the Great White Shark hanging nearby. The sign near the shark said that it weighed 1,478 pounds and was caught in Phillippi Creek on November 14, 1998.

"Is that true, Prez?" Kevin asked.

"I've heard it's an urban legend, but this is the first time I've been here, too–so I'm not sure," Prez replied.

"What's an urban legend?" Nick asked.

Prez answered, "It's a questionable story handed down over time that spreads quickly and is believed to be true by

tons of people. Lots of urban legends get around quickly on the Internet."

"No matter if it's true or not, I'll bet this big shark and this sign get lots of extra business for this place," Governor Ed said.

Chad said, "We've been reading a lot about Sarasota, and much bigger things than this shark have been caught around here."

"Like what?" Governor Ed wanted to know.

"Like back in 1936, there was a manta ray–they called them *devil fish* back then–caught 15 miles out in the Gulf that was over 5,000 pounds," Chad said. "We found a picture of it hanging from the pier down at Bayfront Park, and it was amazing! Nineteen feet long and five feet thick! It took two fishing boats and 13 men from two o'clock in the afternoon one day to five o'clock in the morning the next day to land it!"

Kevin said, "We also found a picture from 1930 where a man named Captain Holmbrook caught a shark off Longboat Key that looked about twice as big as the one in those old *Jaws* movies. They claimed it was the biggest Great White Shark ever caught in the whole world at that time. It was huge!"

Jessie looked at KT, Chad, and Prez, and said, "Are you sure it's going to be safe swimming at your beach?"

"Sorry for all this talk about sharks, Jessie," KT said. "We've talked to the lifeguards at Siesta Public Beach, and they said they've never had a shark attack *anyone* on our beach, and we won't let you be the first."

Governor Ed chuckled. "Please don't mention *sharks* to First Lady Nancy when she comes down to Sarasota."

Everyone had a great time and some excellent food at Phillippi Creek Oyster Bar. To make things even better, they were seated only a few yards from the water. Governor Ed said, "I love eating seafood right by the sea. Somehow, seafood in North Dakota just can't match this."

"I don't know," Nick chuckled. "Those fish sticks at school are pretty tasty."

Everyone laughed.

Prez asked, "When we're done here, do you want to go for a boat ride and watch the sunset, Governor Ed?"

"Are you serious? I'd love to," Governor Ed replied. "I've heard there are people who move down here just to watch the sunset every night."

"It really is beautiful," said KT.

After they got to Siesta Key, they unloaded the luggage, and then Sarabiskota and Governor Ed got aboard the *Rough Rider*.

Governor Ed said, "I heard about your fabulous boat launching invention on the plane ride down here, Prez. I can't wait to see how it works."

Governor Ed was fascinated with gadgets and inventions. He'd even put together a team that won a national competition called *Junkyard Wars*, where they had to develop an invention to throw a refrigerator through the air as far as possible. The gadget had to be made only with stuff they could find in the junkyard. Governor Ed's team designed and built a catapult that threw the refrigerator over 70 feet!

"Would you like to give it a try?" Prez asked, handing the remote control device to Governor Ed.

"You don't have to ask me twice," Governor Ed said, eager to give it a try.

Prez told Governor Ed which button to push, then an engine started, and the trailer and boat moved slowly in reverse down to the beach. All the while, Governor Ed was smiling like a child on Christmas morning.

As Prez instructed, Governor Ed pushed another button. "Oh, wow!" the Governor said as the boat rose above the trailer.

"You're going to like the next part, too," said Prez.

After that, Governor Ed used the joystick to maneuver the boat over deeper water, and he slowly ... gently lowered it to the water's surface.

Everyone applauded!

"Do you have any idea how much fun that was! Thanks, Prez!" Governor Ed exclaimed.

"You're welcome, Governor Ed."

Prez started heading toward Point of Rocks, hoping they might see Jack Lambert on the way.

Less than a fourth of the way there, Jack Lambert suddenly jumped 15 feet out of the water in front of the boat! Governor Ed yelled, "A dolphin!"

At the same time, almost everyone else yelled, "Jack Lambert!"

"Governor Ed seemed confused at hearing his friends say *Jack Lambert*. He asked, "Did you say *Jack Lambert*–as in the great Steelers linebacker?"

"That's right, Governor Ed. He's a friend we met shortly after we moved here," Chad explained.

Prez slowed the boat down, and Jack Lambert poked his head out of the water, looking up at Governor Ed and all the other new faces. Then he made some happy dolphin sounds.

"That's got to be one of the most amazing things I've ever seen!" Governor Ed exclaimed. "I know First Lady Nancy is going to want to meet Jack Lambert, too!"

Then something spectacular happened! Jack Lambert got behind the boat and swam in reverse on his tail fin, with almost his whole body out of the water. From the perspective of everyone on the *Rough Rider*, Jack Lambert was positioned right in the middle of the setting sun! KT and Jessie grabbed their disposable cameras to capture it on film, but by then it was too late. Jack Lambert had settled down into the water.

"Please do that again, Jack Lambert," KT said.

And he *did*–as Jessie and KT got pictures and everyone watched in total amazement!

"That's better than any postcard in the world!" Governor Ed said enthusiastically. "I wouldn't have missed that for anything! Thanks, Jack Lambert!"

Jack Lambert made lots of happy dolphin sounds as he got to know all his new friends on the boat. After that, they watched the sun set slowly all the way into the ocean. As they were driving back to Sunset Beach, Governor Ed said, "I want to walk your beach in the moonlight a little when we get back ... Do you think you can all stop by the Ritz-Carlton and have breakfast with me before I fly back tomorrow morning, too?"

"We wouldn't miss it for the world!" Mike said, speaking for all of them.

Early in the morning, when all the boys were sound asleep at Prez's house, Prez's watch phone beeped. "Prez, are you awake?" Kari spoke in almost a whisper.

"What time is it?" Prez said, still half asleep.

"About three. Are you awake?" Kari asked.

"Uh ... I'm starting to wake up now, Kari. Have you girls been up all night?"

"I guess so," Kari said. "We thought you guys would be up, too."

"Chad needs all the beauty sleep he can get," Prez said. "What's up?"

"We've been talking and eating–also we've been working on the Sarabiskota logo, and we think we've got something cool to share with you."

"Bring it on," Prez said.

"Picture this. The North Dakota Capitol Building on Siesta Key Beach. Sara de Soto is standing on the beach, and Jack Lambert is jumping out of the water. *The Starship Exercise* is nearby. And, to top it off, Governor Ed is standing on top of the Capitol pointing at *The Starship Exercise*."

"Where are we, Kari?" Prez inquired.

"Oh, that's my favorite part. Jessie thought of this. Each of us is represented by a pelican. Your pelican has the Presidential seal on it somewhere and is wearing a Steelers cap. Mike's would have Elvis hair and would be holding a guitar. Kevin's is wearing a Nebraska cap and he's holding a football, and so forth."

"That's terrific, Kari! How about adding a Mall of America sign somewhere to represent Minnesota and KT's favorite shopping place?"

"Great idea, Prez!"

"Thanks. Now, you girls better get some sleep. We're having breakfast with Governor Ed in a few hours, and then we're taking him to the airport ..."

KEVIN KREMER

17

The girls didn't get any sleep at all that night, and they were out walking the beach with bare feet before sunrise. Jan, Jessie, and Kari couldn't believe the powdered-sugary softness of the sand. The moon and the stars above them provided a view that was breathtaking. The soothing sound of the surf meeting the shore, and the vastness of the ocean were extremely special to the three North Dakota girls.

About half an hour later, just before sunrise, the boys came out to the beach and met the girls. Prez asked, "Did you girls sleep at all last night?"

"Not really," Jessie said enthusiastically, "but none of us are tired at all."

Jan added, "We're running on adrenaline now, Prez, and we can't be stopped. We may hit a wall this afternoon sometime, but we were having so much fun last night, we couldn't sleep."

Kari asked, "Are we going to Braden Castle after we have breakfast with Governor Ed and take him to the airport?"

"That's what I'd like to do," Prez replied. "How's that sound to everyone?"

"Fabulous!"

After they'd had breakfast and said good-bye to Governor Ed, Prez's dad took them back to Siesta Key before he left for work. Within minutes, they were on the *Rough Rider*, anxious to get to Braden Castle.

As they headed south to meet up with their pal, Jack Lambert, Jessie said, "This is the best! It's so much better than watching everything on a screen in Kari's basement."

Less than one-eighth of the way to Point of Rocks, Jack Lambert swam near the boat, stuck his head out of the water, and took a good look at his new friends from Bismarck.

Jan, Kari, Jessie, Kevin, Nick and Mike talked to Jack Lambert as if he was another human being. Incredibly, they got the feeling he understood exactly what they were saying, too. Then Jack Lambert disappeared for awhile as Prez turned the boat north and headed for Braden Castle. Within a minute, Jack Lambert reemerged, swimming 30 yards in front of the boat.

Jessie whispered, "Are we gonna mention the *Admiral Flip* thing to Jack Lambert?"

"I don't think we should," KT replied. "We know how smart he is–but it might freak him out, and I don't want to hurt a close friend."

"I agree totally," Chad said, "but wouldn't you like to know all the stuff Jack Lambert did in the Navy?"

"No doubt," said Kevin. "That part about attaching a camera to Jack Lambert is so cool. I'd sure like to see his view of the world."

"Maybe we can rig something up later," Prez suggested.

"KT, how are we doing with all the place names on your map?" Kari inquired.

"Great!" KT replied. "I found out Stickney Point Road

and Stickney Point Bridge were named after a friendly man named Ben Stickney who came to Sarasota to manage the DeSoto Hotel. He used to have some great picnics and parties on Siesta Key."

"I found some information on Egmont Key," Kevin offered. "I guess it was named after the Earl of Egmont, who was the brother-in-law of the Hillsborough guy that Hillsborough County is named after. Hillsborough got a lot of land when England controlled Florida between 1763 and 1783."

Prez said, "I found something that might explain the name Big Sarasota Pass. Apparently, a long time ago, the pass between Siesta Key and Casey Key was called Little Sarasota Pass, but it filled in with sand in 1926–there was a hurricane that year."

"Now the Big Sarasota Pass name makes sense," Jessie said. "How can you have a *Big* Sarasota Pass without a *Little* Sarasota Pass?"

Mike said, "I found out the name Manasota came from the name of a lumber company located on Manasota Key back in 1918, when the railroad ran right through there."

"Didn't they just combine the first part of the word *manatee* and the last part of the word *Sarasota*?" Nick asked.

"For sure," Jan said.

Kari said, "This one's not on your map, KT, but I found a town's name that's actually an anagram."

"What's an anagram?" Nick asked.

"That's where you take the letters from one word, mix them up, and get another word–like *cat* can become *act*," Kari explained.

"Oh," Nick said. "What town name is an anagram?"

"The town of Lipona," Kari replied. "If you rearrange the letters, you get *Napoli*. It turns out the Prince of Napoli, who was the oldest son of one of Napoleon's sisters, was once exiled in the town, near Tallahass–"

Suddenly, Jack Lambert's head popped up out of the water, and he had a small, pink, child-sized flip-flop in his mouth. He flicked it into the boat, and then made some happy dolphin sounds as if he wanted to play catch.

Jan picked it up and threw it out of the boat as far as she could. It landed on the water 25 yards away and floated there for only a few seconds–then Jack Lambert swam over, picked it up in his mouth, swam over closer to the boat, and flicked it back to them again. They played catch like this for a long time as they slowly rode north toward the Manatee River.

When they finally approached the mouth of the Manatee, Kevin asked, "Can Jack Lambert follow us up the river, or does he need to swim in salt water only?"

"It will be interesting to see what happens when we get there, but I know he can swim in the river if he wants to," Prez replied. "If he stayed in fresh water for several days, though, it might cause him some harm, I think."

As they started boating up the river, Jack Lambert continued to lead the way. Prez pointed to the right of them. "Shaw Point or De Soto Point is right over there. Braden Castle is about eight miles up the river from here. This might be a good time to review some of what we know about Braden and other things along this river."

Jessie asked, "The town of Bradenton is named after the family that lived in Braden Castle, right?"

"That's right," Chad replied. "The first post office wasn't too far from where the Bradenton Pier is located. We'll see that about five miles from here. The story of how the town actually got its name is pretty funny, too."

"How's that?" Nick wanted to know.

Chad smiled. "Let's just say there was a little spelling problem involved."

"What do you mean?" Kevin inquired.

Chad explained, "Well, the pioneer family the town was named after was Braden, B-r-a-d-e-n, but the town ended up being called Braidentown, B-r-a-i-d-e-n-t-o-w-n for a long time starting on May 9, 1878. Somehow, an 'i' got in the name."

"How did that happen?" KT asked.

"The people who know for sure are dead, but I read about two possible explanations," Chad replied.

"What are they?" Jan wanted to know.

Chad answered, "Possibility number one–the postmaster's daughter sent the name correctly spelled to Washington, D.C., and a clerk goofed up there. Possibility number two–a lady by the name of Mrs. Cowdrey, who had a little hat shop in the general store where the post office was located, goofed up on the spelling on the application when she confused the spelling of the Braden name with some hat materials she used in her shop."

"I don't get it," Nick said.

Kari said, "You can braid–b-r-a-i-d hair, right?"

"Actually, I can't," Nick replied, giggling. "But I understand the concept of braiding."

"Well," Kari continued, "you can also braid threads and make materials to trim things like ladies' hats. It would be easy for a lady who sold hats to make that mistake, especially if she wasn't a very good speller to start with."

"I get it," Nick said.

Kevin asked, "When did they correct the spelling, Chad?"

"More than 25 years later, in 1905, it was officially corrected to Bradentown–B-r-a-d-e-n-t-o-w-n. In 1924, it became Bradenton, like it is today."

Mike chuckled. "That seems like a long time to change a spelling error."

"No doubt," Jan added. "I hope the government works a little faster when you're President, Prez."

Prez giggled. "I'll put Chad in charge of spelling corrections."

KT asked, "What do you know about the first postmaster of Braidentown, Chad?"

Chad replied, "His name was Major William Iredal Turner."

"Was he a real major?" Nick asked.

"Yup," Chad said, "he fought in both the Second Seminole War and the Civil War. Major Turner grew oranges and vegetables around here. In 1877, he bought seven acres of land on the Manatee River, and he built a large two-story house and hotel called the Mansion House. Across the street from that, he had a warehouse for his store and a wharf."

"What's a wharf?" Nick inquired.

"It's like a pier where you can load and unload boats," Kevin answered.

"Oh."

Prez asked, "Why did Major Turner decide to name the town after the Bradens anyway?"

Chad said, "The place where Turner built his Mansion

House and had his post office was really close to the spot where Dr. Joseph Braden built a log house when he first moved here from Tallahassee. Near the log house, Dr. Braden also had a stockade or fort called Fort Braden and a pier made of pine logs where boats could pick up products and unload supplies."

"Was the fort built to protect against Seminole Indian attacks?" Nick asked.

"That's right," Chad replied. "From what I read, the fort was about a 100 yards by a 100 yards and had walls that were 15-feet high made of pine logs stuck into the ground and sharpened at the ends. There were a bunch of holes, called *loopholes*, in the logs for people to stick their rifles through. The fort had a trading post, a watchtower, several small log cabins for workers to stay in, and a sugar warehouse."

"Was Dr. Braden's sugar plantation located right there, too?" Kevin asked.

"No," Chad answered, "it was east of there several miles, in the area near where Braden River and Braden Castle are. There was a dirt road connecting the fort to the plantation."

"Why would he build his first log cabin, pier, and fort so far west of where his plantation was located?" Jan wanted to know.

Chad said, "Sandbar–there was a huge sandbar downstream from his plantation, so large boats carrying supplies or taking his sugar to customers couldn't get all the way to the plantation. The deeper water was close to shore where he built his first house, the pier, and the fort."

"That makes complete sense to me," Nick said.

"Thanks, Nick," Chad replied.

Prez asked, "What else do we know about Dr. Braden

other than what we learned when we talked about the attack on Braden Castle?"

Kari said, "Actually, there were two Braden brothers–Dr. Joseph Braden and Hector Braden. But the town is probably named after Joseph. Hector wasn't around Manatee very long."

"What happened to him?" KT asked.

"I'll save that part of the story for later," Kari replied. "Let me give you some background first. Remember, we talked about Josiah Gates being the first settler south of Tampa? He came here in 1841, and the town of Manatee grew up around the Gates homestead. Bill Whitaker came to Sarasota in December of 1842. Well, many other settlers came to the Manatee area between 1842 and 1845, mostly from the Tallahassee area, and the Bradens were two of them."

Mike asked, "Why did they move to Manatee anyway?"

Kari explained, "A big bank in Tallahassee failed, and guys like the Braden brothers lost their fortunes. They thought they could get them back by growing things like sugar cane on the good fertile land near the Manatee River. The Armed Occupation Act made it really easy to get land around here, too."

"What's a bank failure," Chad asked, even before Nick could.

"It's a little complicated," Prez began, "but a bank's money comes from depositors who put their money into the bank. The bank makes its money by loaning that money to other people and charging a little bit extra. Now, what would happen if enough of those borrowers can't pay back those loans for one reason or another, and then some of the depositors come in for some money but there isn't enough left in the bank to pay them?"

"I think I understand the concept," Chad said.

Nick asked, "If Dr. Braden was a real doctor, how did he have much time to grow sugar cane?"

"Good question, Nick," Kari said. "I read that Dr. Braden had always been so rich, he didn't have to practice medicine."

"That seems like such a waste," Jan said.

Prez asked, "What was *Hector* Braden's occupation before he came to Manatee?"

"He was a lawyer," Kari replied.

Kevin asked, "Does anyone know if Bill Whitaker was down on Sarasota Bay before the Braden brothers got to the Manatee River?"

"It must have been close," Kari observed. "We know for sure that the Bradens were living in Manatee as early as February 27, 1843, because they signed their names in an old book in Manatee that day. Bill arrived at Sarasota Bay a few months before that, on December 14, 1842."

"Did the Bradens own lots of land around here?" Nick asked.

"That's right," Prez said. "The two Braden brothers eventually bought over 1,100 acres of land running for miles along the southern bank of this river here and along the Braden River. At one time they were producing about 250,000 pounds of sugar a year. I read where this area was once the leading sugar producer in the whole country."

"I can't imagine growing anything along this river back then," said Mike. "Just clearing the land and getting it ready to plant anything without tractors would seem impossible."

KT said, "I read about this, and it must have been really

difficult. The Bradens had 79 slaves to help with all the work around their plantation. It also said they had 50 oxen to do the really heavy work."

"After you clear the land, what else do you have to do to grow sugar cane, anyway?" Chad asked.

"More than I could comprehend," KT replied. "It sure sounded more complicated than growing wheat in Minnesota. Once they planted sugar cane, it took about four years before they even got a first crop. After the crop was harvested by cutting its stalks, it had to be milled and boiled. It took lots of work with lots of machinery before they ended up with grains of sugar. Then they had to put the sugar in large barrels called hogsheads and ship them from the river."

"Did Dr. Braden have the biggest plantation around here back then?" asked Mike.

KT answered, "No, it was one of the largest, but Major Robert Gamble had a 3,500 acre plantation on the northern bank of this river. Remember, Major Gamble was the guy who gave that rapid-firing gun to Dr. Braden that he used during the attack on Braden Castle."

Prez said, "I read that the Gamble Mansion is still standing in Ellenton. They've fixed it up and give tours. We'll have to stop there sometime. That was where Judah Benjamin hid for a few weeks before he went to the Whitakers' house."

"The hiding in the beef guy!" Nick added, enthusiastically. "The big picture is starting to come into my brain."

"Me, too, Nick," Kari said. "It's really fun knowing about the history of this area."

"Did anyone find out yet how Ellenton got its name?" Chad asked.

"I thought you'd never ask, Chad," Prez said. "When Major Gamble left this area, a man by the name of Major George Patton bought the plantation. He had a daughter named Ellen, and he named the post office after her."

"While we're on that subject," said KT, "what about Palmetto? It's north of us right now. Does anyone know how it got its name?"

"I do," Mike replied. "A guy named Joel Hendrix had the post office there. His neighbor was from South Carolina–the Palmetto State."

"Cool," Nick said.

Prez said, "I can almost picture what it must have been like living here on the Manatee River in the 1840's. There were only about a dozen families, most of them on plantations, doing pretty well financially. All of them wanted to be safe against Indian attacks, many of them were raising families, and they all were hoping to make some money, mostly from crops like sugar cane. Getting around was mostly done with boats, but there were also dirt roads between homes for wagon travel. People depended upon each much more than we do now, so neighbors got to know each other really well."

"There's the Bradenton Pier up ahead," KT pointed out. "Dr. Braden had his first house and Fort Braden near there."

They rode by the pier, trying to imagine what it might have been like in the 1840's.

"Whatever happened to the Bradens, anyway?" Jessie asked.

Kari said, "Things were going pretty well for everyone around here until 1846."

"Then there was the hurricane, right?" Jan said.

201

"Well, just before that," Kari explained, "something awful happened. On October 4, 1846, little two-year-old Ella Gates, who everyone around here loved and adored, died–I'm not sure why. Then, on October 14th, the Hurricane of 1846 hit. That's where Hector Braden comes in."

"What happened to him?" Chad asked.

"Well," Kari began, "he was coming back from a trip up to northern Florida on his horse when he got to the Little Manatee River north of here. By then, the hurricane had already hit, and it must have been really tough going. Hector was crossing the river, when his horse somehow wandered into some quicksand or a sinkhole. That's when there was a real Stephen Queen moment. Days after the hurricane was over, after a lot of searching, they found Hector's body still seated up on his dead horse. Hector's eyes were wide open and his hands were still tightly holding his reins and riding whip!"

"Yikes!" Nick said.

"That *is* a Stephen Queen moment!" Chad added.

Mike asked, "Did anything bad happen during the Hurricane of 1848?"

"I'm afraid so," Kari said. "John Gamble, the youngest Gamble brother, was out in the Gulf on board a schooner named *Atlanta*, and it went down in the storm. John Gamble drowned."

Prez pointed out, "We're really close to two places we talked about before. This is near 14th Street East in Bradenton. There was a mineral springs near the south bank of the river here; that's where Branch Fort was located, and many families stayed there during The Billy Bowlegs War.

"Just one block further east is where Gates had his house, and the village of Manatee was mostly south of there. Manatee became part of Bradenton in the 1940's, and some of the old buildings are still there–in a place called Manatee Village Historical Park."

"Could we stop there on the way back?" Chad asked.

"Sure," Prez replied, "if we have time and you want to."

Jan asked, "Does anyone know why Dr. Braden left his log house and decided to build Braden Castle three miles or so up the river from there?"

"No one seems to know for sure," Prez said, "but I guess it might have had something to do with the beauty of the new place and with the great location near the confluence of the Manatee and the Braden Rivers–much closer to his sugar-making operation."

"What's a confluence?" Kevin asked before Nick had a chance.

"It's where two or more streams come together," answered Prez.

Kevin chuckled. "Oh, I knew that."

Prez added, "We'll see how it looks now, but back then, Braden Castle was supposed to have been in a beautiful, thickly wooded area, with oaks and pines and palm trees. Braden Castle was built on a small hill that gradually sloped toward the river. It must have been quite a sight."

Nick asked, "When did Dr. Braden build Braden Castle?"

"In 1850," Prez answered.

"Whatever happened to Dr. Braden?" Chad wondered.

"There was a financial crisis in the country in 1857, so there was no one buying Braden's sugar anymore," Prez replied. "Because of that, he couldn't pay his debts, so he lost his land, his slaves, and all his equipment."

"Where did the Bradens go after that?" Mike asked.

"Texas," Prez said. "Sadly, Dr. Braden didn't live long after that, either. I found an old record that said he died in LaGrange, Georgia, on February 7, 1859, when he was only 48. I didn't find anything yet about what happened to the rest of his family, though."

"What happened to Braden Castle after Dr. Braden left?" KT asked.

Prez said, "A man by the name of General James Cooper, a Seminole War veteran, bought the castle and lived there the rest of his life. After that, though, it was abandoned, and it went downhill. In the summer of 1903, there was a woods fire that did a lot of damage to the castle–it took out the entire roof and part of the interior wall. The Hurricane of 1926 demolished the walls. In 1924, the Camping Tourists of America bought the land, and a huge trailer park developed there. I guess they put a wire fence around the ruins eventually, so at least something from the landmark could be saved for history's sake."

When they got to the location of the Braden Castle ruins, a 750-foot wooden pier extended prominently out into the river. Prez called out to the fisherman at the end of the pier and asked if they could dock the boat on the pier. He said that they could.

Jack Lambert swam up and down the pier, apparently searching for clues. The fisherman seemed shocked to be seeing a dolphin so far up the Manatee River! "Well, I'll be darned!" he said.

They quickly walked down the pier, then through a small park to the ruins of Braden Castle, which were surrounded by a four-foot high fence. Although there wasn't much left of Braden Castle, enough huge chunks of tabby remained so Sarabiskota could get an idea what the home of Dr. Braden once looked like. There were many small holes in the tabby just big enough to poke a gun through.

One huge tabby structure was still standing. It resembled an enormous picture frame and looked like a large entryway had probably been located there. A tall tree was growing right next to that structure.

A narrow street surrounded the park and the ruins, and beyond that were many tidy little houses, some so small they looked like large doll houses. It appeared many of them were actually converted trailers.

As Sarabiskota approached the fence, a caretaker was behind it, pulling some weeds. Kari spoke for all of them. "Hi, I'm Kari Wise from Bismarck, North Dakota, and these are my friends. We're very interested in the history of this area, and we were wondering if we could get a closer look at the Braden Castle ruins."

"Sure, come on in," the caretaker said. "I'm Harry Aumend ... We had a little excitement here late last night."

"What happened?" Kari asked.

"Someone tried to go over the fence, and my German shepherd, Cuddles, ended up taking a nice chunk out of his pants. The guy got away on his boat, but I'll bet he got a good scare."

"What do you think he was doing?" KT asked.

"I have no idea. Some people are just troublemakers, I guess," Harry said.

Sarabiskota opened the gate and walked through, spreading out amongst the ruins, looking for a clue, while Prez

continued talking to Harry. Nick climbed the tree growing next to the huge frame-shaped tabby structure.

While peering into one of the small holes near the top, he spotted what looked like a disk-shaped rock, about one-third the size of a hockey puck. Nick reached into the hole and pulled out the object. He took a quick look at it and noticed two dates scratched into the surface–April 24, 1913, and September 7, 1923! He quickly slipped the object into his pocket!

On the other side of the Manatee River, several hundred yards away, Stephen Queen stood on his boat and peered through his binoculars, watching all the action at the Braden Castle ruins. If only he could hear what the teen-agers were saying! But, then again, now that he'd planted the listening devices on Prez's boat and in his workshop, he'd soon know if they found anything. He rubbed his backside. "That darn dog!" he said, in a loud whisper.

At that moment, Jack Lambert detected Stephen Queen's presence on the other side of the river. He swam at high speed underwater and approached Stephen Queen's boat like a torpedo! Stephen Queen was too busy looking through his binoculars to notice a thing. Suddenly, Jack Lambert exploded out of the water, jumped high into the air, and pulled the binoculars out of Stephen Queen's hands with his mouth! The binoculars fell into the water, sinking to the bottom of the Manatee River!

Stephen Queen quickly started his boat and raced down the river as fast as he could!

18

Sarabiskota got in the *Rough Rider* and started back to Siesta Key, with Jack Lambert leading the way. As soon as they were underway, Prez asked KT, "Would you please drive the boat awhile? I want to take a closer look at that object with the dates on it. That September 7th date looks really familiar. I can check things out on my computer down below."

Prez went below deck for about 20 minutes. When he came back, he was holding the disk-shaped object, and he was obviously excited. "I was right! I know about September 7, 1923, but I haven't found anything about the other date yet ... there's something else pretty interesting about this object, too."

Everyone gathered closer to Prez to get a good look.

"What's that?" Nick asked.

Prez was ready to burst, but he spoke as calmly as possible. "It must have been in the water a long time. Under several layers of matter, there's definitely an old coin of some kind. I can't tell much more about it until I remove all the matter. But notice where I scratched down to the metal here–it's obviously *gold*."

There was some serious celebrating on board the *Rough*

Rider for the next few minutes! Jack Lambert could tell his friends were celebrating something, and he decided to join in. To the delight of everyone on board, Jack Lambert put on a one-dolphin spectacular that topped anything ever seen in Florida or anywhere else!

He did back flips, triple twisting somersaults, and some jumps over 20 feet in the air! Sarabiskota cheered wildly as Jack Lambert continued celebrating!

At one point, a water-skier driving by stared over at what was going on. He was so astounded, he lost his balance and wiped out!

When Jack Lambert's revelry was over, Nick asked excitedly, "Are we rich?"

"I don't even want to guess how much this is worth right now," Prez said. "We can find out everything we need to know about this coin when we get back to Siesta Key. This sure makes me wonder what other surprises Captain Sarasota could have in store for us, though."

Prez handed the object to Nick, and it was eventually passed around to everyone.

"What's the deal with September 7, 1923?" Kari asked.

"It's the date a well-known Sarasota golfer died–right on his own golf course in Sarasota," Prez explained.

"That's unreal," Mike said. "How old was he?"

"He was 71," Prez answered. "I've just been scanning some of the material I read about him before, and it's a good story."

"Please clue us in, Prez," Jan requested.

"All right. The man's name was John Hamilton Gillespie. He definitely built the first golf course in Florida, and maybe it was even the first one in America, back in May of 1886.

It was a two-hole course–just one long fairway with two greens."

"Where was that course exactly?" KT asked.

"They've got streets in Sarasota named Golf Street and Links Avenue near the Hollywood 20 movie theaters. It was close to there. Later, he built a 9-hole course on some land he owned east of there."

"So Gillespie sounds like he should be a pretty famous guy. Why haven't I ever heard of him?" Mike asked.

"I don't know, Mike," Prez answered, "but Gillespie was much more to Sarasota than just a golfer. The Scottish people who came to Sarasota were the ones who started to shape the town of Sarasota, and Gillespie was a real leader of the Scots."

"I don't get it," Nick said. "What do you mean the Scots shaped Sarasota?"

Prez explained, "What I mean is–they were the ones who had a blueprint for the town of Sarasota, and then they actually started building the town."

"Oh."

Jessie yawned and said, "Prez, I'll bet you're going to tell us all about the Scottish people coming to Sarasota, aren't you?"

"Do you think you can stay awake that long? You girls look really tired," said Prez.

"I'm not tired at all," Jessie insisted, holding back a big yawn.

"Me, either," KT added, struggling to keep her eyes open.

"We're still operating on adrenaline, Prez," said Jan. "Get on with your story."

"Where would you like me to start?" Prez asked.

"How about by answering the question of why the Scottish people came to Sarasota in the first place," Kari suggested.

Prez began, "A lot of the people who came to the United States in the late 1800's and early 1900's were looking for a better way of life, and it was the same with the Scots who came to Sarasota. In 1885, Scotland was going through some tough times. Many people didn't have jobs, and they were paying really high taxes. Those who still had some money were looking for a better place to live."

"So, why would they choose Sarasota?" asked Kevin.

"That's a good question," said Prez, "since Sarasota wasn't much in 1885 when the Scots came here."

"What do you mean?" Nick asked.

"The town of Sarasota really didn't exist," Prez began. "It was just a post office in Abbe's general store, an old dirt road running to the bay called Cunliff Lane, plus a few homesteads between Hudson Bayou and Phillippi Creek—"

"Oh, sorry to interrupt, Prez," Jan said, yawning, "but I found out Hudson Bayou was named after an early neighbor of the Whitakers who lived near the bayou, and Phillippi Creek was named after a guy named Phillipi Bermudez, a Spanish fisherman living near the creek. There seems to be another spelling problem in this part of history, too."

"What do you mean?" Chad inquired.

"Well, Phillipi only had one 'p' toward the end of his name, but somehow an extra one got into the name of the creek."

"Interesting," said Nick. "History sure could have used a good spell checker."

"So, why did the Scottish want to come to Sarasota all the way from Scotland?" Jessie inquired.

"Some slick advertisement in the Scots' local newspaper," Prez replied. "The ad said Sarasota not only had a perfect climate, but it was also a modern town, and you didn't have to work hard at all to make a living growing oranges and things."

"Why would the people believe that kind of advertisement?" Kevin asked.

"Partly because they wanted to believe it," Prez replied. "Later, though, they got pamphlets from the company doing the advertising–the Florida Mortgage and Investment Company. They found out the company was owned by some people with good reputations in Scotland. The president of the company was a well-respected man named Sir John Gillespie who owned a large estate near Edinburgh, Scotland. Sir John, by the way, was the father of the golf guy who actually came to Sarasota later. Anyway, the Scots knew some of the other big shots in the company, too, so they started to feel better about the deal."

"What exactly was the deal?" Mike wanted to know.

Prez explained, "Essentially, they sold just about everything they had, and for a 100 pounds sterling, which was a lot of money, they got 40 acres of land to farm, plus a town lot in the town of Sarasota. The pamphlet said the land would be worth a fortune in a few years."

"Then what happened?" asked Kari.

"Well, there were 68 Scots who made the deal, and they eventually sailed from Glasgow, Scotland, on a steamship called *Furnesia* on November 25, 1885. By the way, Chad, they were called the *Ormiston* Colony–named after Sir John

Gillespie's home. They made it to New York City on December 10. Selven Tate, one of the promoters of the company, met them and took them to a hotel. After that, they had three days in New York to sight see."

"Was that Sir John Gillespie guy with them?" Nick asked.

"No, he never came here. His son did, but not yet," Prez replied.

"Oh."

Mike joked, "Did the Scots take in a New York Giants football game while they were in New York?"

Kevin noted, "Believe it or not, Mike, professional football actually started not too many years after this, in 1892, but the Giants didn't start until 1925."

"You're amazing, Kevin," Kari said. "I'll bet you can probably tell us who played in that first professional football game, too."

Kevin smiled. "No, but I'll bet Chad can."

Chad said, "Thanks for the compliment, Kevin ... it was the Allegheny Athletic Association playing the Pittsburgh Athletic Club. One of the Allegheny guys was paid $500 to play, and that's why it was considered to be professional football."

"Who was the guy that got the $500?" Nick asked.

"Pudge Heffelfinger," Chad answered with no hesitation.

"I can't believe Pudge Heffelfinger doesn't get more publicity–maybe it's because no one wants to pronounce his name," Prez said, giggling. "Anyway, getting back to the Ormiston Colony, they left New York, took a steamship called the *State of Texas* from there, and got to Fernandina, up in the northeast corner of Florida, on December 17. After that, they took a train ride on a lousy little train nicknamed *two streaks of rust* and got to Cedar Key on December 18."

"Where's Cedar Key?" Chad asked.

"About 130 miles north of here," Prez answered.

"Except for the train ride, it sounds pretty good so far," Nick observed.

"That's about when the bad news started," Prez explained. "Tate told them they'd have to wait several weeks because the temporary homes that were supposed to have been built for them in Sarasota hadn't even been started yet, so they'd have to stay at Cedar Key for awhile."

"What did they do to pass the time at Cedar Key?" Jessie inquired.

"Mostly, they probably got more and more impatient," Prez replied. "They also toured an Eagle Pencil Company factory and talked to some of the fishermen, but I don't think they were having much fun."

"Then what happened?" Kari asked.

"Can you imagine how anxious and frustrated they got?" Prez said. "When they couldn't stand it any longer, they chartered a side-wheel steamboat called the *Governor Safford* and took off from Cedar Key. The boat was only about 100 feet long and it was packed with people and their luggage. Finally, on either December 23 or December 28, depending on which sources you read, the ship slowly moved through Big Sarasota Pass."

"Why *slowly*?" asked Mike.

"Because the captain had to worry about sandbars, and he'd never even seen the bay before, so he didn't know the depths," Prez explained. "The *Governor Safford* was actually the first steamer ever to enter Sarasota Bay."

"What happened when the Scots saw Sarasota was really nothing?" Jan asked.

"I'll bet it wasn't a pretty situation," Prez said. "You can just picture them out on the steamboat on the bay near where Bayfront Park is today, waiting for the smaller boats to take them to land–looking for that beautiful, new town they'd read about in Scotland."

"And what exactly did they see?" Nick asked.

"Well, not much," Prez offered. "Lots of trees and mangroves and other vegetation and a few old buildings. One building was a deserted fish oil plant that was now the company store for the Florida Mortgage and Investment Company. One building was the place where the fish oil plant workers used to stay. There was also a home down the bay a little where the Willard family had once lived."

"Yikes! Can you imagine how they felt?" said Chad. "What happened next?"

"Of course, they wanted some answers from the local rep for the Florida Mortgage and Investment Company, a guy named A.C. Acton," said Prez. "Acton told them the town was still in the blueprint stage, and they'd arrived earlier than expected, but he assured them the company was going to put millions into Sarasota, and everything would be all right.

"The Scots felt better after that, and then some of the early homesteaders like the Whitakers and the Abbes came along. They'd heard the whistle from the *Governor Safford* and were checking things out. They even helped get the Scots' belongings on a raft and on shore. Then the *Governor Safford* took off."

"How old was Bill Whitaker then?" Nick asked.

217

"About 64, I think," KT replied. "He was born in 1821, remember?"

Nick sighed. "Gee, I remember Bill back when he was our age."

Nick got several strange looks–then everyone laughed.

"Where did the colonists live if there were no houses built for them?" asked Mike.

"Some lived with some of the early settlers," Prez explained. "The Brereton and Lawrie families stayed in an old cedar bucket plant on the bay at the end of Cunliff Lane. Two families lived in that old Willard place. Some, like the Brownings, stayed in tents in the woods."

"Tents aren't the Ritz, but did the Brownings get a good night's sleep?" Nick asked.

"I'm not sure about their quality of sleep, Nick, but before they went to sleep, Mrs. Browning made scones and pancakes and tea by the campfire, and the adults talked with some of the old settlers. I guess some of the Sarasota boys even flirted with some of the cute Scottish girls."

"What would Sara de Sota have thought about *that*?" Jessie said, giggling.

"I'm not sure," Prez said, trying not to laugh, "but the next morning, one of the Whitaker boys, named Hamlin, went out on the bay and caught a bunch of fish and then helped clean and fry them for the Brownings. Another one of the Whitaker boys dropped by with some bread that his mom, Mary, had baked. The Whitaker boys even showed the Browning girls how to make bread in a pan over the campfire."

"I'm feeling better about the whole situation now," Kevin said. "What happened next?"

Prez replied, "The Scots loved to celebrate New Year's Day, so they had a big celebration at the old cedar bucket plant on Cunliff Lane. Some of the settlers like the Whitakers brought game and fish to the party, and they even ate some plum pudding the Scottish colonists had brought all the way from Scotland. It sounds like they had a great time and had tons to eat and drink."

"This sounds like fun," Kari said. "Did things just keep getting better for the Scots after that?"

"Unfortunately, things pretty much tanked for them after that," Prez said.

"What do you mean?" Jan asked.

"You remember the 40 acres of land they'd been promised? Well, to figure out where their land was, each colonist had to reach into a box and pull out a slip of paper with a farm number written on it. That was the farm they were stuck with, no matter where it was located. That system didn't work out too well–to say the least. Some colonists got land up to eight miles out in the woods, a long distance from where they lived. Some colonists couldn't even find their land, and some of the land the Scots got wasn't good for growing anything.

"You can only imagine how they felt once they started trying to clear the land. It was very difficult work, and they weren't used to it. Just imagine cutting down big pine trees, digging wells, and building shacks by hand if you weren't used to it."

"It doesn't sound like it could get any worse," Chad said.

"How wrong you are, Chad," Prez said. "It got much worse. Guess what happened next?"

"It snowed!" Chad blurted out, and then he laughed.

"That's right!" Prez exclaimed and laughed at the look of astonishment on Chad's face. "Not on Christmas, but on January 9, 1886! Even people like the Whitakers, who had lived here a long time, were surprised. They thought the woods were on fire and the wind was blowing around ashes–they couldn't believe it was snow! It even snowed enough so they could make snowballs, but I'll bet the colonists weren't having much fun. Everyone quit working. Everyone was freezing cold, and they were huddling around fires trying to keep warm. Tons of stinky, dead fish even washed into shore. It was a stinky situation all the way around."

"This is getting ridiculous," Mike noted. "The Scots must have been ready to throw in the towel."

"Many of them did," Prez said. "The Lawries took off first–then a bunch of others."

"Where did they go?" Mike asked.

"Some went to states up north where they had relatives or friends," Prez replied. "Most of them had no money left, though, and they even had to borrow money to take a boat up north."

"Did *any* of the colonists stay?" Nick asked.

"The Brownings did–and a few others," Prez answered.

"What happened after most of the colonists left?" Jan inquired.

Prez said, "Surprisingly, even with most of those first colonists gone, the town boomed. The Florida Mortgage and Investment Company started to put lots of money into Sarasota. With help from workers who came from out of town, the colonists who were left helped build a pier, an artesian well, and a roominghouse called the Sarasota

House. They also helped open up Main Street by clearing away all the trees and stuff."

"What's an artesian well?" Nick asked.

"It's a deep well that you dig, and the water pressure forces the water up to the surface," Prez answered.

"How do you build an artesian well?" Nick inquired.

"I don't have a clue, but I did read about how they built the pier, and it must have been tough work," Prez said.

"How did they build it?" Mike asked.

Prez explained, "There was no machinery to drive those huge wooden posts into the ground beneath the water, so here's what they did. The men got into the cold water, up to shoulder deep in some places. Then they grabbed the heavy pine logs and rocked them back and forth for hours until they were buried down to the rock under the sand. That was just the first step."

Jan asked, "How long did it take to build the pier?"

"About three months," Prez answered. "It was really important, too, because then freight and passenger boats started to come to Sarasota."

"When did the golf guy come to Sarasota?" Jessie asked.

"You mean John Hamilton Gillespie," said Prez. "He came over from Scotland in March of 1886. His dad, Sir John Gillespie, sent him over here to get things on the right track and keep them moving after the Ormiston Colony mess."

"What was John Hamilton like?" KT inquired.

"He was tall, built like a defensive lineman, with reddish-brown hair," said Prez. "From what I read, I got the feeling he rubbed lots of people the wrong way, but many men in power do, I guess."

"When you're elected President, are you going to still treat your old friends with respect?" Jan asked.

Prez chuckled. "Everyone but Chad."

Kari asked, "Did Gillespie get a lot done after he took over here in Sarasota?"

"He sure did," Prez said. "Streets were cleared, although they weren't much more than dirt roads. There was tons of construction on Main Street. John Browning, one of the Ormiston colonists who stayed, was an excellent carpenter, and he helped put up many of the buildings. Before long, Sarasota's Main Street had just about everything you needed back then–a doctor's office, a general store, a meat market, a livery stable, and a blacksmith shop. The post office was moved from Abbe's general store to Main Street, and Charles Whitaker became the new postmaster. They even built the first school in town on Main Street, but it wasn't much, and I think the teachers were even more grossly underpaid than Otto Graham was."

"What do you mean?" asked Kevin.

"Well, the school was about the size of Chad's bedroom–16 feet by 25 feet–with some pretty crude furniture. The two teachers, Anna and Sue Whitcomb, got paid absolutely *nothing*. The Whitcomb sisters were good teachers, but they got married after their first year of teaching in the first double wedding *ever* in Sarasota, and they never taught again."

KT asked, "How many kids were in the class, Prez?"

"There were 13 kids–eight girls and five boys. Oh, I forgot to tell you about the best building in the new town of Sarasota, the De Soto Hotel. It cost more to build than all the other buildings in town combined. The De Soto Hotel was the luxury hotel in town, built at the end of Main Street near the bay. It was the center of Sarasota activity, and many people came to the hotel for a couple of winter months each year to hunt or fish, to shoot birds, or to sail the bay."

"It sounds like it was a resort hotel for the new town's first snowbirds," Jan observed.

"That's exactly right," said Prez.

"Things seem to be going so well, Prez," KT said, "but I have a feeling you're going to get to some bad news pretty soon."

"You can almost read my mind," said Prez. "Before the third winter season in 1888, there was a huge yellow fever epidemic that hit the coasts of Florida. Thousands of people got sick and many died. Not too many people came to Sarasota during the winters for awhile, and everything slowed down."

"What's yellow fever, Doc?" Kevin asked.

Jan explained, "It's a mosquito-borne virus that causes a hemorrhagic fever. People get the virus from an infected mosquito biting them, and then the virus replicates in the skin and lymph nodes. From there, it spreads throughout the body to other organs, like the liver, kidneys, and heart. Infected people develop yellow skin or jaundice because of liver damage, and they get a high fever—hence the name *yellow fever*. Thank goodness they have a vaccine for it now."

"Yikes! Sounds totally yummy," Nick observed, grimacing.

Prez continued, "That wasn't the only reason Sarasota's growth slowed down big-time. Sarasota didn't have too many jobs other than fishing and farming, and there wasn't even a railroad between Tampa and Sarasota yet. Then there was a huge national money crisis, and investment in Sarasota almost came to a halt."

KT chuckled. "At least it didn't snow," she said.

"Well, actually it did," said Prez, "but it was a little later, in February of 1894."

Nick suddenly perked up and said, "All this talk about disease and dying and crisis gives me an idea. September 7, 1923, was the day John Gillespie died on the golf course, right?"

"Right."

"Maybe April 24, 1913, is the day someone else died," Nick suggested.

"Nick, I think you may be onto something!" Kari exclaimed.

"Everyone check your minicomputer files!" cried Prez. "See if you can find out where John Hamilton Gillespie is buried!"

After dinner, Sarabiskota rushed over to Prez's workshop. Everyone was anxious to find out more about the coin Nick had found at the Braden Castle ruins. As everyone else watched with tremendous anticipation, Nick assisted Prez in carefully removing all the matter from what turned out to be a beautiful gold coin!

Finding it difficult to hold their excitement in check, Sarabiskota compared the markings on the coin with other old coins pictured on the Internet. Their coin matched others that had been minted by the Spanish in Mexico in the mid 1600's! It was 22-carat gold! Its value was more than $20,000!

At home in his study, Stephen Queen danced around with delight as he listened to Sarabiskota celebrating their good fortune! They were getting closer to a much bigger treasure–he could feel it!

"And I'll be one step ahead of them when it counts," he said aloud.

19

Jack Lambert was already waiting for them in the water in front of KT's house when they got ready to launch the boat the next morning. Sarabiskota was on the *Rough Rider* on the way to Rosemary Cemetery before eight o'clock.

As they started going through Big Sarasota Pass near south Lido Key, they noticed Jack Lambert was swimming close to shore, much further away from the boat than usual. Then he disappeared below the surface for awhile. When he resurfaced, he suddenly began doing everything possible to get their attention—and he succeeded.

"Prez, we've got to go over and see what he wants to show us," KT said.

"My thoughts exactly," said Prez.

Prez maneuvered the boat closer to Jack Lambert. When they got near him, Jack Lambert quickly dove to the bottom, approximately eight feet down. Immediately, KT spotted what he wanted to show them.

"Look!" KT exclaimed as she pointed to what looked like two large gray blobs.

Upon closer examination, everyone could see two manatees right next to each other–a mother and her young calf! Jack Lambert was swimming around them, and it looked like the two manatees were feeding on sea grass on the bottom. The manatees seemed aware of Jack Lambert's presence, but they were totally unafraid.

"This is fabulous!" Jan said.

"I can't believe it!" Mike exclaimed.

Kari asked KT, "How many times have you seen manatees in the ocean before?"

"I've never seen manatees outside of Mote Aquarium," KT replied.

"Chad and I haven't either," Prez noted. "This is fabulous! According to last year's count, there are only about 3,000 of these in all of Florida, so this is a rarity."

"Is Florida the only state with manatees?" Kevin inquired.

"During the summer, some of the Florida manatees go as far north as the Carolinas," KT said, "but Florida is the only place they can be found all year. Even during *Florida* winters, they have to go where the water's at least 72 to 74 degrees, like near power plants or where warm springs feed the rivers."

Jessie sighed. "I wish we had time to swim with them awhile."

Prez looked at Jessie with a big smile. "Your wish is about to come true. I have plenty of snorkeling equipment on board for all of you. I'll stay on board and keep the boat a safe distance from you and the shore, and the rest of you can get a close-up view of the manatees."

That's exactly what they did. For the next 20 minutes, eight Sarabiskota had the time of their lives observing the two manatees from a respectful distance, while Prez maneuvered the boat nearby. Jack Lambert had a super time swimming with his Sarabiskota friends and the manatees, too!

At one point, the mother manatee did a barrel roll. Several times the manatees came to the surface together. When they did, they opened their nostrils and sucked in air, making sounds something like a dolphin makes.

When all eight teens joined Prez back on the boat, there was a lot of excitement about what they'd experienced. As they were drying off, and Prez continued driving the *Rough Rider* through the pass, Kevin said, "I like how they came to the surface to get air. They made a sound a lot like Jack Lambert does sometimes. How long can they stay underwater anyway?"

"I think the lady at Mote said a maximum of 10 or 15 minutes," said Jan. "She also mentioned a lot of manatees get hit by boats when they're coming up for air."

Nick observed, "I can see now why they say the closest relative of the manatee might be the elephant–with those three fingernails on their front flippers."

"That's right, Nick," Prez said. "I think some manatees have four fingernails. They actually think manatees once lived on land like the elephant and those nails probably had more use then."

Mike added, "I read someplace where the Indians thought they looked like beavers. They called them *big beavers*, in fact."

"Where's the *sea cow* nickname come from?" Chad inquired.

Prez said, "They're herbivores like cows and eat mostly plants–but once in awhile they eat little fish, too, I think."

"How fast can they swim?" Jessie asked.

"Up to 15 miles per hour, when it's some emergency, but most of the time they swim really slow," KT replied.

Jan asked, "Did sailors really mistaken manatees for mermaids?"

"I guess so," Prez said, "but I've heard many of the sailors had been drinking too much, weren't wearing glasses, had been out to sea too long, or were too far away to know any better. Columbus even wrote in his log that manatees weren't as *handsome* as he'd heard they were."

Nick asked, "How big can manatees get?"

"I guess about 3,500 pounds and up to about 14 feet long," Prez answered.

"Sounds like a pretty big *mermaid*," Nick said with a laugh.

"How long can they live?" Jan asked.

"Fifty or 60 years, I think," Prez said. "There's one named *Snooty* at a Bradenton aquarium that's the oldest in captivity, and he's about 56, I think."

"I didn't see any ears on the manatees," Kevin noted.

"There are openings behind the eyes, but no ear lobes, so they're hard to see," Prez explained. "I'll show you a picture later."

"What's the deal with the skin?" Nick asked. "They look like they need some Clearasil or something."

"Algae grows on their skin, but they shed the outer layer and get rid of it," KT explained. "I guess they can actually replace teeth continually, too."

"Did you notice the scars on the mother?" Kevin asked. "It looked like she got hit by a boat's propeller or something."

"I saw that," Jessie said. "The baby had a scar on one of her front flippers, too, like maybe a fishing line had been wrapped around it."

"How long do the mother and the calf stay together like that?" asked Mike.

"Up to two years," KT replied.

"Do you know how much the calf weighs when it's born?" Jan asked.

"About 70 pounds, I think," Prez answered.

Jessie giggled. "Even more than Otto Graham did when he was born," she said.

They all laughed.

"Prez, thanks for stopping and letting us have that great experience!"

"Yeah, thanks Prez!"

"Thanks a lot, Prez!"

"You're *all* welcome," Prez said.

Within minutes, they docked at Whitaker Gateway Park and walked about six blocks to the Rosemary Cemetery from there.

By the front gate, there was a sign that gave some historical information about the cemetery. It stated that Rosemary Cemetery was set aside on the Town of Sarasota's original blueprint by the promoters of the failed Ormiston Colony.

As soon as they went through the gate, they quickly spread out and moved through the cemetery, looking for John Hamilton Gillespie's gravesite, stopping whenever they saw a familiar name or noticed an interesting gravestone.

"Here's one of the Whitakers–Robert Hamlin Whitaker. I wonder why he's not buried at the Whitaker Cemetery?"

"Here's where the first postmaster–Abbe–is buried."

"Here's Richard Cunliff, the guy Cunliff Lane was named

after."

"Here's Benjamin Stickney's grave."

"Here's Harry Higel, the former mayor who gave Siesta Key its name and was murdered in 1921. His wife Gertrude is buried here, too."

Prez said, "I've found Owen Burns's grave. He was one of the most important developers in Sarasota. My parents like to go to Burns Court Cinema for movies."

They'd almost walked through the entire cemetery when they found what they were looking for. "Here's John Hamilton Gillespie's gravesite!" Chad called out. Everyone ran over to join him.

When they'd all gathered around the gravesite, Chad pointed out, "There it is on the gravestone–died on September 7, 1923."

Nick wandered over to the large gravesite next to the Gillespies', and he almost yelled when he saw one of the dates on a gravestone there! "April 24, 1913! Isn't that what we're looking for?"

The rest of Sarabiskota rushed over to join Nick! Sure enough, the gravesite next to the Gillespies' was that of John Browning and his wife, Jane! John Browning had died on April 24, 1913!

"Who was John Browning again?" Chad asked.

"Remember? He was the carpenter who built lots of the buildings on Sarasota's new Main Street," Jan said.

"Captain Sarasota's clue has to be somewhere in this area!" Jan whispered loudly. "Let's look around, but remember where we are–be respectful."

They searched everywhere around and between the two gravesites. After searching for 15 minutes, Nick pointed at

the lone palm tree between the Browning and Gillespie gravesites and said, "*Palma sola*. I'm climbing up that tree. It's about the only place we haven't looked."

Everyone else looked around to see if anyone was in sight, but they were apparently the only ones in the old cemetery.

Nick was so strong and nimble, he climbed the tree with ease. When he got to the top of the trunk, he whispered loudly, "You guys! Some letters are carved here. Someone write them down!"

"Go ahead, Nick," KT said.

"T-E-J-G-T-R-W-C-B-R. That's it!"

"Way to go, Nick! Now you can come down!" Kevin whispered.

Nick's tree climbing had triggered a motion-detecting device, which in turn had activated a miniature camera hidden near the top of the palm tree. Someone was watching from afar, but it wasn't Stephen Queen! Mr. Queen was hiding by the side of an old abandoned house just outside the cemetery, keeping a close eye on Sarabiskota's every move!

20

After they got back from Rosemary Cemetery, Sarabiskota walked a mile south of Sunset Beach to Siesta Public Beach. They spent the rest of the day there just having fun.

Soon after they arrived, Jessie got the idea to create a sand sculpture of the Sarabiskota logo using the world's whitest, softest sand. Once they got started, they really got into it. After several hours the nine good friends had created a huge masterpiece on the beach.

At one point, KT said, "Prez, I feel like we should be trying to figure out what those letters mean–not playing."

"You know what happens with all work and no play?" Prez replied. "We need to rest our brains a little. It will do us good in the long run."

"You've convinced me," said KT.

Several times, people walking by stopped to take pictures of the huge sculpture. Many even had their pictures taken in front of it.

In the evening, Sarabiskota was treated to a great kayaking adventure all around Siesta Key. The water was so calm, it reminded KT of a Minnesota lake. Jack Lambert showed up during the kayaking trip, and he had a blast following his friends around Siesta Key.

After that, they all went out for pizza at Demetrio's, where they had a super time. They got back to Sunset Beach just in time to watch a beautiful sunset. Then, Sarabiskota got together at Prez's house to try to solve Captain Sarasota's letters clue. Having no luck after a few hours, they all decided to get some sleep. The girls went over to KT's house, and the boys settled down at Prez's.

At 2:30 in the morning, Prez eagerly pushed Kari's cell phone number! "Hi Kari! This is Prez!"

"Prez?" Kari had definitely been sound asleep. "What time is it?"

"About 2:30. We've been playing around with those letters all night. Guess what? ... Kevin figured them out!"

"What!" Kari almost shouted, waking up the other girls.

"Kevin figured the letters out ... with some help from the rest of us!"

All the girls got close to Kari so they could listen to the conversation. "Give us the details, Prez!"

"I'll let Kevin explain."

Prez handed the cell phone to Kevin. "Kari, those letters are a series of initials. The TE stands for Thomas Edison. The JG for John Gillespie. The TR for Teddy Roosevelt. The WC for Winston Churchill, and the BR for Babe Ruth!"

"That's cool," said Kari, "but what location around here could possibly have all those people in common?"

Kevin said, "We thought the same thing–but all those people and more stayed at what was once one of the best hotels in the country–near here–and it's still there!"

"Where's that?"

"The Tampa Bay Hotel up in Tampa ..."

The next morning, KT's parents treated Sarabiskota to an early morning parasailing adventure. Because of the large size of their group, two boats were necessary.

The boys had gotten no sleep the night before, and the girls hadn't slept since their phone call, so they were all a little tired. But once again, they were so excited, adrenaline kept them going.

When he was way up in the air parasailing, Prez got a call on his cell phone. It was Dickie V. "Prez, how are you?"

"You're not going to believe this, Dickie V! I'm parasailing at this very moment! A bunch of our friends from Bismarck are here in town staying with us. We're having a great time!"

"Awesome! Hey, Prez! I'd like to meet all your friends. Yours truly has to go to Tampa tomorrow for a TV interview, but maybe we can get together sometime after that."

"Dickie V, would you mind some passengers on your Tampa trip? We've got something we want to see up there ..."

Dickie V picked Sarabiskota up shortly after 7:00 A.M. the next day. Soon, they were traveling north on Interstate 75 toward Tampa in Dickie V's RV.

Dickie V said, "Wow! We have a flat out amazing day in store! I've got that interview in an hour with the Channel 8 people, then we're going over to the Tampa Bay Hotel, then I've got a little surprise for you! I mean, it's mind-boggling!"

"What's you're surprise?" KT asked.

"I would love to tell you, KT, but I'm not even going to give you a hint. Let me just say it will be a big-time, amazing, awesome surprise!"

"Just one *tiny* little hint," KT almost begged.

"Not even for you, KT," said Dickie V. "I don't want to ruin it for you."

Chad asked, "Dickie V, what's your TV interview about?"

"I've got an awesome Sarasota Sports Hall of Fame Banquet coming up to raise some money for the Boys and Girls Clubs of Sarasota where we honor a top athlete from the Sarasota area each year! They're going to talk to me about that incredible event!"

"Do you know if Jennifer Leigh is going to be there?" Chad asked.

"Chad likes to watch Jennifer Leigh because she's so *cute*," KT teased. "She's one of the reporters at Channel 8."

"There's a chance Jen will be there, Chad," Dickie V said.

"Who are you honoring at your banquet this year?" Kevin asked.

"We're honoring long-time Sarasota resident–and one of the greatest tennis players *ever*–Monica Seles! She was one of the most intense competitors I ever saw! Heck, I saw Monica beat the great Chris Evert when she was only 15 years old! I knew Monica was going to be a star *then*!"

"My dad likes how she grunts when she hits the tennis ball," said Mike.

Kevin asked, "Dickie V, who are some of the other great athletes from around here?"

"Of course, you've already met Otto Graham. Let's see ... the man who many consider to be the greatest athlete of all time actually played a sport here in Sarasota–but it wasn't even his best sport."

"Who was that, Dickie V?" Chad inquired.

"The great Michael Jordan! He was in Sarasota for base-

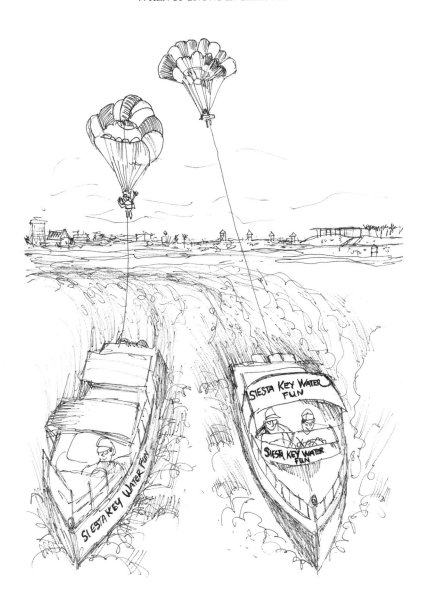

ball Spring Training for the White Sox organization."

"When was that?" asked KT.

"Back in 1994, I think," Dickie V replied.

"How did Jordan do playing baseball?" Kari asked.

"As I recall, he played Double A ball for the Birmingham Barons and hit around 202. Then he went back and won some more NBA Championships with the Chicago Bulls! Michael was the *creme de la creme*! A fierce competitor!"

Prez asked, "Any other great athletes you can think of?"

"Well, Buck O'Neill, one of the all-time great baseball players who played in the Negro leagues, grew up here in Sarasota, and still lives here. Buck also was the first black coach in the major leagues for the Cubs. Buck used to tell me about shagging home runs as a kid in Sarasota when the New York Giants used to hold Spring Training in Payne Park. He said the sound of Babe Ruth hitting the ball was dynamite! Buck only heard that sound two other times in his whole life–when the great Josh Gibson hit them out, and when the amazing Bo Jackson hit a dinger!"

"Isn't Bo Jackson the guy who also played football for the Raiders?" Kevin asked.

"That's right!" Dickie V replied. "He was a monster athlete! Oh! Here's another baseball player I know you've heard of who was down here for Spring Training back in the 1940's. He's considered the greatest hitter of all-time by many. He hit 406 in 1941! His nickname was Teddy Ballgame or the Splendid Splinter. He was a war hero, too! He once landed a fiery jet in Korea seconds before it blew up!"

"Ted Williams of the Boston Red Sox!" Kevin exclaimed.

"That's right! Awesome, Kevin!" said Dickie V.

"Anyone else?" Mike asked.

"Let's see–Tampa Bay's best pro football player of all-time still lives in the Tampa area! Heck, he even has a freeway and a restaurant named after him! He's a Hall of Famer from the Oklahoma Sooners–"

"Lee Roy Selmon," Chad said.

"That's flat out amazing, Chad!" Dickie V said.

"Deb Walker from Sarasota set 16 world records as a swimmer!" Dickie V noted.

"Wow!" Jessie said. "I would be satisfied with *one*."

Dickie V continued, "PGA golfer Paul Azinger lives in Bradenton. Tennis great Martina Navratilova lives on Casey Key. Wimbledon champion Maria Sharapova lives up in Bradenton. Tampa Bay Rays baseball all-star Aubrey Huff is from right around here. Nick Bollettieri up in Bradenton is one of the top tennis coaches in the world. The NFL's all-time interception leader, Paul Krause, lives around here. Heck! There are so many great athletes from this–"

"Wow! Look at that!" Jessie exclaimed.

In a flash, a beautiful, red, 1958 Ford Edsel passed them going at least 100 miles per hour!

"That looks exactly like the car in Stephen Queen's movie *The Edsel That Destroyed Ohio State University*!" Mike exclaimed.

"Could you see who was driving?" Kari asked.

"No," Chad replied. "The car was going too fast, and I think it had dark tinted windows anyway."

Nick asked, "What's an Edsel?"

"Elvis had one," Mike explained. "It's an old car with a funny-looking oval grille in front. They only made them about three years. Now it's mostly a collector's item."

"I have a funny feeling about that car," Kari said.

"I have a funny feeling about who's driving that car," KT added.

"What do you mean?" Dickie V asked.

"Oh, nothing really," Prez replied. "We've been talking about those strange Stephen Queen movies too much, I guess."

"I know what you mean," Dickie V said. "I liked his movie where people started singing with loud opera voices every time they told a lie."

"Me, too," Chad said. "Wasn't that called *You Lie, You Sing Opera*?"

"That's it!" said Dickie V.

After they'd settled down awhile, Jan asked, "Dickie V, have you ever been to the Tampa Bay Hotel?"

"I've been on the campus of The University of Tampa a few times, and I've seen the beautiful building there, but I've never walked through it. This will be a monster experience for me, too! What got you interested in the Tampa Bay Hotel anyway?"

Prez explained, "It seemed incredible to us that so many famous people could have stayed in one hotel."

"Oh! Who are some of the famous people you're talking about?" Dickie V inquired.

Kevin began, "Babe Ruth signed his first major league contract while staying at the Tampa Bay Hotel. They actually had a baseball field on the hotel grounds and some think he hit the longest home run *ever* at that field—almost 600 feet."

"Two football fields?" Nick observed. "That's amazing!"

Chad said, "Thomas Edison stayed there, too. He'd just

barely invented the light bulb, and some of his first light bulbs were even used in the Tampa Bay Hotel. I guess Edison's children liked to visit the hunting dogs at the hotel's kennel, and they also liked to swim in the indoor pool."

Mike added, "John Gillespie, the golf guy from Sarasota, was a guest there a lot, and he even designed the golf course at the hotel."

Kari said, "Mrs. Palmer actually stayed at the Tampa Bay Hotel and planned what she was going to do when she got to Sarasota."

Jessie said, "Winston Churchill, one of the greatest world leaders in history, stayed at the hotel before the Spanish-American War got started."

"Incredible!" Dickie V said. "Wasn't Winston Churchill the leader of England during World War II? It's hard to believe he was even alive during Spanish-American War times."

Prez explained, "Churchill was only about 21 and a young journalist when he stayed at the Tampa Bay Hotel around 1895. Then he went over to Cuba to observe the war going on over there–which eventually turned into the Spanish-American War. On his twenty-first birthday Churchill was in Cuba, and he actually had a bullet shot right through the hat he was wearing! Not long after that, Teddy Roosevelt came to Tampa before he fought in Cuba during the Spanish-American War."

"Hey, Prez?" said Chad.

"Yes, Chad."

"Was Teddy Roosevelt in North Dakota before or after the Spanish-American War?"

"Teddy was in North Dakota *before* he came here to

Tampa. Then he went from Tampa to Cuba to fight in the Spanish-American War. He probably never would've gone to fight in the Spanish-American War, though, if it weren't for his experiences in North Dakota."

"What do you mean, Prez?" Dickie V asked.

"Teddy was a big city guy before he moved to North Dakota. His time in North Dakota really prepared him for his fighting during the Spanish-American War–and even the job of being President. North Dakota toughened him up, and he became a pretty good cowboy there, too."

"What brought him to North Dakota in the first place?" Jessie asked.

Prez said, "He went to the North Dakota Badlands in 1883 to hunt buffalo. Before he was done with that hunting trip, he invested in the cattle business south of Medora and bought the Maltese Cross Ranch. Then something really strange and tragic happened. About five months after his buffalo hunt, his wife died on Valentine's Day, only 11 hours after his mother died!"

"What!" Jessie exclaimed. "Not on Valentines Day!"

"I'm afraid it's true," Prez said. "After such a traumatic experience, Teddy decided to get far away from it all–to leave New York City, and head back to North Dakota to live. When he got back to North Dakota, he even bought another ranch, the Elkhorn."

"How long did he stay in North Dakota?" Kevin asked.

"He actually ranched there until 1887, but continued his ranching interest in the Medora area almost right up until the Spanish-American War," Prez answered.

Dickie V asked, "Is it really true the Teddy Bear is named after Teddy Roosevelt?"

"Sure is," Prez said. "After he became President, Teddy was on a bear hunt when another guy captured a bear and tied it to a tree and then waited for the President to get there to shoot it. When Teddy showed up, he wouldn't shoot the defenseless bear. After that, a cartoonist drew a picture of this event for a newspaper, and it was published all over the country. Anyway, a Russian immigrant couple named Michtom, who had a store in Brooklyn, had seen the cartoon and wrote to Teddy and asked if they could call the small stuffed bears they sold in their store *Teddy's Bears*. The President gave his permission, but he told the Michtoms that he doubted that would help sell them. Well, they sold tons!"

"And now we know ... *the rest of the story*," Dickie V said.

Nick asked, "What's the deal with the Spanish-American War anyway?"

Prez asked, "Just exactly what do you know about it already, Nick?"

"Well, back in North Dakota, our family went to Medora in Theodore Roosevelt National Park. They have that cool musical there where Teddy charges up San Juan Hill and becomes a hero. That happened during the Spanish-American War, right?"

"That's right, Nick," said Prez, "but there's a lot more to the story. I was even surprised to find out how much of the action took place right down here in the Tampa area. It's a great story."

"Like how?" Nick asked.

"How much do you want to know?" Prez inquired.

"Everything you know," Nick replied.

"From the beginning?" Prez asked.

"From the beginning."

"Well," Prez began, "first you should know that long before the United States fought Spain in 1898, everything got started when the people of the Cuba got tired of Spanish rule, very much like we rebelled against British rule in 1776. A major revolution in Cuba started in 1895, but it had been building for many years before that."

"So, why did the United States take sides with Cuba?" Kari asked.

"That's a little complicated, but I'll try to explain," Prez said. "One of the Cuban leaders of the revolution was a guy by the name of Jose Marti, and he came to Tampa and other Florida cities many times to help get support for the revolution, starting in about 1891."

"Why did Marti come to Tampa to raise money anyway?" Jessie asked.

"Well," Prez replied, "lots of people had escaped Spanish rule in Cuba to live in the Tampa area. Many of them worked in one of the 97 cigar factories in Ybor City, and you can imagine how bad they wanted the Spanish out of Cuba. Many of them, in fact, gave one-third of their salaries to support Marti and the revolution. They wanted *Cuba libre* or a free Cuba. The money they donated was used to smuggle guns, ammunition, and men into Cuba."

"How did Teddy get involved in the Spanish-American War?" Mike inquired.

"Teddy was one of the big reasons why the United States took sides with the Cuban revolutionaries against Spain," Prez said. "Back in 1897, Teddy was Assistant Secretary of the Navy and William McKinley was President. Teddy felt it was the duty of the United States to help the people of

Cuba and get the Spanish out of the western world for good.

"Then the big newspapers in New York City started to write stories about the Cuban heroes in the revolution and how cruel Spain was. Lots of the stories were exaggerated or made up. In fact, a new term was used to describe this type of newspaper writing–*yellow journalism*. Those newspaper stories helped get even more people in the U.S. in favor of declaring war on Spain."

"So, did the United States declare war then?" Kevin asked.

"Not yet," Prez replied. "Things started to get more dangerous in Cuba, so our battleship, the *Maine*, was sent to Havana Harbor in Cuba just in case some Americans in Cuba needed to be evacuated. Then something happened that was the last straw, and the United States declared war on Spain."

"The *Maine* blew up!" Dickie V said.

"That's right," Prez said. "268 of the 343 men on board were killed, and that was it. The United States declared war on April 21, 1898, and Teddy came to Tampa. *Remember the Maine* became a war cry!"

"What caused the Maine to blow up?" Nick inquired.

"It's another big mystery in history." Prez giggled at this accidental rhyme. "Some think maybe the coal stored inside the big ship caused the explosion or maybe a submarine mine, but they never found out for sure.

"By the way, you'll never guess who was in Havana when the Maine blew up out in the harbor ... a famous woman, who was in her 70's, who founded the Red Cross."

"Not Florence Nightingale?" Nick guessed.

"Good guess," Prez said. "Florence Nightingale had a lot

to do with making nursing what it is today, but she lived in England a little before this time."

Kari made a guess. "Clara Barton?"

"That's right," Prez said.

Nick said, "I still don't get why Teddy comes to Tampa."

Prez explained, "Tampa was the most important city in the United States during the Spanish-American War, and Teddy came here before he left for Cuba and San Juan Hill."

"Why did Tampa become so important?" Dickie V asked.

Prez said, "A big railroad man by the name of Henry Plant used his influence in Washington, D.C. to have many of the troops come here before they left for Cuba. It definitely helped that Tampa had the railroad to get troops here, a deep river that could handle big supply ships, and it was an excellent port pretty close to Cuba."

"How big was Tampa back then?" Chad inquired.

"Only about 12,000 people," Prez answered.

"Was it the largest city in Florida?" Jessie asked.

"Key West was," Prez replied. "About 18,000 people lived there. Anyway, like a lot of the troops that came to Tampa, Teddy and his troops came there on crowded railroad cars. When they got to Tampa, it was a pretty crazy place. Remember, the town only had 12,000 people, but more than 50,000 troops were stationed there. Thousands of other people came to Tampa just to be part of the action.

"It was June–and really hot. There was no air conditioning yet–and there were lots of mosquitoes. It rained like crazy at times, so it must have been a mess. The lousy food and unsanitary conditions caused lots of disease, so thousands died–way more than the 379 people who died during the fighting in Cuba. Clara Barton called the conditions in

Tampa *horrible*."

"It sounds like it might have been pretty crazy around Tampa!" Dicki V said.

"To say the least," Prez remarked. "Cannons went off every night during patriotic rallies at the courthouse. The theme song around Tampa was *There'll be a Hot Time in the Old Town Tonight*, and there really was. The troops were busy during the day, but at night they were pretty wild. Lots of crazy stuff went on, including tons of fights."

"What about Teddy and his Rough Riders? Did they behave?" Jessie asked.

"Their nickname, Rough Riders, might give you a clue," Prez answered. "They got in all sorts of trouble. One time some of them actually rode their horses into a new restaurant. The newspapers called it 'The Charge of the Yellow Rice Brigade.' I guess the owner didn't even get mad, though.

"By the way, I found out Teddy's soldiers had other nicknames before the name *Rough Riders* stuck. The newspaper people called them the Western Regiment because many of them were cowboys. They also called them the Rustler Regiment, the Cowboy Regiment, and *Teddy's Terrors* before they settled on Rough Riders."

"It seems like the newspapers liked writing about Teddy and the Rough Riders. Why?" Dickie V asked.

Prez replied, "Teddy and the Rough Riders weren't regular army men–they were volunteers. They were also an unusual group of men–colorful to say the least–some with great nicknames, so the newspapermen liked to write about them."

"What were some of the nicknames of the guys?" Chad

asked.

"Well, there was a guy who swore all the time they called Prayerful James ... other guys had nicknames like Cherokee Bill and Happy Jack of Arizona and Rattlesnake Pete. There were even four Methodist ministers in the Rough Riders, but I'm not sure if they had nicknames. Even the Harvard football coach was a Rough Rider."

"Where did all the troops stay in Tampa?" Kevin asked.

"The officers and the newspapermen stayed at the Tampa Bay Hotel; the Rough Riders even trained behind it. The other troops were mostly in tents all over the place," Prez said.

"When did the Rough Riders finally go to Cuba?" Jan asked.

"On June 14, early in the morning," said Prez. "Thirty-five ships carrying troops and equipment left at that time with over 16,000 soldiers and 2,000 horses and mules on board. There were a bunch of other ships in the huge convoy including a hospital ship and several naval escorts."

Jessie asked, "How long did the Spanish-American War last?"

"Just a couple of months–until August 12," Prez explained.

"How long was it after that before Teddy become President?" Kari asked.

"Well," said Prez, "the Spanish-American War was officially over on August 12, 1898, and Teddy was President on September 14, 1901. So it was only about three years."

"Why September?" Dickie V asked. "Aren't Presidents usually inaugurated in January?"

"That's right," Prez said, "but this was one of those special tragic times in U.S. history. Teddy had been elected as McKinley's Vice President in 1900. He had only been Vice President for six months when McKinley was assassinated in Buffalo, New York."

"Did the Spanish-American War affect Sarasota in any way?" Kari asked.

"Lots of ways," Prez said. "By 1895, Sarasota was worried about war, so no one was buying land in the new town. After the *Maine* was sunk, Gillespie even wrote a letter to his mom, telling her he was worried about Spain attacking the West Coast of Florida and burning every house in Sarasota. One time, an unidentified boat was spotted offshore–and the Sarasota citizens panicked, and many ran for the woods. It turned out to be one of *our* ships, though ... Also, because of the Spanish-American War, thousands of people saw Florida and Sarasota for the first time, and many liked the area so much, they moved here."

Dickie V said, "Hey, this has been awesome–with a capital A! I've learned more on this ride to Tampa than my first two years of college! It looks like we're almost to the television studio. I think you'll like meeting all the Channel 8 News people. They're phenomenal!"

KEVIN KREMER

21

When they all got into the WFLA Building, the reception-ist recognized Dickie V right away, and she took them to a conference room to meet with Gayle Sierens and Bob Hite, the co-anchors of WFLA News Channel 8.

Dickie V introduced each of his Sarabiskota friends to Gayle and Bob. Gayle said, "Our meteorologist, Steve Jerve, should be here in the next hour. He's from your part of the country. I know he played basketball at the University of Minnesota Morris."

"Minnesota Morris–the Cougars," Chad noted.

"Hey, Gayle and Bob! My awesome young friends here are huge sports fans! Gayle, do you want to tell them why you're a big-time person in sports history?"

Gayle smiled and said, "Why don't you tell them, Dickie V."

Dickie V put his arm around Gayle. "You're much too modest," he said. "Gayle did something in 1987 that was a first in the history of the National Football League!"

"You were the first lady to do play-by-play for an NFL football game, weren't you?" Kevin guessed. "I thought you looked a lot like the lady I saw on the NFL Channel."

"I was a lot younger then," Gayle Sierens replied, with a

big smile.

"But you've never been more beautiful than you are right now," Dickie V said.

"You're such a charmer, Dickie V," Gayle said, blushing.

Dickie V continued, "And my friend, Bob Hite, here, is an incredible outdoor sportsman himself! Bob is an ocean diver, a Coast Guard captain, a pilot, a horseman, and even a marksman! When Bob got his job here in Tampa, he put all his stuff on an old, wooden sailboat, and sailed right down here from Philly!"

"That's about it," Bob said.

When Prez heard about Bob Hite's boating experience, he had to ask, "Mr. Hite, do you still do a lot of boating here in the Tampa Bay area?"

"Please call me Bob ... I guess I know the waters around here just about as well as anyone–both above and below the surface."

Prez hesitated for a moment. "Bob, we've been reading about Captain Sarasota who lived out on his boat in this area for a long time. Did you ever meet him?"

Bob looked a little surprised at the question. "One time," he began. "We were both about 10 miles out in the Gulf helping a disabled yacht. Captain Sarasota had saved a man a few months earlier when the *Summit Venture* hit the Sunshine Skyway Bridge, and I had a chance to talk to him about it that day."

"What happened to the Sunshine Skyway Bridge?" KT asked.

Bob explained, "The Sunshine Skyway Bridge used to be two parallel bridges really–one for northbound traffic and one for southbound traffic–each bridge had two lanes.

Early in the morning on May 6, 1980, a storm suddenly hit the bay near the bridges. A big 609-foot freighter named the *Summit Venture* was approaching the bridge at this time and somehow it totally lost its bearings during the storm. At 7:34 A.M. the big ship slammed into the southbound bridge support tier, causing about a quarter mile section of the bridge to plunge 15 stories into the bay! A hundred feet of the bridge's roadway collapsed right onto the *Summit Venture*."

"Fifteen stories!" Jan exclaimed. "That's about the height of our Capitol Building in North Dakota!"

"Did the cars on the bridge stop before they came to the missing road?" Kari asked.

"Unfortunately, no," Bob answered. "Several vehicles approached the missing road, and because of the blinding rain, they couldn't stop in time. A Greyhound bus, a pick-up truck, and six automobiles plunged into Tampa Bay. Twenty-two passengers on the bus were killed. A total of 35 people perished that awful morning."

"Did anyone survive?" Nick asked.

"That's where Captain Sarasota comes in," Bob continued. "He was out in the bay somewhere and had apparently seen the bus and other vehicles plunge into the bay. Immediately, he notified the Coast Guard. One of the vehicles that plunged into the bay, a blue Ford pickup, bounced off the side of the *Summit Venture*, knocking out the driver. The truck sank below the surface of the water. Somehow, though, the driver regained consciousness underwater, and he rolled down his window and got out. Then he miraculously struggled to the surface–seriously injured and nearly in shock. He probably would've drown, but Captain

Sarasota somehow maneuvered his boat near enough to grab the man before he went under."

"Was that guy the only survivor?" Mike asked.

"Of the vehicles that plunged into the water, yes," Bob replied. "Another guy up on the bridge in a Buick Skylark hit the brakes just in time and missed going over the edge by about 14 inches."

"Oh, my gosh!" KT exclaimed.

"That's really sad," Jessie added.

"What did they do with the damaged bridge after that?" Mike asked.

"The traffic used the two lanes of the northbound bridge until they finished the new Sunshine Skyway Bridge in 1987," Bob explained. "Then they took some of each of the old bridges and made them into the world's largest fishing pier. The rest of the old bridges they sank out in the bay, and it became artificial reefs."

"Bob," Jan asked, "did Captain Sarasota talk about anything besides the Sunshine Skyway Bridge tragedy when you saw him?"

"As I recall ... we talked about the weather and our boats a little—"

A man walked over and gave Gayle the thumbs-up sign. Gayle said, "It looks like they're ready for our interview. Do all you Sarabiskota want to come in the studio and watch, and then I'll take you on a tour later."

Chad asked, "Uh ... is Jennifer Leigh here today?"

"I think so," Gayle said with a big smile. "I wonder why so many cute young men want to meet Jen?"

After Dickie V's interview and their tour of the WFLA

studios, they went to the Tampa Bay Hotel. When they got within a block of the building, Mike looked out the window, spotted the hotel, and said, "Wow! It looks like something you'd see in Turkey or something."

"That's about right, Mike," Jessie said. "It's a Moorish revival style of architecture–notice the minarets."

"What's a minaret?" Nick asked.

"That's what those tall, slender towers are called," Jessie replied.

"Oh."

After Dickie V parked the RV near the front of the Tampa Bay Hotel, they slowly walked toward one of the main entrances, while marveling at the size and beauty of the building.

Two college men walking nearby spotted Dickie V. "Hey, Dickie V!" one of them said, doing a pretty good impression of Dickie V's voice. "You're awesome, baby!"

"Forget about it!" Dickie V yelled back. The two men smiled and waved.

As they approached the front of the huge hotel, Mike said, "The porch is huge!"

"They call it a *veranda*," Jessie explained. "Notice all the fancy trim everywhere. That's called gingerbread."

"I love the keyhole shape of all the arches and doorways," Kari noted.

Kevin pointed toward the top of the building. "Look at the crescent moons way on top of the minarets."

"Who built this thing anyway?" Nick asked.

Kari said, "I read where as many as 1,000 people were working on building this hotel at one time–without power tools, too, by the way. But the guy who was most responsi-

ble for the whole thing was Henry Plant, the same guy who got the troops to come here before they went to fight in the Spanish-American War. Plant also built a whole system of railways, steamships, and hotels that brought a lot of people to Florida. When this hotel opened in 1891, it was one of the fanciest hotels in the whole country."

"It still looks pretty fancy to me," Mike said.

"Sure beats the Motel 6 in Bismarck," Nick said with a giggle.

"I guess part of it is a museum now, and part of it is still used by the University of Tampa," Prez said.

When they entered the museum part of the hotel, a nice lady named Aundrea Haverlock greeted them at the door. She told them that she'd lived in the hotel 50 years ago as a student, when part of it was used as a dormitory for The University of Tampa.

After that, Aundrea took them on a tour of the hotel. As they walked through the building, Aundrea told them many interesting things about the place. She said, "The hotel had 511 rooms, and it was built on six acres of land. If you walk around the outside of the building, it's exactly a mile; if you walk from one end to the other, it's a quarter-of-a-mile. It took a staff of about 300 people to run this place."

Nick asked, "How much did it cost to build?"

"It cost $2,500,000 to build back then, and another $500,000 for furnishings. Henry Plant and his wife went shopping in Japan, China, and Europe, and eventually had 41 railroad cars full of stuff to furnish the hotel."

Kevin asked, "How much did it cost to stay here?"

"Five dollars per night for a single room, and 15 to 18

dollars for a suite. That might not sound like much, but most people earned only two or three dollars a week back then. The people who stayed here were much wealthier than that, however. By the way, the Tampa Bay Hotel was the first large Florida building to have electricity and electric lighting, and it had the first elevator in Florida. The rooms also had telephones."

Nick asked Prez in a whisper, "When were all those things invented, Prez?"

"The elevator, in 1852, by Otis. The telephone, by Bell, in 1876, and Edison's light bulbs in 1879."

"What about the radio?"

"Not until 1896, by Marconi."

"The airplane?"

"Wright brothers–1903."

"That was a cool time to be alive," Nick whispered.

Aundrea continued, "Eventually there were 21 buildings on the 150-acre grounds here, so it really was a vacation paradise. In fact, we like to call it *Florida's **First** Magic Kingdom*."

"What were some of the things you could do here?" KT asked.

Aundrea answered, "There was a golf course, tennis courts, croquet courts, boating on the Hillsborough River, hunting and fishing, a heated indoor swimming pool, a bowling alley, stables, a horse track, kennels, a casino with a 2000-seat auditorium for entertainment, spa facilities, and card rooms."

Kari asked, "What did the children do when they were here?"

Aundrea said, "You kids would have probably been bored. It was Victorian times, when Queen Victoria ruled Great

Britain, and children were expected to play quietly. Many of them who stayed here had nannies to care for them and help them with their school lessons. They also rode bicycles, read stories–they might have played games like Pin the Tail on the Donkey or Musical Chairs, made puzzles, played with sticks or balls, or maybe some of the boys might have even caddied on the golf course."

Chad asked Aundrea, "This is sorta off the topic, but do you know how *Tampa* got its name?"

"I don't think anyone knows for sure, but many think the word has Indian origins and means either *split wood for fires* or *near it*. The *split wood* thing might have referred to all the drift wood along the shore of the bay, and the *near it* might have referred to how close an Indian village was to Tampa Bay. I think there was a third suggestion that the word Tampa came from the name of an old Spanish city. The Tampa we know today actually grew from a fort built during the Seminole Wars called Fort Brooke. The town that developed here was called Fort Brooke, too, but then it was called Tampa Bay, and finally, just Tampa. Is that a good enough explanation, young man?"

"That's tremendous," Chad replied. "How about St. Petersburg?"

"That's one of my favorite stories, but it might be part legend," Aundrea began. "There were two big shots who lived on the Pinellas Peninsula–one was a Russian railroad promoter named Peter Demens and the other was a wealthy property owner from Detroit named John Williams. As the story goes, the two men drew straws to see who would name the town. The loser got to name the first hotel. Well, Peter Demens won–and he named the town St. Petersburg, after his hometown in Russia. Williams named the first hotel the Detroit Hotel, after *his* hometown."

"Cool story, Aundrea," Chad said.

"I'm glad you liked it."

Prez asked, "Aundrea, are there any rooms in the Tampa Bay Hotel that are just like they were back when it first opened?"

"Oh, my," she replied. "There was just a familiar looking man here less than an hour ago who asked me the same question. As I told him, there's just one room like that, and we'll stop there next. It's called The Reading and Writing Room."

Kari asked, "Do you remember if that man who was here an hour ago had thick dark-rimmed glasses?"

"Why, yes, he did," Aundrea replied. "Was he a friend of yours?"

"Not really," Kari answered. Sarabiskota exchanged many puzzled glances.

When they got to The Reading and Writing Room, Aundrea said, "We've used old photos to make sure this room was restored to exactly the way it looked back in the days the hotel was open. The men used this room the most–for things like reading newspapers and writing letters. Big business deals also got done in here."

Aundrea walked over to one of the walls and explained, "Here we have large, framed photographs of some of the famous men who spent time in this room. The photos were all taken right here at the Tampa Bay Hotel."

Sarabiskota could hardly believe whose photographs were hanging on the wall! There was Thomas Edison, John Hamilton Gillespie, Teddy Roosevelt, Winston Churchill,

Babe Ruth, and one more—John Ringling, who was holding a small porcelain clown someone must have given him!

They had their next clue! It was John Ringling!

"Our next stop is your little surprise!" Dickie V said, after they left the Tampa Bay Hotel.

It wasn't long before they were approaching Raymond James Stadium, home of the Tampa Bay Buccaneers. "We're going to Raymond James Stadium?" Kevin guessed excitedly.

"Our little surprise is a tour of the stadium?" Chad surmised.

"Just be patient for a few more minutes," Dickie V said. "I think you're all going to enjoy this."

As they approached a private entrance, they noticed a familiar face waiting to take them on a tour. It was Jon Gruden–coach of the Super Bowl Champion Tampa Bay Buccaneers! There were some screams from Sarabiskota–and it sounded like a few of them came from the *boys*!

When they parked the RV and got out to meet Jon Gruden, the coach noticed the Steelers caps worn by Prez and Chad right away. He said, "What would it take for you two to start wearing Bucs caps?"

Prez said, "My dad said it has to snow in Sarasota on Christmas before Tampa Bay will replace the Steelers as his favorite team. I think it's about the same for Chad and me–but I have a feeling the Bucs will be solidly our *second* favorite team after today!"

Coach Gruden said, "I'll have to see if I can help make the Bucs number one for you two guys."

266

Coach Gruden gave Sarabiskota a tour they'd never forget! When they got to the famous pirate ship, the coach said, "I thought you might like to take a picture up here."

After they got done with the picture-taking, Jon Gruden said, "I'm going to give you all autographed caps from our latest Super Bowl victory before you leave, but Dickie V told me I should ask you a really tough trivia question about myself before I give them to you."

"Bring it on!" Kevin said. "I've read your books."

"All right, but this isn't even in my books ... I played college football at Dayton my sophomore to senior years, but as a freshman I played for a little college in Ohio by the name of Muskingham College. What was their nickname?"

"The Fighting Muskies," Chad said in less than a second.

"Unbelievable!" said Coach Gruden. "How could you possibly know that?"

"It's a little hobby of mine," Chad replied.

"What's a musky?" Jessie asked.

"It's a fish," said KT.

"Please give us another question," Prez requested.

Jon Gruden thought for awhile. "OK ... I try not to give up *ever*, but once when I was just a kid, I was at the 1979 Cotton Bowl. My dad was an assistant coach under Dan Devine at Notre Dame, and our team was getting killed by the University of Houston 34 to 12. It was a freezing cold, icy, windy day in Dallas, and I just gave up–and got on one of the team buses to warm up. Later, when the game was over, I found out Notre Dame had come back to win that game in one of the most amazing games in football history! Who was quarterback of that Notre Dame team?"

"Joe Montana," Kevin said instantly. "Wasn't the final

score 35 to 34?"

"Yes, it was!" Jon Gruden said, looking surprised.

"Didn't Joe Montana have the flu and get some chicken soup at halftime?" Chad asked.

"He sure did," Jon Gruden replied.

"Did you know there's a town in Montana that changed its name to *Joe*–Joe, Montana?" Jan added.

"*Wow!* You kids are smart!" Coach Gruden exclaimed. "I wish all my football players had your brains!"

They all laughed.

Coach Gruden said, "I'm going to ask you one more question that I heard at a banquet recently when they were celebrating the Tampa Bay Lightning's big Stanley Cup victory ... The Stanley Cup is named after Lord Stanley, who was once the Queen's representative in Canada or something. What was Lord Stanley's full title?"

Sarabiskota was totally stumped.

"What was it?" asked Chad.

Coach Gruden took a deep breath. He said, "It was Right Honourable Sir Frederick Arthur Stanley, Baron Stanley of Preston, in the County of Lancaster, in the Peerage of Great Britain, Knight Grand Cross of the Most Honourable Order of Bath."

Coach Gruden inhaled. Dickie V and Sarabiskota applauded!

22

That night, they all went to the workshop on Higel Avenue to work on *The Starship Exercise* and talk about Captain Sarasota's latest clue.

Prez said, "Before we start, has anyone found any more place name stories?"

"I have one I've been working on for awhile called Arcadia, a town about 50 miles east of Sarasota," Nick began. "It's cool, because the town is named after the lady who baked a birthday cake for one of the town's big shots. The cake maker's name was Arcadia Albritton."

KT said, "So you're saying her cake was so good, she got a town named after her?"

"I guess," Nick replied. "The town of Arcadia also had the world's only rattlesnake cannery built by a guy by the name of George End. You'll never guess how it all ended for George End."

"He didn't get bitten by a snake?" Kari guessed.

"Yup," Nick said.

"That's a good one, Nick," Mike said. "I've got one you might like. There's a creek down by Nokomis called *Shakett Creek*–and how it got its name is pretty cool. There was a pioneer family, the Knights, who lived northeast of Tampa, and they decided to move to the Nokomis area. When they were moving all their stuff, they had a big caravan with eight covered wagons pulled by oxen, three buggies pulled by mules, seven horses, and 300 cattle.

"The mules pulling the first buggy refused to budge when they got to the creek, so the dad tried putting ears of corn in front of them to get them to move, but it didn't work. Then he tried to use the whip, but that didn't work either. Finally, he told his son, Bill, to take deer hide and shake it in front of the mules–I guess it makes kind of a cracking sound, like when you snap a wet towel. Well, he probably shook the hides a little too hard, and the mules got frightened. They jolted forward really fast, dumping two of the buggies and all the stuff from a wagon into the creek. The creek was known as Shake It Creek after that."

"Cool story," Prez said. "Any others?"

Chad said, "I got a couple from two girls who work at Barnie's Coffee in the mall when my dad and I went to pick up his coffee."

"Really, Chad," said Jessie. "Can we trust the accuracy of these girls or were they just *cute*?"

"They might have been cute, but we can trust them, too," Chad replied. "They live south of Sarasota in Englewood and North Port. They told me Englewood was named by three Nichols brothers who came from Englewood, Illinois. North Port used to be North Port Charlotte, but they cut off the word Charlotte. North Port really isn't a port. The girls told me it has a few canals, though."

"Good stuff, Chad," said Prez. "Any other place name stories?" No one had any more to offer. "All right, let's talk about the John Ringling clue next."

Kevin said, "Solving this clue isn't going to be easy. There's a ton of stuff around here that's associated with John Ringling and the Ringling name and the circus."

"Like what?" Nick asked.

Kevin looked at his minicomputer. "This isn't even a complete list ... John Ringling Bridge, John and Mable Ringling Museum of Art, Ringling School of Art and Design, Ringling Museum of the Circus, the Sailor Circus, Circus Bridge, the John Ringling Causeway–"

Nick interrupted. "What's a causeway?"

"It's a raised roadway across the water," Kari answered.

"Oh."

"There are several streets, too," Kevin continued. "John Ringling Parkway, Ringling Boulevard, Ringling Drive, Circus Boulevard. Even the phone numbers around Sarasota started with the letters RI for a long time."

Jessie grinned playfully and said, "Ringling had even more to do with telephones than that."

"What do you mean?" KT asked.

Jessie was trying not to giggle. "Think about the sound a phone used to make when you had a call."

"RING! LING!" several of Sarabiskota said at about the same time, and then they all laughed.

"Which of the brothers from the Ringling Bros. and Barnum & Bailey Circus lived in Sarasota anyway?" KT asked.

"John and Charles were the ones who lived here the longest, but I think a few others lived here awhile, too," Kevin replied.

Prez said, "Let's talk about the Ringling brothers from the beginning. I'd like to get the big picture again."

273

Kevin began, "The mother and father of all the Ringling Circus brothers were Marie and August. They were married in Milwaukee in 1852 and then moved to Chicago. The Ringling family moved to Wisconsin after that, then to Iowa, and then they finally settled back in Wisconsin, in a town named Baraboo."

Chad said, "I like that name. *Baraboo*."

"Why did they move around so much?" Jan asked.

"August made custom-made harnesses and saddles, and he basically had to move to wherever the most work was," Kevin replied.

"How many Ringling kids were there anyway?" KT asked.

"There were eight kids–seven boys and one girl," Kevin answered.

"What were their names?" Mike inquired.

"I'll give you their names from oldest to youngest," said Kevin. "Albert, Augustus, Otto, Alfred, Charles, John, Henry, and Ida. I guess Alfred was called *Alf T.* so they didn't mix him up with Albert. In case you're curious, there were about 22 years between the oldest, Albert, and the youngest, Ida. Albert was born in 1852, and Ida was born in 1874."

"Who was the biggest Ringling brother?" Chad wanted to know.

"As far as the tallest, John was, going somewhere around six-foot four and 245 pounds–built something like an out-of-shape offensive lineman," Kevin said. "Henry was slightly shorter, but he looked even bigger than John."

Chad had a picture on his computer screen that he held up to show his friends. "Don't you think John Ringling

looked a lot like Babe Ruth?"

"He does."

"There *is* some resemblance."

"They're built the same."

"It's the haircut."

"Was the family poor?" KT asked.

"I have that feeling," Prez said. "Imagine just feeding all of those big boys. I saw a picture of their house in McGregor, Iowa, where John was born, and it looked like a little cracker box. It sounded like no one starved, though."

"Were all the brothers in the Ringling family involved in the circus?" Kari asked.

"Henry and Augustus weren't involved much," answered Kevin. "The other five were the Ringling Brothers of the circus."

"How did the Ringlings first get interested in the circus?" Nick asked.

Kari said, "I read a couple of stories that might explain that. The first one said it might have all started when a river-boat show stopped in McGregor, Iowa, and Mr. Ringling got some free passes for doing the harness work for the show people. Another story said Mr. Ringling did some work for a circus man nicknamed Popcorn George, but Popcorn did-n't pay Mr. Ringling for the harness work he did. Mr. Ringling sent two of his sons to wait around until Popcorn paid them, and it got the boys interested in the circus."

KT asked, "Were there lots of circuses and shows around back then?"

"No doubt," Jan said. "There were about 70 small cir-cuses just from Wisconsin."

"How did the Ringlings start their first circus?" Jessie

inquired.

Kevin explained, "They started out with something like a comedy, music, variety show they'd put on in town halls. Then they took the show to other towns in the area by train. After a few years, they got a circus going with a guy named Yankee Robinson, who had lots of circus experience. It was sad, because Yankee died during the first circus season, so the Ringling boys became owners by themselves."

Mike asked, "What did each of the brothers do in the circus?"

"Al was the ringmaster," Kevin began. "Otto handled the money. Alf T. was the leader of the band. Charles was the orchestra leader, and later he was the one in charge of the whole circus crew. John was a Dutch clown at first, but later he became the guy responsible for scheduling and booking the circus all around the country."

"What happened after they got their first circus?" KT asked.

"The circus just kept growing," Kevin replied. "The Ringlings provided good family entertainment at a fair price. They went from a one-ring circus to a three-ring circus. Then they bought the huge Barnum & Bailey Circus. By the year 1910, the Ringling brothers had three big circuses. I read where most circuses lasted just a few years, but the Ringlings were involved in more than 19,000 circus performances in 40 years."

"Which of the Ringlings came to Sarasota first?" Jan asked.

"John Ringling," Kevin answered.

KT asked, "Why did John Ringling come to Sarasota in the first place?"

Jan explained, "By 1910, all the Ringling brothers were rich. During the winter, the circus shut down, and all the Ringlings except Otto were looking for a good place to escape the cold weather."

"What was the deal with Otto?" Nick asked.

"Otto didn't care that much about warm winter vacations, I guess," Jan said. "Anyway, John and his wife, Mable, came down to Tarpon Springs a few winters, but they felt like the people there gave them the cold shoulder. Apparently some people looked down on circus people. One day John and Mable cruised down to Shell Beach in Sarasota on a small yacht named the *Louise II* to visit friends Ralph Caples and Charles Thompson, who lived there. Ralph and Charles told the Ringlings that Sarasota people were more friendly, and they should consider spending winters in Sarasota instead of Tarpon Springs."

"Were Ralph Caples and Charles Thompson rich, too?" Mike inquired.

"Oh, yes," Prez answered, "Caples was a big shot with the railroad, and Thompson was a former manager of one of the Ringling circuses. By the way, Caples even managed the train for the presidential campaign of Warren G. Harding."

"Did those guys talk John and Mable into moving here?" Kari asked.

"They sure did," Jan said. "In February of 1911, John bought 20 acres of land from Charles Thompson, and in October he bought a renovated house from Caples. John and Mable called the house *Palms Elysian*–I have no clue what that means. Surprisingly, this was really the first house John and Mable ever bought, and they'd been married for quite awhile."

"Why didn't they have a house before?" KT inquired.

Jan explained, "Well, during the circus season, mid-March until late November, they spent most of their time in their private railroad car, the *Wisconsin*, or in hotels and apartments while they followed the circus around the country. During the off season, they liked to travel in Europe, especially Italy."

"They had a private railroad car?" Mike asked.

"They had two, and they were both fancy," said Prez. "The first one was the *Wisconsin*, which they also called *The Honeymoon Car* because they bought it before they were married. It was about 75 feet long, and had a large living area, a chef, a maid, a porter, sleeping compartments, bathrooms, and everything."

"What's a porter?" Nick asked.

"It's the guy who handled the luggage and things on the train," Kari answered.

Mike asked, "What was their second railroad car called?"

"The *Jomar*, which was an acronym for John and Mable Ringling," Prez said.

"I don't get it," Nick said.

"Well, you take the letters JO from John and the letters MA from Mable and the R from Ringling and you get *Jomar*," Prez explained.

"Oh, cool," Nick said.

Prez said, "The *Jomar* was the longest railroad car *ever* when the Ringlings bought it–82 feet long! It was like the luxurious corporate jet of the time. When the Ringlings were here in Sarasota, the *Jomar* used to sit way out on the end of the city pier, and some people would stay there when they visited the Ringlings. A queen from Romania even stayed in the *Jomar* once."

"Fit for the queen!" Mike said. "I'll bet Elvis would have enjoyed the *Jomar*, too."

"Anyone would have enjoyed it," Kari said. "When did Charles Ringling come to Sarasota?" she asked.

"Not long after John and Mable bought their home," Kevin answered. "You see, Ralph Caples and John bought some more land in the Shell Beach area, and Charles was the first person to buy land from them. He built a house really close to John's. I guess it's still there, and it's now part of a college called New College."

"Is New College really still a *new college*?" Chad said. "After awhile, shouldn't they have to change their name to Old College?"

Everyone gave Chad funny looks.

"I just think it's dangerous giving a college a name like that," Chad insisted.

"Uh, whatever you say, Chad," Jessie said with a giggle. "Did any of the other Ringlings live in Sarasota besides John and Charles?" she asked.

Prez said, "John and Charles's little sister, Ida, lived in Sarasota a long time after her husband died. Alf T lived here awhile and actually built a nice house, but he died before he had a chance to live in it."

"Who would you say was richer, John or Charles?" Mike asked.

"John probably had the most wealth," Prez replied. "In fact, some magazine said he was the seventh richest man in America at one time. Charles was once one of the 25 richest men in America."

Jan asked, "Did John make all his money from the circus?"

"No," Prez said. "Besides the circus, he was involved in all sorts of things—oil, railroads, even a huge 80,000 acre cattle ranch in Montana. After World War I, Sarasota became his biggest investment."

"What was the deal with World War I?" Jessie asked.

Prez explained, "During World War I, John couldn't travel to Europe much, and he saw lots of possibilities for investing in Sarasota. Then there was a land boom in Florida, and John started dreaming about making Sarasota into a vacation paradise and a great place to live."

"What's a land boom?" Nick inquired.

"It's basically a time where lots of people want to buy land—the demand and the prices boom," Prez answered.

"Oh, cool."

"What exactly was John Ringling's dream for Sarasota?" Kari asked.

"His dream was called Ringling Isles," Prez began. "John Ringling wanted to develop Sarasota into one of the nicest places anywhere to live or vacation. There's so much to his dream, but I can give you some highlights. It included buying Bird, Otter, Coon, St. Armands, Lido, and Longboat Keys and developing them into places with beautiful houses, golf courses, and casinos. He envisioned bridges connecting the mainland to all the keys. St. Armands Key would have a circle of shops and restaurants. There'd be a luxury hotel, the Ritz-Carlton, on the southern end of Longboat Key. He even wanted the mansion on Bird Key called Worcester's Castle to become President Warren Harding's winter White House, but President Harding died before he had a chance to come down to see it."

"What happened to him?" asked KT.

"That's a story in itself," Prez said. "He had a massive heart attack after just two years in office."

"How could John Ringling possibly buy up all that land on all those keys?" Jan asked.

Prez said, "The Hurricane of 1921 made a mess of those keys and there were no bridges to get to them back then, so the land must have been fairly cheap."

"If John was busy with the circus most of the year, he must have had some big-time help with all those dreams of his," Kari observed.

"He had lots of help, but no one helped him more than Owen Burns," said Prez.

"Owen Burns? Didn't we see his gravestone in Rosemary Cemetery?" Nick asked.

"That's right, Nick," Prez replied. "He was a prominent Sarasota developer who also had a construction company and all the ability to put many of John Ringling's dreams into reality. They met on a trip to Chicago, and after that, they worked together on several projects."

Kevin added, "John Ringling's dreams for Sarasota also included building a beautiful dream house for Mable and him, where they could invite possible investors and entertain friends."

"That's the Cà d'Zan, isn't it?" KT guessed.

"That's right, KT," Kevin replied.

Nick asked, "How did you say the name of their house, again?"

KT replied, "I just say *ca*, like I was starting to say *cat*, then *dah*, and then *zahn*. I think that's right."

"CA ... DAH ... ZAHN!" Nick said enthusiastically. "Ca dah zahn! Ca dah zahn! Ca dah zahn!"

"Very good, Nick," Prez said. "It was pretty cool, too, because John could use the circus to promote all his Sarasota dreams. The circus programs and posters had lots of advertisement for Sarasota on them. Millions of circus fans got to know about Sarasota that way. Posters said things like 'Spend a Summer This Winter In Sarasota.'"

"What about Charles Ringling? What did he do around here?" Jessie asked.

"Lots," Kevin replied. "Ringling Boulevard is named after him, and he developed much of the land along that road. He owned a bank; he had a beautiful hotel called The Sarasota Terrace Hotel; he donated the land for the Sarasota County Courthouse and helped arrange for the design of that building. He was really active in the community when he was around here, too."

"Did John and Charles Ringling ever work on projects together?" Chad asked.

"Sure," Kari said. "There's a funny story about that. I guess John liked to stay up all night and work, and Charles used to give him a rough time about that. One night, John was working on the purchase of a huge 66,000 acre chunk of land in this area. To irritate his brother a little, John called Charles in the middle of the night when he knew he'd be sound asleep. John refused to hang up until Charles agreed to go 50-50 on the deal–which Charles did after–"

Prez's cell phone rang. "Hi Dickie V! What's up?"

"I'm so excited! After talking to you and your friends about your *Starship Exercise*, I decided I might get a boat ready for the Creative Boat Parade, too, so I'm talking to a boatbuilder right now! I think we can get it done!"

"What are you going to build?"

"It's going to be a secret for awhile, but I just wanted to call and thank you all for getting me interested in the parade!"

"No problem. Dickie V, we've just been reading about the Ringling brothers, especially John and Charles and all the stuff they did in Sarasota. What's the first place you think of around Sarasota when you think of the Ringlings?"

"That's easy, Prez! That whole complex up on Shell Beach, including the art museum and the Cà d'Zan–it's phenomenal!"

After breakfast the next morning, Sarabiskota got out to the *Rough Rider*, anxious to go to Shell Beach. Even before Prez had finished using his gizmo to launch the boat, Jack Lambert was jumping out in the water nearby.

Prez said, "KT, there's a small camera in my backpack I've rigged so we can attach it to Jack Lambert's dorsal fin–if he doesn't mind. Before we get underway, why don't Jessie and you ask Jack Lambert if you can put it on him."

As everyone else watched, Jessie and KT waded out into the water, and they talked to Jack Lambert. Then they attached the small camera to his dorsal fin. Jack Lambert didn't seem to mind at all what his two friends were doing. By this time, he trusted them totally.

Prez got on the boat, turned on one of the monitors, and said, "The camera is working perfectly. We now have the *Lambert cam*, so we can see the world from Jack Lambert's perspective. The only problem is, we're probably not going to see much when he's moving rapidly through the water below the surface. It should be interesting, though."

It turned out to be extremely interesting! Sarabiskota launched the boat, then watched the monitor as it received pictures sent from the Lambert cam.

"Wow! That looks so cool when he jumps into the air!"

"Look at those big fish!"

"Jack Lambert's taking a picture of us!"

"It's working even better than I thought," Prez said.

As they continued watching the monitor, Jessie said, "We never really finished talking about John and Charles Ringling."

"I'm sure we'll find out more about them when we get to Shell Beach, but where were we?" Prez asked.

"You know," Jessie offered, "John and Charles were building all sorts of stuff around Sarasota. John was working on his Ringling Isles dream, and they started building the Cà d'Zan. What happened after that?"

"Well, it's sad and a little strange, too," Prez said.

"Don't tell me it snowed again," KT guessed.

"No," said Prez, "but another hurricane had some affect on what happened."

"What's the deal?" Mike asked.

Prez explained, "You know that big land boom in Florida we talked about that started in about 1922 that John and Charles Ringling took advantage of? Well, the boom pretty much fizzled out in 1926 when the stock market fell. A few months later, in September, the Hurricane of 1926 made matters even worse. Interest in buying land in Florida was down to about zero. Then Charles died on December 3."

"Oh, no," said Jessie. "How old was he?"

"Sixty-two, I think," Prez answered. "John was 60 at the time, and he became the only Ringling brother left. Since all his other brothers died in their fifties and early sixties, it might have been even tougher for John. On the brighter side, though, John and Mable moved into the Cà d'Zan in

December of 1926 ... but then, on the negative side, construction on the huge Ritz-Carlton hotel on Longboat Key had to stop because of money problems, and John never did finish the thing."

Jan asked, "Whatever happened to that Ritz-Carlton?"

Prez replied, "It just sat there until 1962 and it was finally torn down ... but on the positive side, though, even with all this bad stuff going on in his life, John Ringling did two things in 1927 that probably helped make him the most famous Sarasotan *ever*."

"What?" Kari inquired.

Prez answered, "First, he decided to build a huge museum for his art collection that was getting larger and larger."

"What was the second thing?" Nick asked.

"Well, they were having the annual Sara de Sota pageant in the spring of 1927, and John Ringling announced that the winter quarters of the circus were being moved to Sarasota. People around here were really excited because they knew it would be a huge attraction, and it would help Sarasota's economy, too."

"Where were the winter quarters of the Ringling Circus before they were moved to Sarasota?" Kari asked.

"Bridgeport, Connecticut," Prez replied.

"How long did the winter quarters stay in Sarasota?" KT wanted to know.

"Thirty-three years," Prez said. "That's how Sarasota became known as the Circus City."

"Where were the winter quarters located in Sarasota anyway?" Chad inquired.

"In northeast Sarasota, somewhere east of Beneva Road," replied Prez. "The Glen Oaks development is there now."

"Where did the winter quarters move after they left Sarasota?" Jan asked.

"Just south of here, to Venice, until 1991," Prez answered. "Then they moved up to Tampa–to the State Fairgrounds there. That's where the winter quarters are now."

Kari asked, "What were the winter quarters in Sarasota like?"

"Picture this," Kevin began. "There was a huge 200 acre site John had planned out by himself. There was a three ring outdoor arena, similar in size to the indoor arena at Madison Square Gardens, where the circus performed a lot. There were barns for all the animals, all sorts of buildings and offices, even railroad tracks where they built circus cars."

Prez added, "Before the winter quarters first opened to the public, they had an open house on Christmas Day in 1927, and 6,000 people toured the whole huge complex. That day, John did something else that must have helped boost his popularity in Sarasota even more. He decided all the admission money to the winter quarters, 25 cents for adults and 10 cents for children, would be used for charities in Sarasota."

"How many people came here to visit?" Nick asked.

"That first year the winter quarters were open on Wednesdays and Sundays. In just three months, 65 thousand people visited," Kevin said.

"What went on at the winter quarters anyway?" KT asked.

"Lots of things to get the circus ready for the next season," Kevin began. "Like canvas workers had to build a new Big Top circus tent for the next season. Just imagine–it was made in 18 sections, each one weighing about 1,500 pounds.

There were over three acres underneath the tent! It was the largest tent in the world! I guess there were about 300 other canvas structures that had to be made, too, like tents for the animals and dressing rooms. Apparently, the old tents were pretty much worn out after eight months on the road."

Jessie added, "The circus also had about 70 double-length steel railroad cars to carry the circus around the country, and all of them were at the winter quarters being fixed up and repainted. You can only imagine all the circus wagons, animal cages, circus outfits, and other things that had to be worked on."

"What else was going on at the winter quarters?" Mike asked.

Kevin continued, "You could watch tons of circus performers practicing for the next season. The horses were working out in the ring barns, and the elephants were being trained someplace else. There were animals everywhere! Apparently, everyone who came to the winter quarters wanted to see a huge gorilla from the Congo named Gargantua and his wife M'Toto."

Nick said, "Gargantua—a good name for a professional wrestler."

Nick got some funny looks from several of his friends.

Prez said, "In the spring, huge crowds would gather at the winter quarters in Sarasota as the performers loaded into the railroad cars and left Sarasota for their tour of the country."

"It must have been so cool to live around here at that time," KT said.

"That's for sure," Kari agreed.

Chad asked, "So, what happened in John's life after the circus began wintering here in 1927?"

"Well, Mable and John had just a few more years together," said Jan. "Mable died on June 8, 1929, of something called Addison's disease that was complicated by diabetes."

"What's Addison's disease, Doc?" Nick asked.

Jan explained, "It's a failure of the adrenal glands—the adrenal glands affect the body's ability to maintain blood pressure, blood sugar levels, and things like that. It's interesting, because back then, the leading cause of Addison's disease was tuberculosis."

"That must have been really tough," KT observed. "John had no brothers left and now his wife, Mable, was dead, too."

"That's right," Prez said. "Unfortunately, it seemed to just get worse after that. Financially, it got really messy for John."

"What do you mean?" Mike asked.

"Three months later, the stock market crashed, and John's financial problems got worse. Then, in 1930, he married a lady named Emily Haag Buck. She gave him $50,000 to help him with his money problems, but I don't think they had a good relationship. I got the feeling she really didn't like Sarasota, the circus, or all the art John liked to collect."

"How long did the marriage last?" Jessie asked.

"They were divorced about three years later," Prez answered. "On the positive side, though, Ringling's art museum opened free to the public in 1932, but Ringling's financial situation was so bad by then–legend says he was living off the 25 cent parking fees at the museum parking lot. The management of the circus had been taken from him, too."

"Yikes," said Kari. "Did he have to sell his art collection then?"

"No, he had millions of dollars tied up in his art, but they say he never sold any of it," Prez replied. "In May of 1932, it just got worse, though. John got a bad case of blood poisoning caused from being stepped on while dancing at The Gasparilla Ball in Tampa several months earlier."

"I'm definitely going to continue to avoid dancing," Chad noted.

"No doubt," Prez said, holding back his laughter. "Then, in December of 1932, John lost all control of the circus, and he developed thrombosis."

Everyone looked at Jan. "I'm guessing it was cerebral thrombosis—when a blood clot forms in a major blood vessel to the brain, often causing paralysis," she said.

"That's probably it," Prez said. "John got some paralysis to his right side. He got a second and third blood clot in 1933, the same year he filed for divorce. By then, he was using a wheelchair and his speech was affected by the stroke. His money problems were getting worse, too. In fact, in November of 1936, John found out the Cà d'Zan was going to be taken away and sold to pay off some of his debts, and that may have been the last straw. On December 2, 1936, John Ringling died of pneumonia, a few days before the Cà d'Zan was going to be sold. After that, there were 10 years of litigation where friends, relatives, and the state fought over who would get control of the museum and the Cà d'Zan."

"What's litigation?" Nick asked.

"It's legal stuff, involving lawyers and courts," Prez replied.

"Oh."

"Look at that!" Kevin said, pointing at the Lambert cam

monitor.

They all looked. They could see Jack Lambert swimming near the bottom of the bay, and there were two big loggerhead sea turtles swimming nearby! Jack Lambert swam around the sea turtles for several minutes, while Sarabiskota watched all the action on the monitor.

"This is so cool!" KT said.

"That's for sure," Kevin added. "Jacques Cousteau would be impressed."

"Huh?" Nick said, looking puzzled.

"Famous ocean explorer, Nick," Prez explained.

"Oh."

After they docked at the Cà d'Zan, KT told Jack Lambert what they were going to be doing. After that, they found out they had to run over to the John and Mable Ringling Museum of Art to get tickets for the Cà d'Zan tour. While they were running there, they got a good idea just how big the whole 66 acre Ringling complex was.

They purchased tickets to the first tour, the one at 10:15, and then they ran back to the Cà d'Zan. They entered the house through the Solarium, where several people were already waiting for the first tour.

When Nick saw the *Solarium* sign, he said, "I know this one. *Solar* means *sun*, so the Solarium must be a room to get some sun. That must be the reason for all the cool multicolored windows."

From the Solarium, they went into the Reception Room, where their tour guide was wearing a name tag that said *Ryan Noone*. He said, "I'm Ryan *Noon*. You young people will notice it's spelled like *no one*. Believe me, that could be tough sometimes on the school playground ... Anyway, this is the

home of John and Mable Ringling called the *Cà d'Zan*. *Cà d'Zan* means *House of John* in Venetian dialect, but it should probably be called the House of Mable, since it was Mable who made most of the decisions on the details of its building and furnishing.

"It's estimated to have cost one-and-a-half million dollars to build, which is 15 million in today's money, and another $400,000 to furnish, excluding artwork and tapestries. That's about four million dollars in today's money. The house is 22,000 square feet–four stories high. It has 32 rooms, 15 baths, and one shower. There were seven live-in servants here."

"Who were some of the servants?" Nick asked.

"Let's see," Ryan said. "I know there was Frank, the butler; Hedwig, who was Mable's maid; John, the house man; Sophie, the cook; Eric, the Swedish chauffeur; and Al Roan, who was captain of the Ringling yachts."

Ryan continued, "When John died in 1936, the house stood vacant for about 10 years while the state of Florida and the family fought over ownership. During that time, its condition deteriorated. When the state took control of the house in 1946, it was opened again, but no significant money was spent on it. By 1996, when the remake of the movie *Great Expectations* was filmed here, the place was falling apart from decades of neglect ... by the way, that was just what the movie people needed for that particular movie. The tile roof leaked, the furniture inside was in tough shape, and the wallpaper had faded. When the state came up with money to renovate the place in 1996, they estimated the cost would be 6 million dollars to do the job, but it turned out to take 15 million dollars–and it took them until April of 2002 to finish.

"The goal was to make it look like it did when John and Mable lived here. Keep in mind as you walk through, 99 percent of the furniture and other furnishings are original. Mable had taken many pictures of the interior and they were a big help in restoring things to the way it was in those years the Ringlings lived here.

"John and Mable loved to vacation in Europe, and John would also audition new circus acts while they were there. Later, John also bought a lot of fine art while they were in Europe. Venice was probably their favorite place to visit, and they loved the Venetian style of architecture. As they started to plan building this house on their trip to Europe in 1923, they wanted it to resemble a canal-side palace or *palazzo*. Mable collected pictures, brochures, and drawings of some of her ideas for the house to share with an architect when they got back from Italy. John Ringling's business partner here in Sarasota, Owen Burns, built this house. Dwight James Baum was the architect.

"In 1924, the Ringlings actually moved their other house, the *Palms Elysian*, further back from the water on the property and lived in it while the Cà d'Zan was being built. It took two years to finish."

"What does *Elysian* mean?" Chad asked.

"It refers to a place in Greek and Roman mythology where souls live in perfect joy," Ryan explained.

As they moved to the next room, the Ballroom, they looked up at the ceiling at 22 panels painted by a famous Hungarian artist, William Pogany. The entire creation was called *Dancers of Nations*. Ryan said, "Pogany was a famous illustrator of children's books and a set designer for the

Ziegfield Follies, a famous entertainment extravaganza in New York City. On each panel you'll notice a different couple dancing, each one representing a unique culture and time."

"How did John and Mable first meet?" KT asked.

"That's a good question. We're not sure where or how they met. Some think it was in Atlantic City, New Jersey. There's really quite a bit of mystery surrounding Mable, in fact. We're not even sure when she was born. She gave only one interview in her life, and that was to a Seattle newspaper–about traveling with the circus. Mable never agreed to be photographed by the press, but studio portraits and family photos show how beautiful she was–with dark hair, a slender build, and porcelain skin.

"Mable was not all elegance, though. There's a story about her walking the grounds when the museum was being built. She was dressed in pants, and she was carrying a gun so she could shoot the snakes that had been disturbed by all the construction going on around here. She loved fishing, she was a good shot, and she liked cruising in their yachts or riding in her gondola, which she brought back from Venice, Italy.

"By the way, Mable was from Moons, Ohio, and had four sisters and one brother. Two of those sisters, who were also two of her closest friends, actually lived on St. Armands Key near here."

Next, they moved into the largest room in the house, the Court, with beautifully painted 30-foot ceilings. Ryan said, "The Ringlings handled the interior decoration, and they bought many of their furnishings at auctions in New York City. "

Along one wall under a large painting of John Ringling, Ryan pointed out an Aeolian Organ that had 2,220 pipes hidden behind the tapestries in the second floor balcony. "The organ would cost tens of thousands of dollars to fix, if there is anyone still alive to fix it," he said. "It's said the organ could be heard around the entire bay when it was being played. The antique Steinway piano on the other side of the room cost $40,000 just to fix. The beautiful crystal chandelier hanging here once hung in New York's Waldorf Astoria."

Next, they went into the Breakfast Room, where there was an iron gate in the entryway. Kevin asked, "What was the reason for the iron gate?"

"Good question," Ryan said. "The Ringlings had no children, but a menagerie of pets including a cockatiel, two parrots, some miniature Dobermans, and a German shepherd named Tel who basically had the run of the place. John and Mable also had many nieces and nephews who were frequent visitors. The gate was there to keep the dogs out mostly–not the children.

"The Breakfast Room may look a little unusual with green chairs and a beautiful green crystal chandelier. Mable actually had the chairs painted green to match the chandelier."

When they got to the huge Dining Room, Ryan said, "The Ringlings were busy with the circus from the spring through December, so they didn't move in until December of 1926. They entertained here for the first time at Christmas with a dinner for family members who were still grieving the death of John's brother, Charles, who had died on December 3 ... Many famous people have dined at this very table."

"Like who?" Nick asked.

"Many we'll never know about because they liked their privacy, but there was Thomas Edison, who lived down in Fort Meyers part of the year and came here with his wife, Mina. Edison even gave John and Mable the big Banyan tree out front ... Henry Ford stayed here, and he was actually Edison's neighbor in Fort Myers. Will Rogers, who was a famous movie star, writer, rope trickster, and comedian stayed here ... Have any of you kids ever heard of Will Rogers?"

Prez said, "I've seen his movie *Ropin' Fool* where he actually stood on the ground and threw three lassos at once at a running horse. One rope caught the running horse's neck, the other would hoop around the rider, and the third swooped up under the horse to loop all four legs. I think he's also the guy who said 'I've never met a man I didn't like.'"

"Very good, young man," Ryan said.

"Did any other famous people stay here that you know of?" Chad asked Ryan.

"Yes," Ryan replied, "the mayor of New York City, Jimmy Walker, stayed here. The owner of the New York Giants baseball team named John McGraw stayed here–and John Ringling's friend, Sam Gumpertz, eventually talked McGraw into moving the Giants here for Spring Training. We've had major league baseball spring training in Sarasota ever since. Uh, Ziegfield and his wife, actress Billie Burke–two of the greatest entertainers on Broadway *ever*, stayed here."

"Did any Presidents stay here?" Nick asked.

"There are rumors that Warren Harding and Calvin Coolidge did," Ryan answered.

When they got upstairs to the second floor, they walked through John Ringling's exercise room, which had a barber chair and a massage table in it. Also, there was an old machine with a vibrating belt on it that didn't do much more than vibrate the fat on the backside.

Jessie said, "It doesn't look like much exercise was going on in this exercise room."

Everyone laughed.

Then they walked through John's corner office. Ryan said, "Notice the fantastic view John Ringling had from this office. From here he could see much of his Ringling Isles dream." It *was* a great view!

After that, they went into John's bedroom. They found out John paid $50,000 for nine pieces of furniture–half a million dollars in today's money.

Next, they toured Mable's bedroom and a guest bedroom, before they were about to go downstairs again.

"What's up on the third and fourth floors?" Mike asked.

"Well, I can't take you up there because of fire safety laws, but let me tell you about them. The third floor is the Playroom. The ceiling painting in that room is called *Pageantry of Venice*, also painted by William Pogany, and it shows scenes of John and Mable dressed in costumes with their pets.

"Half-a-flight up from the Playroom, you get to a very nice guest suite, beautifully paneled in mahogany, with fantastic panoramic views from the windows. Will Rogers loved to stay in this room. From there, a door opens to the outside stairway which winds up to the tower. The 60-foot tower was something Mable wanted because it reminded her of the old Madison Square Garden in New York City where their circus used to perform. That tower was lit up when the Ringlings were around."

When they went downstairs into the kitchen, Ryan talked about the cutting edge technology that was put in the Cà d'Zan, including electricity, electric lights, and an Otis elevator, but no air conditioning–since it hadn't been invented yet.

"I think it was invented, but just not in common use then," Prez offered.

"Please tell us more, young man," Ryan said.

"It's pretty interesting. Dr. John Gorrie from Florida was actually trying to come up with a device to keep his yellow fever patients cool, and he came up with a crude air conditioner way back in 1852. Back then, companies made big money by cutting big chunks of ice out of northern lakes and rivers, packing it in sawdust, and shipping it down here. When Gorrie tried to sell his invention, the ice companies got the newspapers to make fun of Gorrie, and his invention never got off the ground. Now, however, he's recognized as one of the great inventors of the twentieth century."

"I thought Carrier invented the air conditioner," Ryan said.

Prez said, "William Carrier is the guy usually given credit for developing the air conditioner, and his first unit was put in a publishing company in Brooklyn in 1902. During the 1910's and 1920's department stores and movie theaters started to put in air conditioners. The United States Congress got theirs in 1928, and the White House got air conditioning in 1929. Cars started getting them in 1953."

"Who was the first air conditioned President?" KT inquired.

"I think that would be Herbert Hoover," Prez said.

Nick smiled, "Was he the first President with an electric vacuum cleaner, too?"

Nick got a lot of strange looks, followed by some giggles.

Next, they went outside to the huge terrace on Sarasota Bay. It was one-fifth the size of a football field, and was made of beautifully colored marble.

Ryan said, "Mable had bridge and tea parties for hundreds out on this terrace. Mable actually brought a gondola back from Venice, Italy, which was docked here. The Ringlings had several yachts around here, too–the yachts just kept getting bigger and bigger as the years went by."

"Could you tell us a little about the yachts?" Nick asked.

"Well, Mable and John first came down to Sarasota from Tarpon Springs in the *Louise II*. After that, they had the first steam yacht called the *Wethea*. Next, there was the *Vidoffner II* with a captain and crew of eight–that one was destroyed by an explosion while docked in Tampa. Then there was the *Salome*, which was actually Henry Ringling's boat. It caught fire, burned, and sank during a thunderstorm in Tampa Bay. Mable got scars on her arms during that incident. The *Zalophus*, which means *sea lion*, was next. It was John's biggest yacht of all at 125 feet. The *Zalophus* had an 11 man crew, and it hit an object off Lido Beach and sunk. Finally, there was the *Zalophus Junior*, which was only 52 feet long."

"Gee, the Ringlings didn't have the greatest luck with yachts, did they?" Jessie said.

24

After they left the Cà d'Zan, Sarabiskota walked through a small garden of flowers, trees, and bushes nearby. Mable Ringling had called this the Secret Garden.

Prez explained, "When John and Mable lived here, the Secret Garden was hidden by lots of trees and shrubs so they could come here to relax in privacy."

They all walked on the path of flat stones through the entire garden until they got to a black iron fence. Behind the fence, they could see three headstones side-by-side—John's, Mable's, and Ida's.

Nick read the common inscription on all three headstones. "*Interred June 4, 1991*–what does that mean?" he asked.

"That means their bodies were buried here that day," Jan explained. "They must have been moved here from somewhere else."

Kari said, "I read somewhere that John and Mable actually thought about being buried in the art museum in a special crypt, but it was never built. This is a much more beautiful place anyway—right on Sarasota Bay."

After they left the Secret Garden, Sarabiskota walked past a huge Banyan tree that Thomas Edison had given to

John and Mable. Then they entered an enormous wagon wheel-shaped garden called Mable's Rose Garden.

Stephen Queen watched Sarabiskota's every move from behind the Banyan tree! Mr. Queen had driven his car to Shell Beach–doing everything he could to avoid Jack Lambert.

Sarabiskota quickly walked through the garden, looking at the hundreds of roses planted there, each one neatly labeled. Mike even found a green rose, and Jessie found one named the *Mable Rose*.

"It would be nice having a beautiful flower named after you," said Jessie.

"That would be OK," Chad agreed, "but I'd rather have a football team named after me like Paul Brown of the Cleveland Browns sorta did."

"Chad, your name is already infamous in recent Florida history ... the election problem in 2000 has you to blame," Prez commented.

Chad looked confused. "Huh?"

"The hanging *chad*," Prez said.

"That's pretty bad," Kari chuckled.

Nick looked puzzled. "I don't get it. What?"

"I'll explain later," said Prez.

As they were walking to the Circus Museum, Kevin mentioned, "I guess this museum wasn't something John Ringling would've been too thrilled with."

"Why's that?" KT asked.

Kevin pointed to the east. "Because he wouldn't have wanted it to take attention away from his huge art museum over there."

"Why was it built here then?" Mike inquired.

As they approached the door, Kevin said, "The first art museum director thought people wouldn't want to come here just to see a bunch of fine art, so they started this museum. Look at the size of this building. It used to be John Ringling's garage!"

When they got into the Circus Museum, they slowly walked around, looking at the beautiful circus wagons, all the colorful circus costumes, many of the props the performers used, the wonderful circus posters—even an enormous mechanized miniature circus, complete with lots of sound and circus action. They also read about some of the greatest circus performers ever.

They even saw a truck with a big cannon attached, used by the Zacchini family, the human cannonballs. Jessie said, "Don't you have to wonder about a whole family that makes their living being shot out of a cannon? Talk about a bunch of big shots!"

They all laughed.

Then they came to a large display called *The Greatest Show on Earth*. KT said, "Look, it says that a famous producer and director by the name of Cecille B. DeMille and his large film crew came to Sarasota in January of 1951 and spent six weeks here filming the movie *The Greatest Show On Earth*. Some of the biggest movie stars of that time were in Sarasota, like Betty Hutton, Dorothy Lamour, Charlton Heston, and Cornel Wilde. Jimmy Stewart was in the movie, too, but he never came to Sarasota. They shot his scenes in Philadelphia at an actual circus performance. There was never a more exciting time in Sarasota!"

Jan asked, "Isn't Jimmy Stewart the dad from the movie *It's A Wonderful Life*?"

"That's right," Kari said. "Our family watches that movie together every Christmas."

"So does ours," Kevin added.

"Charlton Heston is in all those *Planet of the Apes* movies, isn't he?" Nick asked.

"That's right, Nick," Prez said. "He's in tons of movies. I saw him in *The Ten Commandments* not too long ago."

Mike was scanning some more information on the wall. "The movie had 150 circus stars in it," he noted. "At the end of the movie, they had an actual parade down Sarasota's Main Street and up Ringling Boulevard led by Betty Hutton. Wow! She was a beautiful movie star!"

Kari added, "It says the movie won the Oscar for the Best Picture of the Year."

Nearby, there was a small theatre set up for people to watch the movie if they wanted to. All they had to do was press a button to start the movie at the beginning.

"Should we watch it?" Mike asked.

"Why not?" Prez said.

"It will be cool to see what Sarasota looked like back in 1951," KT added.

"I can't wait to see what the winter quarters of the circus looked like," said Chad.

Mike put his hand on the button to start the movie, and spoke in his best Elvis voice, "I want everyone to get comfortable in their seats out there and enjoy this great movie. It may not be as good as some of my movies like *Blue Hawaii*, but I think you'll enjoy it anyway."

Nick asked, "How about some popcorn, Elvis?"

"No popcorn, but I could sing a few tunes before I start the movie if you'd like," Mike offered, still sounding like

Elvis.

"Just start the movie, please," KT said.

"Thank you. Thank you very much. Here goes," Mike said. Then he pressed the button and sat down with his friends to watch the entire 149 minutes of the movie ...

"Now I can see how huge the circus tent was!"

"There's the winter quarters. Cool!"

"That's John Ringling North playing himself in the movie. I think that's Ida's son, right?"

"That's right, Nick."

"It's hard to believe this movie was made in 1951. It's great!"

"Yeah, the story is good–no special effects or senseless violence needed."

"It does have the romance, the bad guys, and lots of great circus action."

"Would you like to try to be a trapeze artist?"

"No way!"

"KT, you look a lot like Betty Hutton."

"That's a compliment, Prez. She's really beautiful."

"Now I see what the circus train looks like."

"Did they say 1,400 people went on the road with the circus?"

"Yup."

"I feel sorry for the circus's Fat Boy having to ride with the hippos because he wouldn't fit in the passenger train cars."

"Look at the lady swallowing the huge sword!"

"Ewwwwwwwwwwww!"

"KT, the star that looks a lot like you plays the Queen of the Flying Trapeze."

"She's standing on her head on that little swinging bar way above the ground!"

"Yikes!"

"Now she's got the two back legs of the chair on the trapeze bar–and she's doing a handstand with her hands on the back of the chair!"

"I can't look!"

"See how the circus stars changed costumes for some of the later circus parades around the arena?"

"Do you girls think that Sebastian guy is cute?"

"Well, yes."

"It's Hopalong Cassidy in the parade!"

"Who's that?"

"He's in a lot of those old westerns. He had a cool horse named Topper."

"Look at them unloading the huge circus train when they get to the next town."

"Yeah, it looks like the elephants did most of the heavy work."

"Did they just say it takes 1,000 people to put up the circus tent?"

"Yup."

"That cotton candy that little girl's eating sure looks good."

"I wouldn't mind being the ringmaster."

"I love the clowns and their little exploding cars."

"Hey, they just did a close-up of Bing Crosby and Bob Hope in the audience."

"Wow! They look so young!"

"I think that's called a cameo appearance."

"Oh."

"That's Emmett Kelly, the most famous circus clown ever."

"That's Lou Jacobs, another famous clown."

"Ouch, that's got to hurt."

"I think Sebastian should have used the net when he did that stunt."

"That guy's jumping rope one-legged on a tightrope!"

"I could do that."

"Sure, Kevin."

"I read that here in Sarasota they actually let high school kids try circus acts with the help of older performers. It's called the Sailor Circus."

"She's bouncing eight little balls at one time!"

"She's walking around with that other girl head first on top of her head!"

"What's your favorite animal act so far in the movie?"

"The cute dogs riding the horses."

"I'm an elephant guy myself."

"Yikes! That elephant's going to crush that pretty lady's head!"

"It's not a good idea to make the elephant trainer jealous, I guess."

"Oh, no! They're going to stop the circus train and rob it!"

"And there's another circus train right behind it!"

"It's going to crash into the other train!"

"The animals are getting loose!"

"Yikes!"

"What a mess!"

"How can they get the circus boss out from under all that wreckage?"

"Wait, the elephant will help get the heavy stuff off the circus boss!"

"Looks like they're still going to have the circus, but they've got to get the people from that nearby town to come to them."

"That's a good idea. Have a circus parade in the town, and the people will follow it to the circus performance."

"That's the Main Street of Sarasota! There's Betty Hutton in the first float, leading the parade down Sarasota's Main Street–riding a trapeze on the float and singing."

"That must have been exciting!"

"This is a great ending for the movie!"

Suddenly, Chad jumped right out of his seat and pointed toward the movie screen! "Look! That guy standing by the float looks just like Khan from *Star Trek*! Oh–he's not on the screen anymore! The movie's over!"

"What?" Kari asked.

Chad said, "I thought there was a guy standing by that float that looked like Khan from the *Star Trek* movies. Dickie V said that's what Captain Sarasota looks like!"

"How old did the guy in the movie look to you, Chad?" Prez asked.

"I just got a quick look," Chad replied. "I'm guessing 60 or so."

"The movie was made in 1951, Chad," Jan said. "Maybe it was Captain Sarasota's grandpa."

"If we have the time, we can rent the movie sometime, and take a closer look," Prez suggested. "Right now, let's get something to drink at the Banyan Cafe."

The Banyan Cafe was just a few steps from the front door of the Circus Museum. As Sarabiskota sat at two adjoining

tables, drinking their beverages, Kari said, "We've seen so much Ringling stuff in the last several hours, it's unreal, but I have no idea what the Ringling clue could be. What should we do next?"

"Let's at least take a quick walk-through of the art museum," said Jessie. "We can come back tomorrow if we don't find anything."

Sarabiskota was amazed at what they saw at The John and Mable Ringling Museum of Art! They walked quickly through more than 20 art galleries, with hundreds of beautiful paintings, sculptures, and art objects on display. After that, they walked out into the museum's massive courtyard.

"Oh, my gosh!" Jessie exclaimed. "The museum is huge–now look at this courtyard!"

"I think you could get a football field in here if they'd just remove some of the trees and statues and things," Chad commented.

"This is even more impressive than I would've dreamed!" KT exclaimed. "This has to be one of the best art museums anywhere."

"That's for sure," Mike said. "And I'm not even a big art person–although I do have that cheap painting of Elvis playing cards with some dogs."

Everyone laughed.

Jan asked, "What are we going to do next?"

"Look, I don't know about you, but I'm tired," said Prez. "I say we head back to Siesta Key. Tonight we can get together and talk about our next move."

25

As soon as the boys got to the kitchen for breakfast the next morning, Prez's dad handed Prez the morning paper and said, "Looks like they had some excitement at the Cà d'Zan last night."

Prez glanced at the headlines and read them out loud, almost yelling! "**Mysterious *Break In at the Cà d'Zan*!**"

"Are you serious?" Chad asked loudly.

"Read it to us, Prez!" Kevin exclaimed.

"OK," Prez said anxiously. "It says:

> **It doesn't get any stranger than this! There appears to have been a break in last night at the Cà d'Zan, yet nothing seems to be missing. The Cà d'Zan has state-of-the-art motion detectors which were installed during its multi-million dollar renovation, yet none of them functioned. The second story window in John Ringling's office was left opened by the intruders, yet, because of its small size and location, there was no possible way that window could have been used**

as their entry point.

Most perplexing is the fact that the lights in the 60-foot tower of the Cà d'Zan apparently came on about the time the break in occurred, and that's what prompted a call to the police in the first place. Cà d'Zan officials, however, weren't even aware the lights in the tower were still functioning. They didn't even know where the switch to turn them on was located.

Ringling historian David C. Weeks told the *Bradenton Herald* that the lights in the tower were illuminated only when John and Mable were at home. The last time the famous Sarasota couple was at home in the Cà d'Zan together was in 1929, the year Mable died!

When Dr. Weeks was told of the circumstances of the break in, he said, "It's almost as if John and Mable returned for the evening. They went up to John's office, opened the window, and they saw how all of John's dreams for everything out on the keys turned out. If that's what happened last night, I'll bet both John and Mable liked what they saw."

During Florida's land boom, John Ringling had dreams of developing many of the keys near the Cà d'Zan into a first class place to live and vacation, but his dreams were never fully realized during his lifetime.

Since his death in 1936, however, many of the things he envisioned have come to fruition.

What's next in this case? Braydon Huschka, Sarasota's Police Chief, told the *Bradenton Herald*, "It's the strangest case I've ever been associated with or even heard about! All we can do now is keep checking to see if anything's missing and look for any other evidence—and maybe dial a psychic."

"Amazing!" was all Mike could say.

"I can't believe it! We were just at the Cà d'Zan!" Nick said. "By the way, what does *fruition* mean?"

"It means the achievement of something you've been working on," Prez explained.

"Oh."

"We've got to tell the girls about this!" Kevin said excitedly.

"I'll call them right now!" Prez exclaimed.

Prez immediately called KT on his cell phone. "KT, this is Prez! Could you girls meet us on the beach in a few minutes?"

"Sure, Prez. We're just having a little breakfast. What's up? You sound pretty excited."

"I'm beyond excited, KT! We'll fill you in at the beach in a few minutes!"

Ten minutes later, the girls met the boys on the beach, and the boys shared the front page story. Suddenly, Jack Lambert appeared down by the beach, and Sarabiskota walked out into shallow water to meet their friend.

As they were playing with Jack Lambert, Kari said, "This is Captain Sarasota's work, isn't it? I think he's trying to tell us the John Ringling clue we're looking for is somewhere out on one of those keys that were part of John Ringling's big dream."

"If it's Captain Sarasota's work, wouldn't that mean he's still alive?" asked Nick.

"After all that's happened the last couple of weeks, I don't know what to think anymore," Chad replied.

"Let's just assume Captain Sarasota's Ringling clue is somewhere out on one of the keys," Jan suggested. "That's a lot of territory out there. Where would we even start looking?"

"I think I know!" KT almost yelled. "I'll bet the Ringling clue is out at St. Armands Circle! In fact, John Ringling *himself* is out at St. Armands Circle!"

"Now you're scaring me a little, KT," said Kari. "What do you mean John Ringling is out at St. Armands Circle? ... And what's St. Armands Circle?"

KT spoke much faster than usual–she was so excited. "There's this place called St. Armands Circle on St. Armands Key where my mom and I like to shop. There are all kinds of little shops and restaurants built around a circular road. It's cool. Anyway, there's a park in the center of that circle, and my mom and I bought some ice cream at Scoopdaddy's once and took it across the street to the park to eat it. I'm almost sure there was a statue of John Ringling in that park!"

"KT, I think that's it!" Prez said, finding it impossible to remain calm. "It's a quick boat trip to St. Armands! Let's go there now!"

"Should we ask Jack Lambert if we can put the Lambert

cam on him again?" KT asked.

"Good idea," said Prez. "I'll go get it off the boat."

Prez got the Lambert cam and gave it to KT. Then Jessie and KT waded into the water and asked Jack Lambert if they could attach it to his dorsal fin. He let the two girls know it was OK.

They were on the *Rough Rider* in a matter of seconds–on the way to St. Armands Key. Jack Lambert was leading the way and the Lambert cam was sending great video images to the boat.

Prez asked, "Can you guys find any information about St. Armands Key?"

Kevin got on his minicomputer and said, "Here we go. The first homesteader was Charles St. Amand from France, who fished and farmed there. He didn't have an 'r' in his last name, but someone misspelled it on a land deed and it stuck."

"Another spelling problem in a place name story," Chad noted.

KT said, "Have you noticed sometimes they put an apostrophe on *St. Armand's* and sometimes they don't?"

"I think I read someplace that they've discouraged apostrophes in place names for a long time," said Prez. "Apparently, mapmakers say apostrophes look like rocks when the names end up in the water on the map."

"That's extremely interesting," said Nick.

"I thought you might think so, Nick," Prez said, smiling.

Kevin continued, "St. Amand started to buy property on the key in 1887–that's just a few years after the Scots came here. Anyway, he called the key *Deer Key* when he lived there. He bought 132 acres for $21.71."

"That would be about 16 cents for a football field," Jan calculated mentally. "Not a bad deal."

"Does everything have to be about sports with you, Jan?" Chad asked with an impish smile.

Jan smiled, then made a face at Chad.

"A football field-sized piece of land there now would cost you several million," Prez noted.

Back at home in his study, Stephen Queen had been listening to the conversation on board the Rough Rider, and he knew he had to get to St. Armands Key as fast as he could! There was no way he could beat those Sarabiskota kids there now—but he had to get there as quickly as possible, and that meant taking his boat. He'd have to watch out for that darn dolphin, though!

"St. Amand died during the Hurricane of 1921," Kevin continued reading information from his minicomputer. "After that, the land was bought by a guy named Arbogast from West Virginia, and by that time, the key was called St. Armands. Then Owen Burns bought the land in 1913, and he sold it to John Ringling's company in 1924."

Kari referred to her minicomputer, and added, "And John Ringling wanted St. Armands Key to be a big part of his whole dream for all those keys–all those hotels, nice homes, golf courses, and stuff we talked about before. Remember, John even wanted President Harding to live on nearby Bird Key during part of the winter, but the President died."

"That's right," Kevin said, "and from what I'm reading here, it sounds like St. Armands Circle has turned out a lot like John Ringling planned, except he wanted it to be called

Harding Circle. I guess it was actually called that until about 1969, but then it became St. Armands Circle for some reason. Anyway, John wanted upscale shopping available, and KT says there's plenty of that. He wanted a large park in the middle of the circle with plenty of palm trees and flowers and things, and I guess that's pretty much the way it is."

"That's for sure," KT said.

Kevin continued, "Ringling also wanted well-lit, wide streets approaching the circle, with statues of all the Presidents along them. He wanted the connecting streets to be named after Presidents–like Cleveland and McKinley."

"I don't remember any statues of Presidents, but the streets were definitely wide with lots of street lights, and they were named after Presidents," KT confirmed.

"Here's something pretty interesting," Kari added. "When they were building the bridge to get out to St. Armands, the circus elephants actually did some of the heavy lifting."

"Does it say anything about all the plaques honoring the great circus stars?" KT asked. "They're all the way around the sidewalk around the park at St. Armands Circle. I think it's called the Circus Ring of Honor or the Circle Walk of Fame or something."

"Yup, here it is," Kevin said. "They call it the Circle Walk of Fame here. It says new memorial markers are still being added to it periodically."

"We're going to dock the boat just west of St. Armands Circle–right up there in that canal," Prez pointed. "Get the ropes ready."

Jack Lambert swam next to the boat as they entered the canal. After they docked the boat and got off, KT told Jack

Lambert, "We'll be back in a few minutes."

Sarabiskota jogged toward the park they'd just been talking about. On the way, they passed a store named Kilwin's, and KT made quick mention of the great fudge she had eaten there. "They make it right here on those huge tables, and then you can buy it right away. It's so fresh it melts in your mouth," she said.

"It looks like most of these places open at ten o'clock," Prez noted. "That'll give us some time to investigate before it gets crowded around here."

After they got to the west end of the sidewalk around the circle, KT led them 90 degrees clockwise around the circular sidewalk to the northern-most point.

"There!" KT pointed to the bust of John Ringling mounted on a stone pedestal, about 10 yards from the sidewalk.

Jessie observed, "John Ringling appears to be looking toward Longboat Key, and he's probably wishing that Ritz-Carlton he was building out there got finished."

"Hey, you guys," Nick said. "Here's the plaque honoring the Five Ringlings."

Sure enough. Nearby, on the ground, was the bronze plaque, shaped like a circus wagon wheel, honoring *The Five Ringling Brothers*. Around the circumference of the wagon wheel, there were several symbols of the circus–including animals, trapeze artists, and circus clowns.

Jessie said, "Hey, doesn't that circus clown look a lot like the porcelain clown John Ringling was holding in the picture at the Tampa Bay Hotel?"

"It does!" Kari whispered loudly.

Before anyone else could move, Kevin took a quick look

around to make sure no one was watching, then he got down on his knees so he could get a close look at the clown on the circus wheel.

"I don't see anything here," Kevin said. "I'll get out of the way so someone else can take a look."

As Kevin was helping himself up from his knees, he placed his right hand firmly on the clown symbol, and that's when everyone got a huge surprise! A small compartment slid open in the back of the large plaque– and inside was a piece of paper!

Kevin quickly grabbed the piece of paper and handed it to KT. KT opened it up and whispered excitedly, "*July 5*! That's all it says!"

"That's the day of the Suncoast Offshore Boat Festival!" Chad whispered loudly. "That's less than two weeks away!"

As soon as the small compartment opened, a radio signal was sent many miles away to a workshop hidden on an isolated key off the Gulf Coast. After he received the signal, the old man smiled. "July 5 will be a day to remember for these young people!" he said to himself.

Meanwhile, Stephen Queen drove his boat into the same canal where the *Rough Rider* was docked. Jack Lambert watched Stephen Queen's boat approaching. He knew exactly who was on board and what he had to do!

Jack Lambert swam up and down the narrow canal, creating as much commotion as he could! For the next few minutes he acted like a hyperactive dolphin in fast motion as he jumped, splashed, and swam with unbelievable speed, attracting as much attention as possible!

People who were working on their boats in front of the houses that lined the canal gathered to watch this dolphin show! More people started coming out of their houses to watch the amazing performance!

Several spectators recognized Stephen Queen in the boat as it came down the canal, and they waved and called out his name! Mr. Queen waved back hesitantly, and he became extremely uncomfortable about all the attention he was getting. It didn't take long before he turned his boat around and drove out of the canal, putting a safe distance between himself and Jack Lambert.

When Sarabiskota got back to the *Rough Rider* ten minutes later, Jack Lambert greeted them by the dock. Many people were still standing around, talking about the incredible dolphin show and the appearance by Stephen Queen they'd just witnessed in their little canal. Sarabiskota got eyewitness accounts from several people before they got on the *Rough Rider* and headed back to Siesta Key.

Kevin asked, "Prez, can you play back the digital tape from the Lambert cam so we can see what happened?"

"Sure," Prez replied. In less than a minute, Prez found the place on the tape where Stephen Queen's boat started entering the canal. They all stared up at the monitor as they watched the incident unfold!

"Oh, my gosh!" Jessie exclaimed.

"I've had a strange feeling about Stephen Queen since he was watching us on the way to Spanish Point," KT said.

"I'll bet it was him who passed us in that Edsel on the way to the Tampa Bay Hotel, too," Jan added.

"Remember that noise at Shaw Point?" said Chad. "That

was probably him, too."

Prez said, "How could he possibly know every move we make, unless–"

"Are you thinking what I'm thinking?" Kari asked.

"I sure am," said Prez. "Stephen Queen has probably been following us since the very beginning using electronic listening devices–and who knows what else?"

Chad was wide-eyed. He whispered, "Do you mean he might have bugs on this boat right now, and he might be listening to us this very second?"

"I wouldn't doubt it," Prez replied, finding himself whispering all of a sudden, too. "There are lots of other surveillance techniques he could also be using."

"What should we do?" KT asked.

Prez suggested, "We can start by doing an electronic sweep of the boat, the workshop, my house, and maybe KT's house the next couple of days to see if we can find anything. For now, we've got to assume Stephen Queen knows everything we know about Captain Sarasota."

"Even the July 5th clue–" Nick tried to catch himself, but it was too late!

26

Sarabiskota accomplished tons the next week and a half. Most importantly, they finished building *The Starship Exercise*, and they tested it to make sure it was seaworthy.

Although Sarabiskota worked extremely hard during this time, they never had more fun in their lives. Being together, working toward a common goal, and anticipating how this whole Captain Sarasota mystery was going to turn out on July 5, was an awesome experience. Sarabiskota also found time to swim and play with Jack Lambert.

Prez rigged up a device to do an electronic sweep of the *Rough Rider*, the Siesta Key workshop, his house, and KT's house. They found two small electronic listening devices on board the boat and four more in the workshop. Their suspicions had been confirmed. Stephen Queen probably knew as much as they did about Captain Sarasota's mystery. They could probably expect just about anything on July 5!

Sarabiskota discussed what to do with all the listening devices they discovered. Finally, they decided to put them all in a small soundproof package along with a CD player playing Mike's favorite Elvis songs—sung by Mike himself. They made sure the CD player was set so it would play the CD over and over again. Sarabiskota laughed just thinking about Stephen Queen listening to their special music!

Because *The Starship Exercise* could only handle six people, Prez tried to come up with a way to accommodate the rest of his friends so they could all take part in the Creative Boat Parade together. He got a brilliant idea, and he estimated they probably had just enough time to get it done.

Then, with only a few days left before the Suncoast Offshore Boat Festival, Sarabiskota was working on *The Starship Exercise* at the Siesta Key workshop. Suddenly, Prez had yet another one his brilliant ideas. They'd be pushing it to get this one done in time–but it would make their Creative Boat Parade entry so cool! Jack Lambert would get to be part of the fun, too!

Finally, the big day arrived! The weather was perfect–like almost every day in Sarasota, with a clear blue sky, a light breeze, and warm temperatures. The waters off Sarasota were even calmer than usual, almost like glass.

The excitement in Sarasota was incredible! Nearly a million onlookers had been expected to line the parade and race routes, but more than twice that many showed up!

Although many spectators were excited about the powerboat races later in the day, most had come to see the parade of the unique boats that would start the day's festivities. Nearly 200 boats were entered in that event!

Even Congresswoman Katherine Harris had returned to Sarasota for the occasion, and she had a viewing stand like no other. A small replica of the White House had been constructed on a barge which had been anchored in the calm waters off Siesta Public Beach. The Congresswoman and her guests would view the festivities from the second floor of Siesta Key's own White House!

Governor Ed and First Lady Nancy decided to fly down from North Dakota for the event. When Congresswoman Harris heard of this, she invited them both to be guests on the floating White House to view the parade.

Four members of the Channel 8 News Team were covering the event. Bob Hite and Gayle Sierens had a viewing area on the ground floor of the White House. Jackie Barron was out in the middle of the huge crowd on Siesta Public Beach. Jennifer Leigh was on board a small boat that looked just like a hammerhead shark, and she was driving around, getting a unique perspective of the parade.

Sarasota's SNN Channel 6 and ABC 7 reporters were helping the Channel 8 news team in covering the occasion from every angle. Their reporters were stationed all along the parade route.

Covering the event from the air were FM radio personalities MJ and Uncle Fester from the *MJ Morning Show*, riding on a two-man powered parachute. The crowd stared up at the powered parachute and gasped as they noticed it was leaning to the left significantly. That happened to be the side where giant-sized Uncle Fester was seated. His partner, MJ, was holding a microphone and piloting the powered parachute while broadcasting live, and Uncle Fester was taking video of the amazing scene below them.

At 9:30 in the morning, The Creative Boat Parade got started. Channel 8's Gayle Sierens and Bob Hite began telecasting from the White House out on the barge.

"This is Gayle Sierens."

"And I'm Bob Hite. We're here to cover one of the most exciting events ever to take place in this area–or anywhere else for that matter!"

"That's right, Bob, it looks to me like almost everyone on Florida's Suncoast is here to watch this incredible event, plus about a million others from all over the world! But just in case you're not here, we'll describe everything from a great vantage point. As you can see, we're on the ground floor of this unbelievable floating White House. If you look just above us, you can see Congresswoman Katherine Harris and other dignitaries watching everything from what has to be the best seat anywhere–right from the second floor of the floating White House."

"Yes, Gayle. Congresswoman Harris is just one of many prominent people we'll be seeing today. Our viewers are in for many special treats and definitely a few surprises. The day's going to start out with a most unusual parade—the Creative Boat Parade. This event allows entrants to come up with some type of creative boat—but it must float and have a motor that works. Boats will be judged during the parade, and winning boats will receive some nice cash prizes and trophies. As a sea captain myself, Gayle, I've had a peek at some of these so-called boats already, and there really are some unusual entrants. Frankly, I'm wondering how some of them even float."

"Well, just in case they don't, Bob, we've got plenty of United States Coast Guard boats and helicopters watching that can help out if needed. Right now, though, I'd like to turn it over to our own Jennifer Leigh, who has tied her *Hammerhead Shark* boat up to another boat, and she's now on board. Jen, where are you?"

"Gayle and Bob, I'm on board the ship called the *Super Bowl XXXVII*. You'll notice the ship is shaped like a huge football! Around me right now are some of the great Bucs of all-time including Coach Jon Gruden, Derrick Brooks, John Lynch, Brad Johnson, and probably the most famous Buccaneer of all-time, Mr. Lee Roy Selmon–the first Tampa Bay Buccaneer ever to be inducted into the Pro Football Hall of Fame. Lee Roy, could I ask you what you think of all this?"

"It's pretty amazing to me, Jen! I've been to a Rose Bowl Parade before, but this beats it. Look at all the unbelievable boats lined up all along here!"

Jennifer Leigh turned to Coach Gruden and asked, "Coach Gruden, is this even more fun than coaching Keyshawn?" The expression that suddenly appeared on Jon Gruden's face would easily have frightened a ghost!

"Oops, bad question, I guess," Jennifer Leigh said. "Back to you, Gayle and Bob."

Gayle Sierens said, "Now, let's check in with Jackie Barron, who is somewhere on Siesta Public Beach."

"Hi, Gayle and Bob! I'm in the middle of tens of thousands of people here who've brought their coolers and have pitched their tents for this wonderful day of fun and excitement. Many of them even have their televisions tuned to Channel 8 so they can watch our coverage of this event, too. As you know, there are an estimated two million spectators up and down the parade route. All of us are ready for what is likely to be one of the greatest parades ever!

"Standing next to me is a group that's traveled all the way from Nova Scotia, Canada, to be here today. To my left, there are people from North Dakota, Minnesota, Iowa, Ohio, and Michigan–even a couple from Australia and a whole family from England. Throughout the day, I'll be wandering around this huge crowd, asking them for some free drinks and food when possible and getting their reactions to everything going on. Back to you, Gayle and Bob."

"Thanks, Jackie. Well, Bob, I think we're about ready to go. Right now our own beautiful Miss Florida, who is up on the second floor of the White House, will sing the *National Anthem* ..."

After the *National Anthem*, Bob Hite said, "Governor Bush, who is in the first boat, will officially get the parade started. The Governor and the First Lady are in a boat built to look like the Fountain of Youth. As many of you know, Ponce de Leon was supposedly looking for such a fountain when he discovered Florida in the 1500's."

Governor Bush said, "Ladies and gentlemen, start those engines, and may all of you float safely all the way to the end of this fabulous parade!"

"Well, Gayle, we're off!" Bob Hite said. "The boat behind the Governor's is approaching us right now, and the crowd is going absolutely crazy! It's the *Stanley Cup-Hockey Puck* boat with many of our Stanley Cup Champions riding on board! There's Dave Andreychuk holding the Stanley Cup up over his head!"

"You pronounced that so well, Bob. Also riding on this amazing float are Ruslan Fedotenko, Martin St. Louis, Nikolai Khabibulin, Vinny Lecavalier, and Brad Richards, who's holding his MVP trophy!"

"Gayle, don't forget Coach Tortella. He's also on the boat. Wow! I've never heard such cheering and screaming! We love our Stanley Cup Champions ... "

Bob said, "The next boat looks just like one of the area's prominent landmarks, the St. Petersburg Pier. Riding on

board are many citizens of St. Pete including Mayor Rick Baker, the city council of St. Pete, and their teacher of the year, Robin Ladd ..."

Gayle said, "We're blessed to have so many famous and talented people living in this area. The next boat is being driven by a famous cartoonist who lives right here on Siesta Key–Mike Peters. Mike's boat looks just like the dog, Grimmy, the main character from his cartoon strip, *Mother Goose and Grimm*–which I read every morning, by the way ..."

Bob said, "Sarasota Jungle Gardens has entered this next boat which is a huge pink flamingo. Sarasota Jungle Gardens is a fabulous zoological gardens located right here in Sarasota, and it has everything from pink flamingos, to exotic birds–even some Florida gators ..."

Gayle said, "Tampa is represented by this next entry, a cigar-shaped boat, reflecting Tampa's early cigar making industry–still going on in Ybor City. Tampa's mayor, Pam Iorio, is actually driving the boat ..."

Bob exclaimed, "Oh my! *The Sunshine Skyway Bridge* boat is floating by us right now! This floating masterpiece, built to look like the area's most famous landmark, was designed and built by many of the engineers and shipbuilders that call the Tampa Bay area home."

"That's amazing, Bob ..."

Gayle said, "Bradenton is responsible for this next boat, called the *Hernando de Soto*. It's built to look just like one of the boats that landed in west Bradenton at De Soto Point approximately 500 years ago ..."

"The wonderful town of Venice has built a large gondola-shaped boat like you might find in its namesake in Italy ..."

"Wow! It's the *Busch Gardens Boat*, complete with a small roller coaster on board ..."

"The next boat is really four smaller boats connected to look like a circus train. Of course, everyone living around here knows all about the rich circus tradition we have in this part of Florida. Many of the performers who have retired from the circus and live in the area are riding on this beautiful boat ..."

"Marie Selby Gardens in Sarasota has entered a boat that looks exactly like a giant orchid. Marie Selby is one of the best botanical gardens anywhere in the world ..."

"The area's most enthusiastic resident, Dickie V, is riding in the boat passing by us right now that looks exactly like a huge basketball. Dickie V and his family are riding in the boat ... and let me just say ... it's awesome, baby!"

"Bradenton's Aquarium is represented by the *Snooty* boat, a boat shaped just like the world's most famous manatee. Wow! Snooty himself is riding on the boat! The people at the Parker Manatee Aquarium in Bradenton have actually built a small pool of water on the boat for Snooty! Look! He's used his front flippers to lift himself out of the water so he can watch the people! Everyone's cheering wildly, showing Snooty their appreciation ..."

"The *Historic Spanish Point* boat is passing us now. This boat is actually supposed to look like the *Phantom*, a boat that was used for hauling cargo like oranges and produce from the Webb's packing house at Spanish Point when John Webb and his family lived there starting in the 1860's ..."

"I knew we would get a Florida gator somewhere in the parade. This *Gator Boat*, entered by Myakka River State Park near Sarasota, is over 40 feet in length, and it looks too much like the real thing for my comfort! Myakka River State Park, the largest state park in Florida, has hundreds of gators you can view from the safety of two of the world's largest air boats ..."

"Sarasota's Classic Car Museum has a boat that looks just like Beatle John Lennon's Mercedes convertible ..."

"Oh, wow! It's the *Rhino Boat* entered by Tampa's great Lowry Park Zoo! Is that an orangutan driving the boat ..."

"G. WIZ Hands-On Science Museum from right here in Sarasota has entered this next boat. My gosh! It looks exactly like the Mars Rover ..."

"The next boat is a called the *Governor Safford*, built to look like the old steamer which brought a small group of Scottish colonists here to Sarasota in 1885. I just love the two cute bagpipe outboard engines on the boat! We actually have some Riverview High School bagpipers playing Scottish tunes on board ..."

"This is great! The Mote Marine Laboratory has entered the gigantic *Sea Turtle Boat*, and it looks like all the scientists and their families on board are having a great time. Bob, you know all about the great things that go on out at Mote Marine."

"I sure do, Gayle. It's truly a world class facility ..."

"Sarasota's famous writer of strange and scary stories, Stephen Queen, has built an elaborate boat resembling the monstrous, evil hot dog from his book and movie thriller *The Hot Dog That Ate The New York Yankees*. Stephen Queen himself is driving the boat ..."

Bob said, "The next entry going by us right now is really something to see! First, they've got a large boat that looks just like the Starship *Enterprise* from the *Star Trek* movies, but they call theirs *The Starship Exercise*. That boat is towing another smaller boat that looks like the shuttlecraft from those same great *Star Trek* movies. Then, if you can believe it, a beautiful bottlenose dolphin is playing catch with a small football that some of the young people in the shuttlecraft are throwing to him!"

Gayle added, "To top it all off, a small Goodyear-type blimp is flying above them, but it's shaped a lot like the dolphin! I think there's a young man on board *The Starship Exercise* operating the dolphin blimp with a remote control device."

"Oh, there's even more, Gayle. You can probably see the small camera attached to the dolphin's dorsal fin. The dolphin is named Jack Lambert, so they call it the *Lambert cam*. Right now, Jack Lambert's sending his own version of this parade to anyone who wants to see it at www.lambert-cam.com."

"Amazing, Bob! The whole thing is apparently the work of nine ambitious kids from Sarasota and North Dakota ..."

Bob said, "I love this next boat! It looks exactly like a baseball, and it's called the *Tampa Bay Rays Baseball Boat*. On board are Coach Popeye Zimmer, Manager Lou Piniella, and some of the stars of the Rays including all-star Aubrey Huff ..."

"Our next entry is the *Super Bowl XXXVII*, with all our hometown Buccaneer heroes riding on board. Right now, we're going to go back out to that boat to our own Jen Leigh, who is going to interview a few of the Bucs' players."

"Hi again, Bob and Gayle. I'm here with the winning quarterback of Super Bowl XXXVII, Brad Johnson! Brad, what do you think of this parade so far?"

"I'm just amazed at watching that dolphin throw a football with his head. I wish I had the accuracy and dexterity he does—it's the most incredible thing I've ever seen! I hope Coach Gruden doesn't try to sign him up for next year, 'cause he'd probably beat me out!'"

Jennifer giggled. "I don't think there's any chance of that happening, Brad," she said. "The only Dolphins you'll have to worry about are on that team in Miami."

Brad laughed and said, "I hope you're right. As a *Star Trek* fan myself, I've got to tell you, those two boats in front of us are fabulous! It's amazing to see what young people can do when they're motivated!"

Jen Leigh interviewed Coach Gruden as they slowly moved north along Siesta Key. Suddenly, Coach Gruden's smiling face changed to a big surprise-face! As he and millions more watched, a 20-foot manta ray-shaped submarine came to the surface 30 yards directly seaward from the *The Starship Exercise*!

A small canopy on the submarine popped open for just a few seconds, and Captain Sarasota appeared! He yelled, "Good job, Sarabiskota! This is all yours!" Then he tried to throw a small blue sphere, not much bigger than a softball, as close as he could to *The Starship Exercise*! The submarine, now a boat, sped away into the Gulf of Mexico!

Dickie V, who turned around in time to catch a glimpse of the action from his basketball boat, was shocked when he saw Captain Sarasota aboard the manta ray submarine boat!

Unfortunately, from his poor throwing position sitting in the sub, Captain Sarasota's throw had been short and wild, and it landed closer to Stephen Queen's boat than *The Starship Exercise*. Stephen Queen reacted in a flash and quickly maneuvered his hot dog boat near the blue sphere and retrieved it!

In the next few seconds, several more incredible events occurred!

The crowd cheered wildly, thinking the manta ray submarine boat was just another amazing parade entry!

KT, who was riding on the shuttlecraft, was about ready to yell something to Jack Lambert—but he was already gone!

Chad yelled to Brad Johnson and Coach Gruden to please throw the footballs they were holding at the blue sphere Stephen Queen was now holding above his head in celebration! Coach Gruden threw a wobbly pass that hit the side of the hot dog boat. Brad Johnson threw a perfect spiral, but it was slightly off the mark! It hit Stephen Queen in the back of the head!

Dazed, Stephen Queen was still somehow able to hold on to the blue sphere! Then, Rays all-star Aubrey Huff fired a perfect fastball–hitting the sphere and knocking it out of Stephen Queen's hands and into the water! Stephen Queen raced his hot dog boat over to get it back!

Jack Lambert jumped high into the air and smacked Stephen Queen in the shoulders with his tail, knocking him into the water! Then the dolphin swam over to the blue sphere, balanced it on his beak, and swam over to the shuttlecraft, flipping the sphere into *The Starship Exercise*!

Stephen Queen let out a bloodcurdling scream, as he dog-paddled back to his boat!

Uncle Fester leaned over a little too far in the powered parachute, trying to get video of the amazing action going on below! He fell off and screamed as he fell 120 feet into the water below, creating a huge splash—a splash that would

later appear on many satellite photos! Uncle Fester quickly came to the surface. He waved to the crowd, obviously OK!

Prez asked Kari to take over control of *The Starship Exercise*! He got the remote control device for the dolphin blimp from Mike–and flew the blimp toward Captain Sarasota's manta ray boat at top speed!

The dolphin blimp caught up with the manta ray, then Prez maneuvered the blimp above the manta ray's closed canopy to get Captain Sarasota's attention!

Captain Sarasota popped open the canopy!

Using the communication devices on board the dolphin blimp, Prez said, "Captain Sarasota, who are you?"

Captain Sarasota yelled up at the blimp, "You'll learn all you need to know when you read the message inside the sphere! Thanks for one of the most fun, exhilarating experiences of my *very long* life!"

Prez called back, "You *did* find the Fountain of Youth, didn't you, Captain Sarasota?"

"It's all in the blue sphere!" Captain Sarasota yelled up at the blimp. "Now, I've got to go, Prez!"

Prez called, "Will we ever see you again?"

Captain Sarasota said, "I have a feeling we'll meet again, Prez. I've got lots of time–*lots* of time!"

Then, all of a sudden, Captain Sarasota's boat took off into the air at tremendous speed! A sonic boom was heard throughout the area! Stephen Queen's glasses shattered!

Gayle Sierens turned to Bob Hite, looking totally perplexed. "Would you explain to me what just happened?"

Sarabiskota watched from the deck of the salvage ship *Judge Silvertooth*, and hundreds of millions more watched on television from around the world as a large treasure chest was being slowly raised from the ocean floor in 80 feet of water off Longboat Key. The event was being covered by all major networks worldwide, as the Captain Sarasota story had captured the imagination of everyone!

Jack Lambert was watching all the action both above and below the water. The Lambert cam was sending out video images to millions of viewers on the Internet.

Veteran TV personality Geraldo Rivera, who had more than his share of bad experiences unveiling treasures on live TV, was nervous, yet excited, as he reported from the deck of the *Judge Silvertooth*. Small beads of sweat were forming on his upper lip.

Geraldo droned, "As you all know, the Captain Sarasota story has now taken us to this place. Captain Sarasota, who most of us think actually found the Fountain of Youth, staged his disappearance, and then left a series of clues to be solved that have led to this treasure chest and whatever is inside.

"Captain Sarasota might have made his first clue too tough. Stephen Queen figured out there was something at

Spanish Point, but that's as far as he got. Mr. Queen became obsessed to find the clue and solve the whole Captain Sarasota mystery.

"When Stephen Queen found out Prez had moved to Sarasota, he devised a devious plan to get the precocious Prez's help in solving the mystery–without the young man knowing he was helping. That's when he secretly followed KT, Chad, and Prez to Selby Public Library, and put the Captain Sarasota story on the microfilm reader.

"It worked. Prez and his friends got intensely involved in the Captain Sarasota mystery, and unlike Stephen Queen, they had success in solving the clues. All Stephen Queen had to do was spy on Sarabiskota and let them do the work.

"You see, Stephen Queen had learned some pretty good surveillance techniques while doing the research for some of his books. With the help of some bugs he planted a few places, he was able to follow Sarabiskota all the way up to the Creative Boat Parade—and you all know what happened there. We understand Stephen Queen has since apologized for his actions. He's even going to put Sarabiskota and Jack Lambert in his next movie based on his latest book *The Dolphin That Became Governor of California.*

"The note Sarabiskota recovered from Captain Sarasota in a blue sphere gave them the exact GPS coordinates of the treasure chest now being raised here off Longboat Key, where we are right now. In that note, Captain Sarasota also said he'd found a Fountain of Youth, but it had been destroyed just months after he found it–during a hurricane *hundreds of years ago*! That's *hundreds* of years ago! Captain Sarasota is *hundreds* of years old at least! In that note, Captain Sarasota also asked Sarabiskota to use half the money from the treasure we're about to reveal to help support sports and educational activities around the whole Tampa Bay and Sarasota Bay region. They are to keep the other half! It shouldn't be long now before we find out just how much that's going to be!

"The mystery still remains where Captain Sarasota is today. We may never know the answer to that question. But, just in case you're watching this, Captain Sarasota– please give me a call."

Geraldo was sweating profusely now, obviously quite nervous! He said, "Oh, my gosh! The people here on board are suddenly cheering wildly as a huge treasure chest about the size of a compact car just popped out of the water. There are several experts on board to get the treasure chest open as quickly as possible as soon as we get it on board... It shouldn't be long now!"

The TV camera crews got a close-up as experts hurriedly opened three massive locks. As the world watched, Sarasota's Mayor Lou Ann Palmer helped Sarabiskota slowly raise the huge lid off the treasure chest...Geraldo's eyes got huge and he fainted! Jan rushed over to give him aid!

The whole world was amazed at what they saw! The huge chest was full of gold coins, silver, jewelry, and large precious jewels! It was unlike anything anyone had ever seen outside of the movies! The value would later be determined to be almost two billion dollars!

After that, Jack Lambert became even more famous, and the Lambert cam was the most popular web cam on the Internet by far. After his appearance in Stephen Queen's movie, Jack Lambert became the most popular actor in

Hollywood.

Although richer than any of them had ever dreamed, Sarabiskota was determined to continue living as normal a life as possible. KT, Chad, and Prez were having a great year in school at Brookside Middle School in Sarasota, and so were Sarabiskota in Bismarck. Prez was even elected president of his eighth grade class, and KT was elected vice president.

Sarabiskota got together at each Tampa Bay Buccaneers home game during the next NFL season and also at several Steelers home games. Governor Ed was even able to join them a few times.

Jon Gruden insisted that Sarabiskota stand on the sidelines with the team at Raymond James Stadium during each Bucs home game, thinking they might bring the Buccaneers good luck, and it seemed to work. The Bucs were undefeated going into the Christmas weekend and seemed destined to play the Steelers in the Super Bowl. Jon Gruden, who was not one to usually look ahead, had already asked Sarabiskota if they would consider cheering for the Bucs during the Super Bowl–if the Bucs made it there.

When Chad answered, "Only if it snows in Sarasota on Christmas," Jon Gruden laughed, but then he got a determined look on his face.

A few minutes before midnight on Christmas Eve, a mysterious looking aircraft flew high over Sarasota, and then released a fine crystalline substance into the air, which slowly fell to earth. As the crystals fell to the ground, they produced the largest snowflakes imaginable. They melted almost instantly once they reached the ground.

Word spread quickly! Within minutes, most of Sarasota was outside, watching it snow on Christmas morning—a miracle made more amazing by the fact that it was over 55 degrees outside!

Prez ran out to Sunset Beach to watch the snow falling all around! Within minutes, KT and Chad had joined him! Jack Lambert popped out of the water nearby, and the Lambert cam captured the incredible occurrence!

Soon, all the news and weather channels in the United States were reporting this Christmas miracle! Kari quickly called all of Sarabiskota in Bismarck and they conference-called Prez.

"Do you think Jon Gruden had anything to do with this?" Kari asked.

"I was thinking more in terms of Captain Sarasota," Prez replied.

Jessie said, "Somehow, this doesn't seem fair. You're getting a white Christmas in Sarasota, and we don't have any snow on the ground at all in Bismarck."

Nick giggled. "Do you think Sara de Soto would have enjoyed this moment?" he asked.

Mike started singing, "I'm dreaming of a white Sarasota Christmas. Just like the ones ..."

Note from the author regarding books and other sources used in writing this book:

When I moved to Sarasota, I read two outstanding books by Janet Snyder Matthews:
1. *Journey to Centennial Sarasota* (1997)
2. *Edge of Wilderness* (1983)

After that, I read the exceptional book by Karl Grismer, *The Story of Sarasota* (1946). Next, I read the following books, in this order:
1. *The Lures of Manatee* by McDuffie (1933)
2. *Venice* by Matthews (1989)
3. *The Mangrove Coast* by Bickel (1942)
4. *Florida Place Names* by Morris (1995)
5. *Ringling: The Florida Years 1911-1936* by Weeks (1993)
6. *The Ringling Legacy* by Buck (1995)
7. *Historic Sites and Buildings: Sarasota-Venice-Bradenton Area* by Reynolds (1996)
8. *Tampa Triangle* by Miller (1997)

I was interested in all the articles written by the Sarasota County History Center that were published by the *Sarasota Herald-Tribune*. Then, as I started to think about writing a book, I visited some of the historic sites in the area and read other books, including the following:
1. *Who's Buried in Grant's Tomb* by Lamb (2003)
2. *Dolphins, Whales, and Manatees* by Reynolds (2003)
3. *It Happened in Florida* by Wright (2003)
4. *Dreamers, Schemers, and Scalawags* by McIver (1994)
5. *Railroads of Southwest Florida* by Turner (1999)
6. *Oddball Florida* by Pohlen (2004)
7. *200 Quick Looks at Florida History* by Clark (2000)
8. *The Spanish-American War in Tampa Bay* by de Quesada (1998)
9. *Florida Curiosities* by Grimes and Becnel (2003)
10. *From Calusas to Condominiums* by Hunter (2002)
11. *Manatees-Our Vanishing Mermaids* by O'Keefe (1993)
12. *Florida's Past (Vol. 1-3)* by Burnett
13. *A Treasury of Florida Tales* by Garrison (1989)
14. *Florida's Seminole Indians* by Neill (1956)
15. *Venice in the 1920's* by Turner (2000)
16. *Sarasota and Bradenton Florida* by Wilpon (1999)
17. *Sarasota ... A Sentimental Journey* by LaHurd (1991)
18. *Twenty Florida Pirates* by McCarthy (1994)
19. *Florida Fun Facts* by Kleinberg (1995)
20. *Florida Hurricanes and Tropical Storms* by Williams (2002)

Chapter Notes:

Chapter III: A copy of Sarasota's actual post office application was provided to the author by Adam S. Westcott, a Volunteer Research Assistant at the Sarasota County History Center.

Possible explanations of the origin of the name Sarasota are from Grismer's book *The Story of Sarasota*, pp. 19-21.

The "Legend of Sara de Soto" can be found in Grismer's book on p. 27.

Chapter V: The Buccaneers' curse is talked about in *Tampa Triangle*, p. 105.

Chapter VII: Smallest police station story comes from *Florida Curiosities*, pp. 6-8, and *Oddball Florida*, p. 5.

The Bardin Booger story is on the Internet, and in *Florida Curiosities*, pp. 29-32, and *Oddball Florida*, p. 34.

Place name story for Fargo is from *Florida Place Names*, p. 86.

Fort Armistead information comes from *Journey to Centennial*.

Snow and weather facts come from *Florida Fun Facts*, pp. 67-68, and National Weather Service Web Site.

Chapters VIII and IX: Most of the Spanish Point information came from all the excellent people on site, especially all the super tour guides!

These pamphlets and booklets were also helpful, and they are available at the gift shop at Spanish Point:*Historic Spanish Point; Guide to Prehistory of Historic Spanish Point; Mrs. Potter Palmer-Legendary Lady of Sarasota*.

Horse and Chaise/Venice place name information is from the book *Venice* by Matthews.

Chapter X: Otto Graham information came from articles in the *Sarasota Herald-Tribune* and from various sites on the Internet.

Chapters XI and XII: Most of the Hernando de Soto information in these chapters was available on site at the De Soto National Monument in Bradenton. The film, the historical markers, and the pamphlets were most helpful.

Also used in these chapters: The books *The Mangrove Coast, The Story of Sarasota*, and *From Calusas to Condominiums*.

Anna Maria place name information was obtained at the Anna Maria Island Historical Museum.

Cortez information is from the book *Cortez-Then and Now*.

Chapters XIII and IV: Whitaker story is from Grismer's *The Story of Sarasota*, pp. 27-46.

Chapter XV: Letter from Sarah Gates to Janie Gates is in the book *The Lures of Manatee*, pp. 91-92.

Chapter XVI: Mote Marine Laboratory information was gathered on site, and from the excellent information they send to their supporters.

The story of the 5,000 pound devil fish was obtained from Pete Esthus at Pete's Lock and Key Shop in Sarasota.

Chapter XVII: The Bradenton history is mostly from *The Lures of Manatee* and numerous historical markers.

Other Bradenton information sources used:

Gamble Plantation State Historic Site

Manatee Village Historical Park

South Florida Museum and Bishop Planetarium

Braden Castle

Eaton Room, Manatee County Library

The wonderful Libby Warner from Bradenton

Chapter XVIII: Gillespie and the Scots story from Grismer's *The Story of Sarasota*, pp. 92-121.

Chapter XIX: Manatee information from the book *Manatees, Our Vanishing Mermaids*.

Chapter XX and XXI: Most of the Tampa Bay Hotel information was obtained from the video and people on site.

Sources used that were available at the Tampa Bay Hotel gift shop:

Moments in Time -(booklet)

Through the Keyhole-(booklet)

The Tampa Bay Hotel -(video)

Florida and the Spanish American War-(video)

Also very helpful: The book *River of the Golden Ibis* by Jahoda (1973).

Chapters XXII, XXIII, and XXIV: Ringling informational sources:

Ringling: The Florida Years by Weeks

The Ringling Legacy by Buck

Cà d'Zan- a special news section in the *Sarasota Herald-Tribune*

The Greatest Show On Earth -the movie

The great tour guides at the Cà d'Zan!

Chapter XXV: *The History of St. Armands* by Hartig

Index

About the Artist:

Richard Capes decided he wanted to be an artist at age six or seven, and he worked toward that goal from that point on. Richard says that he learned much of the discipline it takes to become an artist from working at his parents' restaurant and on their family farm.

Since moving to Sarasota in 1974, Mr. Capes has captured many past and present Sarasota scenes, and has also done abstract work and paintings of lighthouses. During that time, he has had over 85 exhibitions of his work throughout the United States. His works can be found in over 150 private and corporate art collections throughout the United States and Europe, including the White House in Washington, D.C.

Richard has been a member of The Florida Artists Group, Inc., for over 20 years. In the past 10 years, he's been listed in *Who's Who in American Art*, and he's been elected to the Community Video Archives Hall of Fame. In addition, he's published a book featuring Siesta Key, and created the artwork for a U.S. Postal Service cachet holding the first 33 cent stamp–an image that became part of the Smithsonian Institution Archives.

Richard Capes was a teacher at Morehead State University in Kentucky and the University of Southern Mississippi before he started his own business. He has both a bachelors and a masters degree in art education.

To contact Richard E. Capes:

2116 & 2120 Florinda St.   Phone: 941-924-8250
Sarasota, FL 34231   FAX: 941-922-0230

www.snowinsarasota.com

About the Author:

When he was teaching fifth and sixth grades, Kevin Kremer never planned to write a book. But after years of writing stories with his students, he wrote a book to help him deal with the loss of a beloved family member, a shelty collie named Jamie. That book, *A Kremer Christmas Miracle*, was published, and three more books followed.

When Dr. Kremer moved to Sarasota from Bismarck, North Dakota, he brought some of his old characters with him, but he's met many new ones while living in Florida. Kevin has now started his own writing/publishing company to help people fulfill their dreams in these areas.

Kevin has never met a Pittsburgh Steelers fan he didn't like! He's become a fan of the Tampa Bay Buccaneers, the Tampa Bay Rays, and the Stanley Cup Champion Tampa Bay Lightning since moving to Florida!

To contact Dr. Kevin Kremer for booksigning information, writing or publishing projects you need help with, school author visitations, etc., go to:

www.snowinsarasota.com
e-mail: snowinsarasota@aol.com

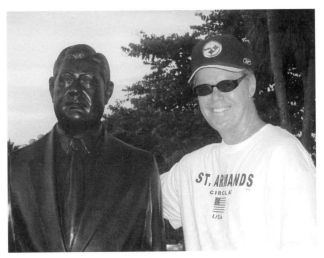

The author with a John Ringling statue at St. Armands Circle.